THE SECRETS OF SOLOMON'S SEAL: SINAI

By

J. Michael Corley

Published in Sweet Home, Oregon by Natisk Publishing.

Table of Contents

Dedication

For Lynetta, whose laughter heals me.

NOTE

All the archaeological sites and places named in this novel are real. The identities of some persons involved in the events described have been altered.

CHAPTER ONE

TEMPLE OF THE MOON

"Time fell asleep here, and the husks of ancient civilizations were buried in deep sand, preserved like flowers between the leaves of a book."
Wendell Phillips

Ma'rib, Yemen
1952

Jamil Ahmed's steely gaze penetrated the thick, swirling dust that enveloped the excavation site. Then fixated on the lone figure before him. With the nonchalant grace of a gunslinger, his calloused hand inched towards the grip of the revolver holstered at his hip as he presented an ancient leather pouch to the man before him.

"Murad Buckshan," he said, "I will ask you once more: where did you find this bag?"

The man lowered his gaze, shaking his head, his figure a stark contrast to the towering, burly form of Jamil. Murad's mustache was wispy, and a hint of gray crept into his beard, camouflaged beneath the layers of dust that clung to his weathered clothes. Though he resembled the other laborers, Jamil had enlisted for this archaeological dig. There was an aura about him, a mystery begging to be unraveled.

Jamil turned away, wiping the perspiration from his brow as he surveyed the dig site. Eighteen grueling years had led him to this point, the pinnacle of his career as a dig supervisor. He couldn't help but wonder if it was only after adopting Western attire to appease the foreigners that he had finally earned this position.

His gazed shifted briefly to a Yemeni guard standing nearby with a rifle slung over his left shoulder. The man was being paid to keep watch. He'd missed Murad's theft. A nagging doubt gnawed at Jamil's mind. Was it the guard's eyes or his motives that were bad? He'd uncovered Murad's treachery himself with no help from the man. He would deal with the slacker later.

Jamil had hired Murad, a man whose demeanor had set him apart from his peers. Given his earlier air of smug confidence, Jamil found it odd that now Murad would not speak to him or even look him in the eye. Instead, he stared at his sandals as if imagining they would answer for him. His shame was obviously an unbearable burden.

"If a rich man steals, it is dismissed as a mistake," Murad finally mumbled, his eyes clenched shut, his words heavy with the weight of truth. "But if a poor man makes a mistake, he has stolen." Then he resumed studying his feet that shifted vaguely, his demeanor loaded with guilt.

Jamil released his grip on the gun and ran his fingers through his hair. If the dig were back home, he would teach Murad a harsh lesson. But Yemen's political climate was treacherous. So, instead, he opted for a different strategy, seeking further evidence to support his growing suspicion.

"Quoting this proverb to shift blame is a clever ploy." Jamil's eyes bored into Murad." But I'm tired of hearing excuses. I should have you arrested. But because this is your first day, I shall refrain from reporting your thievery. We will categorize this incident, as you so elegantly put it, 'a mistake.'

"But hear me well, it is my job to know the location of every artifact we uncover. This knowledge is essential to our work. Every object is vital, regardless of size. If you tell me now where you found this bag, I will let you keep your job. If not—" he patted his revolver and jutted his chin to punctuate his unspoken threat.

Murad's eyes squeezed shut again. Then, after a long pause, he pointed toward the temple's entrance hall.

Jamil opened the leather pouch and peered inside. His eyes widened in astonishment. Nestled at the pouch's bottom lay a breathtaking gold and grayish-black ring. Its round-cut center stone glimmering with an allure that bespoke of royalty. Despite the tarnish marring its silver surface, the craftsmanship and sheer beauty of the ring left Jamil spellbound.

Dragging his gaze away, Jamil struggled to keep his voice level. "How did it get there?"

Murad shrugged.

As he tore his gaze away, struggling to maintain his composure, Jamil's mind raced. How had this artifact come to rest here? Could this be it—the evidence they needed to prove the Marib was home to the Queen?

Dr. Charles Fallbright, the eminent archaeologist and scholar, supported by local folklore and religious texts, had ardently championed the theory that Ma'rib was the capital of Sheba.

Lenard Jones, the Trust's Director, had pinned his hopes on uncovering proof. Hoping to validate Fallbright's hypothesis. The realization that he might now hold that proof sent a shiver down Jamil's spine. His pulse thudded in his ears.

He glanced up. His thoughts retracing Fallbright's words. He shared tales of the Queen of Sheba intertwined with Solomon, the exchanges of gifts, and the legendary ring. His eyes returned to the ring, and a surge of excitement coursed through him. If this was Solomon's Seal, it could immortalize a man's name, bestowing fortune and fame for generations. Jamil understood the urgency—this discovery had to be safeguarded from opportunistic Westerners. They might seize the credit, just as Howard Carter had done in 1922. Carter discovered Tutankhamun's tomb and had died wealthy and world-famous. The arrogant pig.

While Carter's name and face had splashed across the front pages of newspapers worldwide, no news report ever mentioned an Egyptian name. My father and my uncles did the hard work. We should have given Tutankhamen his voice. Not some foreigner. He was our ancestor, not theirs.

Determination edged his voice was as he demanded, "Show me exactly where you found this!"

CHAPTER TWO
THE WATCHER

"Nothing makes us as lonely as our secrets."
Paul Tournier

Ma'rib, Yemen
1952

As Jamil and Murad walked toward the temple's entry, Jamil's grip tightened on the bag in his hand. There was an etched pattern branded on one side. Despite his expertise, the significance of the enigmatic design only added to its mystique, its meaning concealed in the annals of time. The cream-colored leather was in excellent condition, considering that it might be three millennia old. There were no signs of cracking. No severe deterioration visible in the tanned antelope hide—just a general shrinking and stiffness caused by centuries of drying.

To be the first—at least one of the first—to hold this pouch after hundreds, maybe thousands, of years sent shivers down Jamil's spine. It was the same sense of wonder that had attracted him to archaeology in the beginning. When he was seventeen, he'd cradled a scarab amulet that may once have been touched by Pharaoh Djer. He was hooked.

His eager eyes searched inside the pouch again and refused to release their hold on the ring.

The diamond was as radiant as the sun reflecting off the sacred waters of the Nile. It sparkled and winked despite its narrow confines. The jewel was enormous. A frown clouded Jamil's face. What if it's just a white topaz? Not possible. If anyone had worn a topaz, it would have gotten scratched and lost some of its sparkle. This had to be a diamond. If so, it would still be remarkable and quite valuable. Jamil couldn't imagine Solomon using an inferior stone. It had to be. He tentatively reached into the bag. As his fingers encountered the ring, an electrifying shock coursed through his body, and he jerked his hand back, gasping. Something extraordinary had just occurred.

When he regained his composure, he noticed Murad studying him, his expression revealing a hint of recognition and amusement. A silent exchange passed between them, filled with unspoken knowledge.

His hand instinctively found the grip of his revolver, knuckles white with tension.

Murad pivoted and resumed walking.

Is he strutting? Jamil pondered, analyzing Murad's stature. I will handle him when the time is right. Caution was necessary, for the locals were quick and formidable with their jambiyas—curved daggers ever-present and at the ready. A plan was forming in Jamil's mind. He didn't doubt the outcome of their inevitable confrontation.

Murad showed the way down the steps, past the eight massive pillars, and through the entrance into the temple. Ancient stairs led to lower levels of the dig and the south arcade. The columns bore the scars of long-lost bronze plaques, victims of looters.

Jamil's hands shook with a heady mix of anticipation and anxiety. How could the centuries of treasure hunters have missed such a treasure? Above the ancient flagstone staircase, there was a series of false windows with intricate stone latticework. Murad pointed at a niche between the massive stone blocks forming the foundation. A small corner of one of those colossal foundation blocks had broken off, creating a niche.

"Find here," Murad said as he pointed to the cavity. "Bag here."

Suppressing a jubilant grin, Jamil raised his bushy eyebrows. Deliberately concealing his excitement. Jamil worried he would jeopardize everything if he didn't keep a straight face. Fallbright had already associated this level of the dig with the 10 Century B.C. That was the level just above the ancient Sabaean inscriptions on the foundation's cornerstone. The current theory about Solomon's reign dated it as 970-951 B.C.

The location where Murad had discovered the ring was perfect. Jamil issued Murad a final, ominous warning, "If you ever try that again." His hand slid serpent-like for his weapon, then pointed his jutting jaw at the digger. "I have warned you."

Several other workers gathered around, drawn by the commotion. Jamil turned and glared at the two in front. They had influence with the others. He asked, "Does anyone else have items they have discovered but not reported?" The one who always wore a black keffiyeh and was missing the little finger on his right hand turned and gazed at the crowd. Then he looked back and shook his head. No one else stepped forward or spoke. Jamil sent them all back to work with an empty threat. If he shot anyone, it would undoubtedly draw too much attention from the authorities at the Yemeni King's court in Sanaa. He especially wanted no more attention drawn to this find that had already resulted from his confronting Murad. Mentioning a small reward for any artifacts found should help deter further thefts, and the excitement would distract.

"Theft from this dig is a crime. If I catch you stealing, I will punish you. However, I understand times are hard. So, from today forward, I will pay baksheesh for any artifact you find—one zakat for any item you discover. But you must not move it from the place you find it. Call your foreman. He will record your find and report it to the paymaster. If you do move it, you will receive nothing. Do you understand? Nothing!"

The diggers nodded eagerly and murmured approvingly.

"Now get back to work! In the future, if I catch anyone stealing any other artifacts from this dig, I will take great pleasure in shooting you on the spot!"

The diggers looked away and found that they had urgent business elsewhere. Jamil smirked when no one seemed interested in testing his resolve or his marksmanship. They all slinked away. All of them except one—Murad stood his ground and watched.

Jamil's gaze remained fixed on Murad, who alone defied his authority, his eyes harboring secrets. A promise of reckoning hung between them

"Tahiem, watch these thieving Arabs," Jamil raised his voice while addressing his assistant overseer. "The success of this excavation could mean steady work for us for many seasons—no more thefts. Understand? If their king hears about any trouble here, he will cancel his permission to dig. Then will send us packing. I'm holding you responsible. I will send you back to Cairo with no bonus. I don't care who your cousin is. Keep your eyes open!"

"I will not fail," Tahiem stammered.

"Don't you mean you will not fail again?" Jamil did his best to hide his disgust. "Very well. But keep a sharp eye. I will notify the foremen and the paymaster about the baksheesh payments."

Jamil turned and stalked toward the makeshift storeroom, where they kept all the unearthed artifacts. He needed to study this new treasure. The tingle he felt when he touched it made his brain race. With his awareness heightened, he put together the puzzle pieces in rapid succession. Fallbright had already declared that level tenth century BCE. The locals called this ruin "the Sanctuary of the Queen of Sheba." The size and stunning beauty of the ring and everything else pointed to only one conclusion. This magnificent ring had to be Solomon's Seal. But he needed confirmation. As soon as possible. Overwhelmed by the prospect of wealth and global recognition, Jamil grinned at the thought that his name might soon eclipse Howard Carter's. He mulled over the place where he would build his estate. Perhaps along the Nile above Giza. No! He decided it had to be Alexandria. He loved the coast of the Mediterranean.

Putting on a stern face, he waved aside the guard who stood at the entrance of the artifact storeroom. "You can take a break. I will add this pottery shard to the artifact inventory. Be back here in ten minutes."

When Jamil put his hand on the doorknob, he felt the tiny hairs on the back of his neck standing at attention. He turned and surveyed the dig. Someone is watching.

.

CHAPTER THREE
LEGENDS

"Oh, the mother of Yemen, the beloved Queen of Sheba You are the root of our civilization. You who gives life and brings peace, The Mother of Yemen"

Traditional Yemeni Song

Ma'rib, Yemen
1952

Jamil Ahmed stepped into the dimly lit artifact storage building. His every move marked by a sense of unease. As the door closed behind him, he leaned against it, flipped on the lights, and let out a ragged breath. It was Murad. Who else could it be? He must have touched the ring. He knows! The weight of the realization clenched Jamil's jaw, his mind racing to plan. He needed to deal with Murad.

As his eyes adjusted to the dim light, a sudden sensation against his boot sent a shiver up his spine. Startled, he glanced down spotting a black scorpion scuttling into the shadows. Panic momentarily gripped him, and he jerked his foot away. Then calmed. These fat-tailed demons were not nearly as lethal as the green deathstalkers back home.

Wiping sweat from his brow, he turned his attention to the task at hand—he needed to create a diversion in the meticulous cataloging system. He surveyed the cramped room. His thoughts cursing the low ceiling that seemed to press down upon him, the relentless heat intensifying his discomfort.

"They built this place for puny Arabs, not for normal-sized people," Jamil grumbled.

Stacks of latex impressions of inscriptions gathered dust in one corner. The team archived smaller bone and pottery fragments, along with a smattering of coins, alphabetically in brown string closure envelopes. A row of larger statues lined one wall, while miniature statuettes, some made of bronze, others of stone, stood on the shelves against the back wall. Bones, pottery, larger fragments, and eating utensils sat nearby. For a moment, he rested his eyes on his favorite item they had uncovered, momentarily soothing his anxiety. It was a translucent bust of a young woman with a Mona Lisa smile. Lenard Jones affectionately dubbed her "Miriam". The Arabs insisted she was "Aliya," the Queen of the Sabaean Empire.

Seeing her, a faint smile crossed Jamil's lips. Despite feeling confined and tyrannized by the heat, the musty scent of the Sabaean artifacts was a tantalizing reminder of the wealth they represented. It was also a poignant testament to Murad's discovery. Retrieving the small leather pouch from his pocket, he marveled at the ancient, shrunken leather's velvety texture. Gingerly, he retrieved the prized possession, and the moment it contacted his fingertips, chaos erupted in his mind.

A cyclone of thoughts swirled in a maddening vortex, making concentration difficult. Jamil sank into a chair at a nearby desk, studying the mysterious ring. Could this be Solomon's Seal? Had Queen Aliya herself once worn it? His heart raced as he blinked, struggling to regain focus. Despite chewing khat that morning, a substance known to heighten his senses, his mind was now engulfed in a fog of confusion. Alarmed, he hastily returned the ring to its pouch. When he did, relief washed over him. His thoughts ratcheted back a few notches.

After some thundering heartbeats, he withdrew an envelope. There was no way he would report this extraordinary discovery. Instead, he retrieved a broken shard of pottery from his pocket. Then scrutinized it for a moment, placed it in a numbered envelope, and meticulously recorded its size and shape on the outside. He also filled out an inventory card, then sat in a mental haze, gazing at the card.

His mind drifted to Ethiopian claims that the Queen of Sheba ruled from their side of the Red Sea. But everyone in Yemen asserted that the Queen of Sheba was their esteemed ancestor, Aliya al Sharih. Ascending to the throne after her husband's passing. The sparse records of their excavation had unearthed so far claimed she had ruled with integrity and wisdom for a little more than two decades.

El Sharih Yahdhib called himself the Unifier of the Tribes. His enemies knew him as The Suppressor. But her subjects held Queen Aliya in great awe. They loved and respected her, appreciating her generosity and admiring her steady hand in ruling, surpassing the grace of her late husband.

The locals believed Aliya went to Jerusalem to meet the illustrious King Solomon. She returned with a determination to construct a temple rivaling the one she had witnessed in that holy city.

Several minutes slipped away. Jamil finally completed his ruse with the envelope and inventory card. Suddenly, a loud noise outside jolted him. He pulled the drawstring tight on the precious pouch and stuffed it in his pocket. Outside, he shielded his eyes from the punishing sun and scanned his surroundings. As usual, diggers carried baskets of sand on their heads to the dumping site. The daily routines were on track. Weren't they?

Up the hill, beyond the wadi that meandered into the vast Rub' al-Khali desert, the ancient five-storied apartments of Ma'rib rose into view. When he squinted, the skyline reminded him of Cairo, leaving him in awe of the ancients' ability to erect towering edifices with nothing but mud bricks.

Everything looked normal. But since Jamil had taken possession of the ring, nothing felt quite right. Murad's peculiar behavior, the strange sensations Jamil felt every time he touched it, and now unexplained noises. I need to put it in a safe place. His heart pounded like a galloping camel as he hurried across the compound toward his living quarters. Along the way, he berated a digger, shouting, "Get back to work!" The man scurried away like a startled scorpion exposed to the harsh sun, as if worried Jamil might shoot.

Inside his cramped room, a semblance of security washed over him as he retrieved the pouch from his pocket, pouring its contents onto his bed. Using his pencil to pick it up. He examined it from every angle. Tarnish marred the silver shank, while the gold head, hazed by the ages, formed a multi-pointed sunburst. In the center of the sunburst, a scintillating diamond sparkled. Wiping away the accumulated dust with his handkerchief, he noticed smaller green gems near the tip of each point, reminiscent of emeralds. As he scrutinized the ancient artifact more closely, a faint inscription emerged.

It was difficult to decipher because of the subdued lighting and the encrusted tarnish of centuries. But the inscription appeared to be Hebrew. The implications of a Hebrew inscription inside a ring found at the Queen of Sheba's capital sent a shiver down his spine. He flipped the precious relic back over. When he counted, he found twelve points. Twelve points? Twelve tribes!

It suddenly clicked in Jamil's mind, and he gasped. The design was not a sunburst but a 12-pointed star, composed of four overlapping equilateral triangles, forming a double Star of David. "Could this be right?" he murmured.

Suspicions of a hoax gnawed at him. Despite his doubts, he could not deny the inexplicable sensations that coursed through his mind whenever he touched the ring. There was one problem. Many Seal legends mentioned a pentagram, not a twelve-pointed star. To be sure, legends often distorted details. Besides, there were just too many clues seemed to affirm that the Queen of Sheba had indeed ruled her empire from Ma'rib.

One legend forced its way into mind. Jamil stopped short. It spoke of a blessing and a curse tied to the Seal. Trouble would plague those who sought to steal its power, while those with noble hearts would receive blessings. Jamil reasoned with himself - what could be more noble than ensuring the recognition of the Egyptian workers' achievements? Hadn't they crafted the Seal in the Middle East for people from the Middle East? A triumphant smile curved his lips as he envisioned the tales he would recount in the days, no, the years, to come.

Regardless, he could not continue carrying such a valuable object around in his pocket.

A knock on the door startled him. Panic surging as he scanned the room for a hiding place. Finding none better, he dropped the ring into yesterday's mug of thick Arabica coffee, still perched on the dresser. It vanished into the murky liquid. Hidden from prying eyes. Satisfied, he stuffed the pouch in his pocket, turned, and opened the door.

CHAPTER FOUR
ALL THAT GLITTERS

"This life is hard. It's even harder when you're stupid."
Jackie Brown

Ma'rib, Yemen
1952

Jamil Ahmed fixed a piercing gaze on Murad Buckshan, whose hand casually rested on his jambiya—an emblem of status and power in Yemen. Murad's glistened in the harsh sunlight. The jambiya, a symbol of a boy's transition into manhood, was an opulent dagger adorned with intricate designs, usually unsheathed only in times of peril or during festive celebrations.

When Jamil's eyes fell on Murad's ornate knife, his eyebrows shot up in incredulity. It didn't fit. How could a mere laborer afford a weapon with a handle carved from rhino horn and a sheath adorned in silver? Something was amiss, and his suspicion deepened when he noticed the unnatural smoothness of Murad's hand. How had he missed these inconsistencies before? Murad's sly smirk only deepened Jamil's unease. Swallowing hard, Jamil moistened his dry lips, his thick fingers unconsciously wiping his mouth and chin. "Yes?"

"Mr. Jones wants to see you at the Temple," Murad replied casually, his tone indifferent.

A parched sensation gripped Jamil's mouth. "Why does he want to see me?" he asked, his voice strained.

Murad shrugged, leaving Jamil to grapple with his escalating anxiety. "Tell him I'll be there soon. I have a matter to attend to first. I'll come right after that," Jamil stammered, his words tumbling out in haste.

As he closed the door, Jamil's eyes darted to the cup of coffee, his secret still safely hidden within. But he knew he couldn't stay at the dig any longer; he needed to leave without arousing suspicion. If he left without a valid reason, Mr. Jones would certainly suspect foul play. "I must get the ring to someone who can confirm its authenticity," he muttered. Recalling the expedition physician's warning, he smiled. That just might work, he mused.

Stepping out into the blistering sunlight, Jamil shielded his eyes. The relentless sun blazed overhead. Although spring had arrived in the Yemeni highlands, the heat was already oppressive. The coming summer's heat would be brutal. The silver lining was that the excavation season would conclude soon, well before the furnace-like temperatures of summer descended.

Jamil headed to the kitchen and paused briefly to fill his canteen. He dipped it in the barrel of questionable water standing outside the back door. Once it was full, he took a few quick swigs. Then he hurried on his way to Mr. Jones. While he looked for his boss, he watched for Murad. A wave of relief washed over him when he spotted Mr. Jones at the surveyor's transit aimed at the Temple's pillars at the entrance.

To Jamil's right, dozens of Yemeni men and boys carried away baskets of coarse sand on their heads, like ants moving a mountain. They deposited their loads in a pile overlooking the wadi that stretched between the temple complex and the ancient city of Ma'rib. From his vantage point, the ravaged ancient buildings appeared even taller than their five stories. The scene resembled a post-apocalyptic Manhattan perched on a hill.

Lenard Jones, president of the American Anthropological Trust, incongruously looked more like a cowboy than the head of a research foundation. In his early thirties, he sported a Colt 45 slung low on his right hip. He wore a folded back checkered scarf. The traditional Arab head covering, typically worn to protect against the sun, held in place with a braided headband. One reporter had recently described him as America's Lawrence of Arabia. It was strange, but up to that moment, Jamil had had a genuine affection for the young man. But as he approached, he realized that here was just another westerner poised to claim glory and fortune. But not if Jamil could make a clean getaway. He drained the last of the canteen.

"Yes, sir, Mr. Jones," he said, feigning nonchalance. "Murad said you needed me?"

Jones an inquisitive eyebrow, a quizzical expression in his eyes. "Pardon me?" he queried, cocking his head to one side.

Jamil's heart sank as he panicked. "Never mind," he muttered. As he spun to leave, he felt a hand on his forearm stopping him.

"Jamil," Jones said, his grip firm, turning Jamil back toward him.

When Jamil glared down at his hand, Jones released the beefy arm and stepped back. Looking uncomfortable, the American smiled nervously up at Jamil, and asked, "While you are here, may I ask you a question?"

Jamil softened his scowl, calmed himself, and scanned the surroundings for any glimpse of Murad. Seeing none, he replied cautiously, "Go ahead."

Jones asked, "Are you aware of our other project—cataloging manuscripts in the Sinai?"

Jamil nodded, his mind racing furiously, "My cousin, Kadir, is part of the staff at St. Catherine's. That's how I found out about this expedition and contacted you." Jamil saw movement over Jones' right shoulder and glanced at a passing worker. It wasn't Murad. Where is that vermin?

Jones seemed satisfied, but his tone shifted subtly. "I'm glad you reminded me of your connection at St. Catherine's. Yesterday, I sent the courier back prematurely. I hadn't received word yet about the trouble brewing with the King."

Curiosity piqued within Jamil. "What trouble?" he asked.

"His cousin is the local head-man; you've met him, I think."

"Yes, Nabeel Ibn Khaldun? I don't trust him," Jamil replied.

Jones nodded in agreement. "Neither do I. In fact, I've heard a rumor that he's been giving negative reports to the king. I have to send someone to St. Catherine's with a message about how shaky the political situation has gotten. I need someone I can trust and who understands the gravity of the situation. Would you mind going?" Jones asked, a glimmer of hope flickering in his eyes.

Surprised by his good fortune, Jamil fought to contain his excitement. "You want me to leave the dig?" he asked, careful not to sound too eager.

"Yes, this is most urgent," Jones said. "The dig is well in hand. Your assistant can manage, can't he?"

Jamil's mind revved into high gear, an internal motor fueled by both anticipation and apprehension. He berated himself for drinking the tainted water. The looming specter of dysentery gnawed at him. But a glimmer of hope encouraged him that maybe he wouldn't get sick. But in a moment of clarity, he realized that either way, he might elude Murad if he could just leave. Masking his enthusiasm behind a façade of calm, he said, "Ghadi is a good man. That's precisely why I hired him. For the last six months, he has walked in my shadow every day. I have trained him well. He can handle things." Then he added, "Of course, he doesn't have my years of experience. But he will do."

Jones, sporting a playful glint in his eye, stroked his chin, "Perhaps I should send Ghadi. He's Egyptian too, isn't he?"

Jamil, on the verge of protest, paused. Jones's humor was a surprising twist in the conversation.

Jones laughed. "I was joking. Ghadi will do just fine. I'll have Dr. Fallbright keep an eye on him. In the morning, leave for Aden. Just be sure to return promptly."

Jamil hurried back to his quarters and stopped by Ghadi's room. "Ghadi, Mr. Jones asked me to return to the Sinai with an urgent message. I will leave in the morning. After that episode with that pilfering Murad Buckshan, I want you to keep a close eye on him."

Ghadi nodded in agreement. "I will. But why not just fire him?"

Jamil weighed his response, understanding the complexities of the situation. "If you must. But we don't want trouble with the locals. The boss tells me that there are already negative reports circulating. Besides, times are hard, and he has a family to support. How about this? Early tomorrow morning, put him on the job of cleaning the latrine. It's nasty work. See how he does."

"Good idea," Ghadi winked. "Maybe he'll just quit."

"Maybe, but for the first couple of hours, keep a close eye. I want him to pay for what he tried to do."

"I will see to it. By the way, I hope you didn't drink any of the water I saw you put in your canteen."

Jamil feigned ignorance, his expression a mask of innocence. "Why do you ask?"

"Weren't you there when the doctor warned us about the local water?" Ghadi pressed.

Jamil frowned and shook his head, pretending confusion. "I don't remember that."

"I thought sure you were there. Anyway, he informed us that those of us who are not native to this area and not accustomed to the local bacteria will probably contract dysentery."

Jamil grimaced. "Wonderful."

“Did you drink it?” Ghadi asked, concern furrowing his brow. "Are you feeling okay?"

“I am right now. But look at this.” Jamil uncorked his canteen and turned it upside down. Two drops dribbled out. “I’m an idiot.” He’s buying this. I should be an actor.

He turned to leave and heard Ghadi call after him, “Rinse it out with boiling water, my friend. Maybe it’s not too late.”

Rushing back to his room, Jamil found the door ajar that he’d left tightly shut. When he burst into the room and looked around, he could see that someone had searched his belongings. His heart stopped. It had to be Murad! He rushed to the dresser, grabbed the cup, and fished out the ring with his pencil. Relief washed over him as he plopped on the bed and wiped off the coffee residue. He made sure he did not allow his skin to come in contact. He was still wary of the mysterious artifact, unsure of why or how it was affecting him.

Surprised and pleased, he saw that the coffee’s acidic contents had worked its magic, removing the silver and gold tarnish. The center stone flashed and glittered. It was exquisite. The gleaming gold of the star contrasted with the diamond. The other stones were a gorgeous green. In a lesser treasure, each could have been the centerpiece. It was an stunning marvel. Jamil couldn’t help but smile, returning the artifact to the pouch, pocketed it, and started to pack his travel bag.

CHAPTER FIVE
EGYPTIAN CHARIOT

"The feelings that hurt most, the emotions that sting most, are those that are absurd—The longing for impossible things, precisely because they are impossible. And nostalgia for what never was."
Fernando Pessoa

Sinai Peninsula, Egypt
Present

Rahm Khalidi surfaced, removed his mask and snorkel tube, then waded toward the beach. He found a refuge in the waters of the Red Sea from the harsh realities that plagued life in Palestine's West Bank.

Dive equipment in hand, he waded ashore as his wetsuit shed water. Obeying gravity, salty rivulets traced their way back into the sea.

Lulled by the gentle lapping of Gulf of Aqaba waves, Rahm made his way to the beachside showers, a choreographed ritual that felt like a sacred dance. He cleansed his fins, snorkel, and facemask of the briny remnants of the deep blue, the symphony of seawater and sunlight composing a peaceful overture.

As he toweled off, he turned and faced the Gulf. His gaze fixated on a windsurfer navigating the tumultuous waves, a portrait of grim determination hanging on to his sail for dear life. His craft raced ahead of an unforgiving southwesterly wind. Waves churned, their whitecaps serving as a reminder of the sea's unforgiving might. In the distance, a black cigarette boat tore through the morning chop. Its high-speed race threatening to break the spines of its hapless passengers.

Rahm preferred the view beneath the waves and was glad he had gotten into the water early. His mission each morning was to be out of the water before the crazies took over. Activity on the surface would only pick up as the temp warmed. He wove his way through the shore's forest of thatched shade umbrellas. The sand, still warm from the heat of the previous day, felt good underfoot. Stepping onto the sidewalk, he brushed off the sand, slipped on sandals, and dried his buzz-cut hair.

A contented smile found its way to his face. He thought of his favorite author, imagining that Hemingway, too, would find solace in Nuweiba's coastal haven.

The breeze carried an earthy scent of brine, the sharp tang of iodine, and a hint of kelp mingled in the air. To his left, the Hejaz Mountains on the Saudi coast, only ten miles away, tugged at something deep inside. He loved this view of the Gulf and wondered why this place was so magnetic and why the Hilton had selected a south-facing beach. It was certainly beautiful here.

Up the hill to his right, he could see the majestic peaks of the coastal range of the Sinai Mountains. The pass that led toward the interior and south to Dahab, and Sharm el-Sheik, split the range.

His focus pivoted back to the Saudi coast. Maybe the attraction he felt was genetic, like the impulse felt by salmon. His Khalidi bloodline traced its roots to the Saudi Kingdom's Eastern Province. Or maybe it was religious. His mother's faith had immigrated from there. Regardless, the caress of waves on both shores whispered secrets of Arabia, secrets Rahm found difficult to ignore.

Absentmindedly, he unzipped the front of his wetsuit. Far enough for his fingers to follow an involuntary compulsion. They found the silver chain around his neck and closed his eyes in a moment of silent contemplation.

Ramallah
Three years earlier

Rahm stood over the bed and watched his mother. Her peaceful dozing at odds with the emotions that swirled within him. It was already 11:30. She hadn't stirred all morning.

"Mama," he whispered softly, "I have your breakfast."

She turned away and waved weakly. "Not hungry," her voice so low it was barely audible.

"Please Mama. You need to eat something. I made your favorite scrambled eggs with goat cheese."

She kept her back to him. "I don't feel like eating."

"You need to keep up your strength."

With a resigned sigh, she relented, "Leave it on the nightstand."

"That's what you said about last night's dinner."

"What's the point? I have nothing to live for."

"You have me," Rahm said.

She turned back and looked up at him, her eyes puffy and red. "They've taken everything. "Your father, and mine too, and now they have taken the villa."

"But—" Rahm began, unable to quell the rising tide of helplessness.

She reached up and held the key and silver chain in his face. "Take it! Promise you will return."

"But, Mama, they plowed it down. It's gone."

"The land is ours. Promise me."

He knew that reasoning with her, was useless. He tried anyway. What else could he do? "How can a person return to something that doesn't even exist anymore? All that's there is the wall. They won't even let me near it."

She held up the key and chain and shook it. "Swear it."

Rahm wiped a single tear from his eye and reached out to accept its weight.

She pulled it back, "Promise me you will return to our land."

Taking it and slipping the chain over his head, he let it hang around his neck. "On my father's grave," he vowed.

She turned over and waved him away. "Please go. I want to rest."

When the ambulance took her to the hospital that afternoon, the eggs were still on the nightstand. By the next morning, his mother was gone.

Nuweiba
Present

Rahm pulled on the chain until the ancient key was in his hand. He kissed it reverently, then put it back inside his wet suit. He looked up, sighed, and headed toward their room.

When he rounded the corner, he discovered Professor Schwalm stepping through their casita's sliding door to the patio. The older man waved.

"What?" Rahm yelled.

"Hurry! I want you to see this."

Schwalm, known for his stoic demeanor, seldom got excited. Many mistook the history teacher's calm exterior for coldness. But Rahm knew it had more to do with his Mennonite gravitas. That upbringing left him reserved to the point of appearing aloof. But Rahm had never met anyone with a warmer heart.

When Rahm enrolled as a freshman, he'd met the Professor at the Friends School in Ramallah. Schwalm had just moved to the West Bank from the States and was teaching history and joked that they were both freshmen.

The Professor's gracious attitude and credentials immediately impressed Rahm. Despite their age difference, over the next four years, a friendship grew between them. When Rahm applied to the American University of Beirut, the Professor helped him locate and apply for scholarships. Rahm applied for five scholarships and was awarded four of them. The Professor chipped in and covered the shortfall himself.

"Why all the excitement, Professor?" he called out as he jogged up to their patio where the Professor sat.

Schwalm stroked his meticulously trimmed beard with his age-spotted hand. "For years, I have wanted to visit St. Catherine's Monastery to see some of their biblical manuscripts, climb Mount Sinai, and watch the sunrise from the top. So, this latest finding has me baffled."

Rahm's attention wandered momentarily. His gaze drifted toward the palm fronds waving near the Coral Resort's lobby. Its graceful curve, brilliant white by day, had earlier glowed rosy-orange in the sweet light of dawn. The property was well-named—the Hilton Coral Resort.

The stunning sunrise took his breath away. The painted canvas of the sky tells me something is right with the world. No matter what they're like in the West Bank. "Vitamin Sea," he mumbled.

"Pardon me?" Schwalm asked.

"Talking to myself."

"We have our best conversations that way," Schwalm said.

"My mother said that it was fine to talk to yourself, even to answer. But if you ever ask, 'What did you say?' then they come and take you away."

The poolside sound system played an old Simon and Garfunkel song. Its haunting lyrics striped the gears in his head. Synapses sparked, and an anguished memory burned through gray matter. His mother rocked herself to the rhythm of that song and wept over the theft of their home in Safa. In a weird amalgam, that pain mingled with the enchantment of the sun's warmth on his face. Despite the jangling dissonance, he closed his eyes to soak up the moment like a father hearing his child's first prayer.

Schwalm cleared his throat, "As I said, this is puzzling."

"What?" Rahm turned, suddenly curious. "What is it, Professor?"

Schwalm held up his iPad and pointed. "Last night, I found this web page. It says that there is a granite pillar here in Nuweiba. They date it from the reign of King Solomon to mark Nuweiba Beach as the site of the Red Sea crossing during the Exodus. It alleges that at one time, there were two pillars. One here in Egypt and the other on the Saudi side."

Rahm clicked his tongue in skepticism. Dismissing the tale as another online fabrication. "Fairy tales! Haven't you always said we can't believe most of what you read online?"

The smile lines around Schwalm's eyes scrunched up. "Disregard those old lectures. While you were diving, I went for a stroll along the beach searching for the pillar."

"You found it?"

"No, I did not." Schwalm shook his head.

Rahm, seizing the opportunity for playful banter, asked, "What is so thrilling," Rahm chuckled, "about a non-existent pillar? Even if it's alleged to have been placed by Prophet Sulayman." He relished the opportunity to challenge the Professor's vast knowledge, enriched by his doctoral studies in history.

Schwalm's grin remained steadfast. "I have wanted to make this trip to St. Catherine's for many years because Moses received the Ten Commandments at Mt. Sinai. But there's a twist." Schwalm's forehead furrowed as his eyes squinted.

"Intriguing," Rahm responded, his attention fully captured. "What's the twist?"

"Well, if there is really a pillar here in Nuweiba marking the Exodus crossing." Schwalm pointed toward the mountains beyond the Gulf, his eyes alight with excitement. "Then Mount Sinai and the split rock might well be over there."

Rahm couldn't understand why the Professor was so consumed with that rock. "Really?" Rahm started putting his wetsuit back on, "This is a sign. There is clearly no need for this outing." A big grin split his stubble. "It must be Allah's will that I go back to diving the reef."

At that moment, a middle-aged Bedouin man hurried up to them from the direction of the lobby. Between gasping breaths, he said, "Zhe trip to monastery leave soon. Five minute early today. Must hurry! Zhe van she not wait."

Schwalm grabbed his green Oregon Ducks backpack and said, "Rahm, please don't get sidetracked by your love of diving. This revelation makes our trip even more tantalizing. Let's go."

Rahm stripped off his wet suit. The exquisite silver chain hung around his neck. Suspended from its elegance was that fatigued skeleton key, the kind that opened heavy doors. Toweling off, he shrugged on a black t-shirt that showed a swimmer diving into the water. The message below the diver in bold red letters stated, "I Parted the Red Sea."

CHAPTER SIX
AL-NAKBA

"The only thing worse than being blind
is having sight but no vision."
Helen Keller

Nuweiba, Egypt
Present

Rahm slipped his favorite khaki shirt over his thick shoulders, pulled on the new jeans he'd bought for the trip, then stepped into his boots. As he tied his laces, one broke. "You go ahead, Professor. I'll catch up." He dug around in his red backpack for the spare laces he brought along. They were a small but an essential part of the toolkit he carried in anticipation of life's unpredictable twists. When he finished relacing, he locked the doors and hurried after Schwalm, who was favoring his left knee again. Rahm's brow furrowed. We'll need to hire a camel to climb to the summit of Jabal al Musa from the monastery below.

When they got to the lobby, a sleek white van with the Hilton logo emblazoned on the door sat idling, motor purring.

Abdullah, the driver, grinned as he loaded the luggage into the van with practiced ease. He measured only five feet tall, even with his Tony Lama cowboy boots. Muscular, he made quick work of the bags.

When he finished, he swept his hand toward the van and bowed low. "Who enters fine Egyptian chariot first?"

Schwalm moved toward the open door, favoring his left leg. Rahm hurried over to assist. His gaze narrowing with concern as he noticed his friend looking sickly, jaundiced even. We might need more than a camel for what's ahead.

Schwalm's gaunt frame slid into the seat behind the driver. He scowled at Rahm. "I'm old. But not an invalid. Not yet, anyway." Then smiled and nodded. "But thank you."

Rahm poised to follow, stopped short when he heard a voice.

"Good morning! My name is Chaim, and this is Adi." An Israeli man wearing a black kippah approached the van. His hands featured two cabalistic rings. Arriving, he pointed at the third-row bench seat. "We can sit back there."

Rahm backed away to give him room. He spied the Israeli's companion, a beautiful blonde woman. Rahm guessed her to be Israeli, too, from her Star of David necklace. Rahm's eyes widened as she climbed in after Chaim and sat next to him.

Abdullah picked up the bags the couple had dropped and repeated his loading routine.

Meanwhile, Rahm studied the mismatched pair. He had seen them at the resort acting like honeymooning newlyweds, but they seemed an odd match. She looked at least a decade older than the man.

The night before, Rahm had listened to the woman bark orders at the man like a drill sergeant. He had obeyed like a lapdog. As Rahm had listened to the exchange, every journalistic instinct inside his head tingled.

Rahm's expression hardened. Something is not right.

"Are you coming?"

Schwalm motioned for him to get into the van.

Rahm shook his head as his scarred right hand drifted to the center of his chest. He reached inside his shirt, and his fingers found what they sought. Tugging at the key, Rahm turned away.

Moments later, he felt a tap on his shoulder. He turned to see the white-haired professor's worried expression.

"Rahm, what is the problem?" His voice carried genuine concern.

Rahm looked over his shoulder and then back at his friend. "I'm not traveling with them."

"The Israelis?" Schwalm's confusion evident.

"That's right."

"But you've been staying at the same hotel."

"That's different."

Schwalm's shoulders slumped, "How?"

"In my experience," bitterness seeping into his tone, "Israelis breathe death and mayhem. I won't be forced to inhale it."

"There's Jewish blood in your veins," Schwalm countered gently. "What is troubling you about those two?"

"Why do Israelis hate us so much?" Rahm asked. "For centuries, we lived together in the land, Jews and Arabs, Muslims, Druze, and Christians. Then 1948 happened, and everything changed."

Schwalm nodded, acknowledging the history. "In those days, people saw the others as neighbors. Right?"

"Yes. My mother's grandfather was a Jew. He and his Arab neighbors helped each other and celebrated each other's weddings and birthdays. His best friend was the imam at the local mosque. When he commented about Israeli history since 1948, he said, 'We are living by the sword.' My father's grandfather was a devout Muslim. When he was dying from an Israeli bullet, he kept asking why Jews shot him when they had always supported each other. He called Israel's becoming a nation a disaster."

Profound sadness lingered in Schwalm's eyes. a shared grief for a world fractured by hatred and fear. The echoes of history reverberated in Rahm's words, painting a vivid picture of a land scarred by conflict, where neighbors turned enemies, and humanity was lost amidst the rubble of broken promises and shattered lives. "Al-Nakba, right? Then why don't people go back to viewing everyone else as neighbors rather than as enemies? Has it ever occurred to you that what Israelis suffer from is not hate but fear?"

Rahm's jaws clenched, his hands trembling with suppressed rage. "Israeli settlers steal our land. Their army guns down our youth and elders. They abuse us, occupy our land, and steal our water. They killed my father, my grandfather, and my great-grandfather. I can't do it. I won't ride with them!"

CHAPTER SEVEN
PRAYER IS BETTER THAN SLEEP

"King Solomon gave the Queen of Sheba all she desired and asked for, besides what he had given her out of his royal bounty. Then she left and returned with her retinue to her own country."
1 Kings 10:13

Ma'rib, Yemen
1952

Under the tapestry of a million shimmering stars, the desert night embraced silence as thick as secrets. Despite how warm it had been that afternoon, at this late hour, Murad shivered in the night air.

He counted on the darkness to cloak his movements. Few dared to wander in the murky small hours for fear of encountering the Arabian cobra. Yet, there was Jamil Ahmed scurrying toward the latrine. His guts were probably churning. The kitchen's tainted water was having its expected result.

Murad leaned into the shadows by the artifact storehouse and held as still as death.

"Who's there? What are you doing?" Jamil demanded. His voice etched with suspicion.

Murad stepped into the dim starlit, meeting Jamil's accusing tone head on. "Just taking a walk."

"You did not answer my question," Jamil Ahmed pressed, his figure looming. "I cannot allow you to go roaming around the Queen's Temple in the middle of the night. What do you think you're doing out here?"

Murad Buckshan looked at the ground in silence. He contemplated eliminating the brutish overseer for good. But he needed information. Where had the big Egyptian had hidden the Seal? Jamil was fortunate. Murad was under strict orders from King Hamid to keep a low profile.

With a faint smile, he looked up at Jamil, "As the muezzin says, 'Prayer is better than sleep.' "

"It's two in the morning." Jamil's skepticism hung heavy in the air. "You cannot ask me to believe you are out here, praying."

"Have you never had a sleepless night when the moon is full like this?" Murad gestured at the sky.

"Listen, you little jackal," Jamil reached for his low-slung holster, "I know you were in my room. I should. . ."

In the stillness, Jamil's belly rumbled a loud complaint. His eyes widened, fear flickering within them, and he shot a quick glance toward the latrine. "I am watching you!" he warned, his voice a mere growl before he staggered away, the discomfort evident in his gait

And I am watching you. Murad's eyes narrowed. You shouldn't have tried that ruse with the water!

The next morning, Murad's expectations turned into reality when Taheem Ghadi, Jamil's assistant, called for the doctor. "Jamil is very sick. He has a terrible fever. Please come."

Doctor Cunningham's grim-faced diagnosis was, "A severe case of dysentery. He needs better care than I can give him here. I should send him to Aden for intravenous fluid replacement. He's taken some antibiotics and salt pills to treat the fever. But if he doesn't get better care, his condition could be fatal."

Turning to the director, he asked, "What do you say, Jones?"

"Bring a truck," Lenard Jones said to his driver, concern furrowing his brow. "But get back here as soon as possible."

The doctor rested his hands on Jamil's slumped shoulders. He looked into the Egyptian's watery eyes, "Jamil, be sure to drink lots of fluids, understand? And for God's sake, take a bath!"

Mr. Jones reassured Jamil, "The fastest way to get to St. Catherine's is through Aden, anyway. Don't worry. As soon as you are well, you can leave for St. Catherine's on the next boat. Return here as soon as you have delivered these," he handed Jamil three letters.

Jamil gave Jones a weak smile and nodded. With the doctor's help, he headed for the green and black Dodge Power Wagon that would take him to Aden.

As Jamil struggled to climb into the truck's cab, Murad saw the coveted pouch's drawstring protruding from Jamil's pocket.

He was about to follow when he heard Ghadi shout, "Buckshan! Grab a bucket and follow me."

He feigned compliance. "Yes, sir. There are buckets in the toolshed. I'll be right back." He had no intention of losing track of Jamil or the treasure. Stealth and patience would be his allies, just as they had always been in this dangerous game of secrets and ambition.

Aden, Yemen

Murad Buckshan arrived just in time to see Jamil stagger into Aden's Republic Hospital and watch the Dodge pull away.

When he was sure that the Jones's driver had left, Murad entered the Emergency Room. He rubbed his nose at the overwhelming smell of alcohol. Evidence of the unnerving British compulsive cleanliness. He approached the information desk wearing a mask of concern. "My friend Jamil Ahmed was coming here. Has he arrived? He was quite ill."

"Doctors are with him now," the older man at the desk looked up from a book, then picked up a clipboard, "Yes, they checked him into room 222. The nurse just called down. You won't be able to visit for at least an hour."

"Can you tell me how long he will be here?"

"I am not a doctor," the man behind the counter revealed, "but these cases usually take a couple of days. He may be ready to go home tomorrow."

"One more question, please. I can't stay. I am very concerned about Jamil's safety and would like to arrange a ride for him. I will return tomorrow, inshallah. Could you tell me what time of day they might release him?"

"I'm not sure." The man tapped a piece of paper on his desk with thinly veiled impatience. "Our normal procedure is to have the doctors make their rounds and check on patients and then sign their release if all is well. Come back tomorrow afternoon for updates, but not before 4:00," he insisted dismissively. Then made a show of returning to his book.

The next afternoon, Murad checked at the desk and confirmed that Jamil was still there, so he went outside for a smoke. He watched the exit from the shade of an overhanging tree. The coastal breeze felt wonderful.

The thin broth of daylight was leaking from the Western sky when Jamil Ahmad stepped outside. His enormous frame seemed shrunken, and his usual swagger was gone.

Murad's eyes narrowed as he watched the big man move slower than usual. Good. Jamil looked in one direction and then another before heading west on Main Street toward the port.

Murad followed him soundlessly.

When a British patrol rumbled by in a turreted armored car, Jamil retreated to the gathering shadows beside a warehouse. Then leaned against it, striking a casual pose.

Murad busied himself sharpening his jambiya and keeping one eye on Jamil while making sure the British patrol minded their own business. He hated the stench of their diesel exhaust and almost everything else about the English. They should just go home. His resentment toward King Hamid bin Yahya for his self-absorbed and weak leadership simmered just beneath the surface. But bubbled up when he realized the king cared more about his own comfort and wealth than freeing their homeland.

CHAPTER EIGHT
SUSPICION

"He (Jesus) is not just nice, he is brilliant.
He is the smartest man who ever lived."
Dallas Willard

Nuweiba
Present

"The Israeli government may have mistreated your family—"

"May have?" Rahm's voice rumbled. The veins on his forehead pulsating with anger. Then, looking around and lowering his volume added, "Last year, I was subjugated to hours of interrogation by an Israeli soldier for hours at the airport in Lod. Do you want to know what he said?"

Schwalm shook his head, his eyes reflecting concern. "Was that when you went to Paris?"

"Yes. In Paris, I was treated like a hero for my reporting in a war zone. But at the airport, they interrogated like a criminal. What's more, the soldier was a colonel, not some 18-year-old recruit. I confronted him about the land seizures. He said, 'We're going to take it all, you know that, right?' "

"Your family's property in Safa?" Schwalm's brow furrowed with concern. "That is a terrible thing to say."

"Right. But when I asked for clarification, the Colonel said, 'From Dan to Beersheba, it all belongs to us, and we're going to take it back.' Since 1948, that's just what they've been doing, piece by piece, settlement by settlement. Our family is one example. A decade ago, the IDF drove a bulldozer through our family's three-hundred-year-old villa."

"I remember seeing footage of it on Al Jazeera," Schwalm said, his voice heavy with sorrow. "It was heartbreaking."

"They didn't just destroy our house. They destroyed our family and our way of life. How can you go home to a place when there's no *there* anymore?"

"I am so sorry for your loss," Schwalm said with a heavy sigh.

"I will never forget that IDF sergeant," Rahm's nostrils flared. "He was completely heartless. When I showed him the Israeli court ruling saying that the demolition was illegal, he brushed it aside without a second thought.

"They arrived at 6:30 in the morning. Just before sunrise, they woke us with shouted orders. It was an invasion complete with soldiers and heavy equipment rolling down the street. A crowd gathered to protest. It was chaos. It took a while before I found the sergeant in charge. When I presented the court document, he mocked us."

Safa, West Bank Territory
Three years earlier

"What is this?" the sergeant snarled. "Some judge meddling in security issues again? That's not enough. You were notified

yesterday that at 8:30 this morning, this building would be removed. You have one hour to vacate the premises."

"You can't do this," Rahm said. Rahm protested, desperation creeping into his voice.

"I have my orders."

"But your own courts ruled it illegal."

"My paperwork says this building is a security risk. There are no building permits on record. You now have," the sergeant glanced at his watch, "fifty-nine minutes."

"Permits? Are you insane? It was built in 1795."

"Where will we live?" Mrs. Khalidi wailed. "Where can we go? Are we animals that you can drive out into the streets?"

"This is your final warning. Whether or not your belongings are removed. In," the sergeant pointed at his watch, "fifty-eight minutes, that excavator will start removing this building."

"No!" Mrs. Khalidi screamed. "Where are we to go? Have you no shame? No fear of God?"

"I had to drag my mother away from the scene before she got hurt," he said, his voice thick with emotion. Rahm wiped a moist spot from the corner of his eye. "I couldn't stop them. In just thirty-five minutes they wiped out three hundred years of Khalidi family history. I vowed I would return to our family's land. She insisted I take the key to the house and said I should wear it as a constant reminder. I pointed out the obvious to her. 'How can I return to a place that had been plowed down?' Two weeks later, she died in my arms. The hospital called it stress-induced cardiac arrest. She just gave up. I felt helpless and incompetent."

Schwalm said, his voice gentle yet filled with empathy, "I moved to Ramallah because I heard about the Palestinian people's plight. They have demolished nearly 50,000 homes. I'm not sure this has anything to do with competence. But I can certainly understand why you would feel that way."

"I know." Rahm's face reddening in frustration. "They shouldn't get away with this."

"I came to Ramallah to see if there was any way to help bring peace." Schwalm reached out and put his hand on Rahm's shoulder, a gesture of support. "I understand. But we both know that there would be no need for a wall if the Israelis weren't afraid of Palestinian violence."

"You were crazy to come here! How can you make peace in a place where there is none and no one who knows how to make it? What made you think you could be that person."

"Exactly," Schwalm said. "I would have to be delusional to think it would be me, wouldn't I?"

"Yes," Rahm looked up at Schwalm and nodded. "Just another meddling outsider, like all the others who come here with their grandiose ideas, plans, and treaties."

"When Jesus sent out his twelve disciples, he gave them explicit instructions. He told them that whatever town they went to, they should look for a person of peace. That's what I have been doing since coming to Ramallah."

"I've never heard you mention this," Rahm said. "Have you found such a person?"

"That is part of the difficulty. When Matthew and Luke report those instructions, there is very little detail about how one recognizes a person of peace."

"I'll take that as a no."

"Listen, my mother used to say, 'A spoonful of honey will catch more flies than a gallon of vinegar.' Rahm, I understand. You feel violated, but your must sense of outrag must not control you. You are only a victim if you accept the lie."

"What lie?"

"That there is nothing you can do to change the future."

Rahm bowed his head. "But what can one person do against a well-armed and well-funded army of oppressors?"

Schwalm studied his young friend's eyes. "Have you never heard of Gandhi? Martin Luther King, Jr.? Nelson Mandela?"

"Great men of peace. Not one outsider among them. So, what do you think you—"

"I came here knowing I was an outsider and not the solution. But you are not an outsider. Don't get stuck in the past. Let it go. Release the resentment and the hate. See that couple?" Schwalm nodded over his shoulder, "Neither one of them killed anyone in your family, did they?"

"If I ride with them, I would be betraying blood—my family's, my people's."

"Those two are not their government," Schwalm continued. "They are just two young people in love."

"Maybe they are what you say, but I doubt it. There is something off about them."

"I am not sure what you mean," Schwalm said. "But Rahm, please take a proactive approach to this. Do not give them the power to ruin our trip. Besides, traveling with them in the van should give you lots of opportunities. You could either confirm your suspicions or discover that your reporter instincts are sometimes off. How can you do that while diving the reef?"

Rahm glanced back at the van. His gut told him there was a story in whatever was going on with the pair in the back seat. With a sad sigh, his eyes met Schwalm's, "Okay. That is a good point. But I ride up front."

"Think about this. Discovering that the world has misplaced Mt. Sinai would make a big splash. If you then discover its correct location, it could earn you a Pulitzer." The Professor winked. "Instead of reporting an exposé about Israel or Israelis, you could spread real news. Something exciting and positive."

"I know there's a story here." Griited his teeth. "Let's go. I intend to find out what it is."

CHAPTER NINE
THE BUBBLING SPRINGS

"The road to the promised land leads past Sinai."
C.S. Lewis

Coral Resort, Nuweiba, Egypt
Present

Saeed Qatal's eyes snapped open, a sudden surge of adrenaline pounded through his veins, leaving him drenched in sweat. The luxurious bedding of the Coral Resort's king-sized bed became a tangled web around his legs. His haunting dream, a recurring specter from the depths of his past, griped him in its unsettling embrace. The room, shrouded in an oppressive darkness, permitted only the faint glow of the digital clock. It cast eerie red numerals on the ceiling. Once again, the disturbing nightmare had awakened him too early. Annoyed, he kicked his way out of the sheets that clung to him like a burial shroud. His heartbeat echoed in his ears, a relentless reminder of the vivid details imprinted on his brain.

Turning on the bedside lamp, he rose and paced around the room, abandoning any hope of getting back to sleep. Though the apparition recurred less frequently than in his youth, its impact lingered. but every time the nightmare invaded his peace. It would shadow him until late into the day.

Seeking a semblance of productivity, Saeed meticulously laid out his clothes. He selected a white shirt laundered with heavy starch and considered which tie would best go with his beige suit. He chose an emblem of subtle power, the Ricci red and gold paisley.

He showered, shaved, and groomed his thick mustache, then got dressed. Success was a reward reserved for those who understood the value of thorough preparation. Saeed, acutely aware that his was a righteous cause, harbored unwavering confidence. Reviewing the plan, he dismissed the possibility of failure. Too much hung in the balance. He gazed approvingly at the reflection in the mirror—a dangerous but impeccably dressed leader of men smiled back at him.

His brain stored the neural firing patterns of his past, much like music is stored in the grooves of a vinyl record. The recording played the scene once more.

Sitting in the wicker side chair, he delved into a book, allowing the memories to flood back like a tsunami. Putting the book down, he closed his eyes and let the neurons replay that fateful day—September 8, 1978.

Tehran's Jaleh Square materialized. A chaotic collage of rioting students whirled around them like frenzied Sufis, protesting the Shah's tyranny. They drew pictures of the old tyrant on signs, threw the images on the ground, and wiped their feet on his face. Consigning him to hell, they lit his likeness on fire.

Placards picturing the black-turbaned Ayatollah Khomeini held high in reverent hands. Banners, hung on the surrounding buildings, proclaimed hatred for the implacable Shah and America for backing him.

When the shooting started, his father dropped their bag of breadcrumbs. Grabbing Saeed's hand, he dragged his son away from their ringside seat at the sidewalk cafe. But helmeted soldiers blocked their way. The choking smoke filling the air tasted like burning rubber.

They dodged left to escape past an overturned Pepsi truck and a flaming pile of debris. But a soldier rushed at them through the pandemonium and pushed his father to the ground. The embodiment of cruelty—the man shot his father in the chest, shattering the idyllic scene.

Blood gushed from the wound.

"Baba joon! Nah, Baba joon!" Saeed shouted. But his father's empty eyes told him he had not heard—would never hear again. Crushing despair him engulfed him. Baba was gone—sent behind the sun by infidels. Tears flowed, and his arms hung limp at his side. Young Saeed's soul shriveled, leaving an icy inner void.

Then the soldier turned his weapon on Saeed. A sinister sneer twisted the man's face as he took aim at Saeed.

Saeed's legs went weak, and his heart stopped. Out of the swirling melee, a demonstrator's rock unexpectedly smashed into the soldier's face, erasing his sneer.

The soldier fell. A nasty cut on his cheek below his left eye gushed blood. Rage boiled up, overwhelming Saeed's fear and stirring something deep and dark. He bent, grabbed the soldier's gun, and pulled the trigger. Twice.

He watched the life drain from the soldier's eyes. Conflicting emotions heaved—first, regret. Baba was gone. Then a rush—a sense of power that swelled his chest. Avenging his father tasted as sweet as his mother's zoolbia.

The sweetness evaporated when he looked up to see two soldiers sprinting toward him, bent on revenge, their weapons at the ready. Out of nowhere, powerful hands snatched Saeed by the arms. Students dragged him out of the line of fire and away from the massacre. They had seen what happened and cheered his bravery. Whisked away, they fled through a maze of fallen bodies.

Reflecting on the dream, Saeed recalled seeing the soldier's stunned expression had distracted him from the loss for an instant. He still felt that same delicious buzz every time he stood over a godless enemy of the revolution.

That day in Jaleh Square had been his best and worst. Worst because of Baba's death—best because a new Saeed was born. He arrived at the plaza Saeed Amani, a naïve thirteen-year-old boy. Ironically, his first name meant "happy." He left as Qatal, a soldier of the revolution with a new name, "Assassin!"

People throughout Iran still referred to that day as Black Friday. The body count was just over one hundred. Thirty soldiers died, and sixty-four demonstrators murdered. Over two hundred others wounded. It was the pivot moment in the battle between the Shah's brutal regime and the Islamic Revolution.

The plaza, once Jaleh Square, was now Martyr's Square. It remained a somber reminder of the sacrifices made in the name of revolution. Dealing with that soldier had made Saeed the insurgency's youngest hero and forever sealed his loyalty to the Ayatollah. He would become Iran's most decorated secret agent in his homeland's history. In return, the service had rewarded him with frequent promotions and an affluence that his father had never achieved. The dream was a haunting echo of the past, a reminder of the choices he had made, and the price he had paid.

⁂

When Rahm got back to the van, a hulking figure with no discernible neck arrived. The man's salt and pepper stubble hinted at his age, likely in his late forties. With a massive chest and disturbingly muscular arms, he looked like he might have been an Olympic weightlifter in his younger years. His pugilist's face and bullet-shaped scalp were the color of a boiled lobster.

Abdullah, acknowledging the newcomer, extended an invitation. "Mr. Danilov, would you like to ride up front with me again?"

A thickly accented affirmative rumbled up, "Da. I vould like so much." When he brushed past, Rahm instinctively stepped aside. Even at arm's distance, the big man's breath suggested that his breakfast came from his room's minibar.

Danilov handed his backpack to Abdullah, opened the door, and climbed in.

Rahm, seizing the opportunity, stepped forward and studied the man's bleary eyes. "If you don't mind," he said. "I would like to ride in the front."

Abdullah looked up into the big Russian's face. "Okay?"

"I vant ride front!" Danilov bellowed, slamming the door.

Rahm mimicked the big man's accent, "I vant go home." Then turned and stalked away, shaking his head.

"Rahm Khalidi," Schwalm shouted. "Rahm! Please! Come with me. It's just a two-hour ride."

Rahm stopped and glanced back, momentarily swayed by the Professor's plea.

Schwalm smiled and motioned for him to come and patted the seat next to him.

Schwalm's gesture triggered an image of Rahm's mother sitting on their apartment couch, smiling. Patting the cushion, she motioned him to come and show her the award he received in Paris. "I'm so proud of you, Abni, Best Reporter in the Written Press!"

He smiled wistfully, steeled himself, and walked back toward the van. "Grow up, Khalidi. You're better than this."

Seating himself deliberately next to the door, leaving a vacant space between himself and the Professor, Rahm secured his seatbelt. He glanced over his shoulder at the Israelis behind him, his suspicion growing. He shook his head and bent over to cinch up his boots. Something about them wasn't quite right.

"Are they okay?" Schwalm asked, pointing.

"The boots? Sure. I saw you limping on the way to the van. Are you going to make the climb?"

"I'm not an invalid. Not yet, anyway."

Not yet? That's the second time he's used that phrase. I wonder what that's about.

When Abdullah opened the driver's door ready to climb in, someone shouted from the hotel lobby. He closed the door, hurried around the front of the van, and trotted inside.

Inside, Abdullah conversed with a tall man in the lobby whose appearance made him look like he could have just stepped off of some movie set. A black mustache reminiscent of Saddam Hussein, and mirrored Ray-bans, completed the GQ image.

Rahm could see that the man was not an Arab but was unsure if he was Iranian or Turk. Not Iraqi, he decided.

When Abdullah shook his head, the tall man jerked off his aviators, bent forward, jabbed his finger in Abdullah's chest, and glared. Angry words poured out, and Rahm worried he might rip Abdullah's head off.

Although Abdullah appeared alarmed, he stood his ground. Rahm admired the man's spunk. The day was young, yet already filled with David and Goliath confrontations.

Moments later, Abdullah waved the man in the expensive suit away and came running back to the van. He jumped in, moved the driver's seat forward, adjusted the rearview mirror, and with a smile that looked forced, said, "Everybody ready for adventure?"

There were murmurs of approval, and the young Bedouin pulled away at a sedate pace.

Rahm saw a nervous tic at the edge of Abdullah's smile that hinted at unresolved tension from the confrontation in the lobby. Through the window, Rahm observed the man in the lobby studying the back of the van and then keying something into his phone. He wondered if there was a connection to the Israelis in the backseat. Ominous suspicions jangled in his head.

The van slid away as Abdullah began his well-rehearsed spiel, "In Arabic, the word Nuweiba," he gestured at the view ahead, "by itself, means, 'bubbling springs.' Our seven-kilometer-long settlement developed from barren desolation, with no infrastructure, into the thriving tourist destination you see today."

Rahm mused. Once they left the Hilton resort, it looked more like Nuweiba was struggling rather than thriving. What he noticed was crumbling stucco, boarded-up buildings, and pot-holed asphalt. Stubborn sand grass poked up out of potholes poised to swallow Volkswagen Beetles whole. He tuned out.

Abdullah's conversation with the man in the beige suit niggled in his brain. What were they talking about? Why was he studying the back of the van? What was he doing with his phone? Rahm's intuition said there was a story in the conversation that he had witnessed. Perhaps a conspiracy? Rahm's eyes narrowed to slits as he studied the back of Abdullah's head, pondering the meaning of it all.

Regret clawed at Rahm as the van rolled forward. A feeling lingered that he was facing something more sinister than a friendly tour of a remote monastery.

CHAPTER TEN
THE RUSSIAN

"It is in the admission of ignorance and the admission of uncertainty that there is a hope for the continuous motion of human beings in some direction that doesn't get confined, permanently blocked, as it has so many times before in various periods in the history of man."
Richard P. Feynman

Nuweiba, Egypt
Present

"Just sixty-one kilometer sous of Castle Zaman," Abdullah's voice droned on as he eased the van away from the Hilton's lobby.

Abdullah slowed his pace as a thunderous convoy of Egyptian police vehicles roared past, bristling with mounted machine guns.

"Nuweiba is sree part. From zhe sous, we have zhe ferry port, zhe city, zhen zhe Tarabin—our Bedouin camp and beach is where most backpackers stay. Nuweiba City has a small strip of affordable restaurants, Internet cafe, and some souvenir shops. Along zhe beach, in zhe city, some resorts and more camps are—"

"If it is so peaceable," Schwalm interrupted, "why are the police in such a huge hurry? And why all the weaponry?"

"Sorry," Abdullah glanced up in the rearview mirror, "Abdullah driver, not prophet. Not know why zhe police do zhis."

"Abdullah. Vat is dat tree?" the Danilov asked. "I see many."

Abdullah turned and pointed, "Zhat is acacia. Zhe little yellow sings is blossom."

"We haff none in Moscow. Is very strange."

"We sink acacia beautiful. We eat zhe seeds. Our woman make perfume from bark. Bedouin healer use to cure rabies too. We rest in shade. Now, where I was? Oh, yes. Nuweiba has come at the edge of zhe desert, like wild grass after winter rains. My people settle in zhis place after many years of visiting. Each year in zhe spring and the fall. Bedouin love beauty and zhe gift of zhe food sea provides."

"When we were snorkeling yesterday," the Israeli woman said from the back, "we saw what you mean. The reef here is full of fish. We even saw some Lionfish, and Chaim spotted a gloriously red Frogfish. The place is enchanting!"

"Da!" Danilov laughed, "Dat is true. I am here tree days. I see new fishes each day when I am eatink dem. I very like!"

Abdullah resumed his monologue, guiding the van toward the main road that hugged Sinai's east coast. Rugged, the mountains clawed at the sky—a sky so blue it seemed like the latte-colored mountains were painted on an indigo canvas. Behind them, the Gulf of Aqaba, the eastern arm of the Red Sea, lapped the coasts of four countries; Egypt, and Saudi Arabia, shared the bulk of its beach. Israel had less than ten miles. Jordan occupied twenty-five miles along its shore.

Rahm leaned forward, curiosity gnawing at him. "Mr. Danilov, what brings you to Egypt?"

"I am vork in Arabia. Come here for some days avay," Danilov gestured vaguely toward the van's rear. "Danilov engineer. Cannot tell more."

Rahm smelled a story unfolding. "Do you work in the Saudi oil industry? Or something else?"

Danilov faced forward and said nothing.

The Russian's silence made Rahm even more convinced there was a newsworthy story. "So, if you're a Russian engineer, and you're not in oil, perhaps you're involved in the Kingdom's missile system. Hughes had a missile site in the Hejaz before the Prince bought the mobile THAAD system from Lockheed Martin."

The Russian growled, "Vhy you ask so many question?"

"My name is Rahm Khalidi," he offered. "I'm a freelance reporter for the The Breaking News Digest. You might have seen my recent piece about the Saudis' alarm at developments in Iran. It was delivered to your room yesterday."

"Not see story. But I know Saudis have dis fear. I can smell dem when dey talk about Tehran in office," Danilov replied curtly.

"Maybe," Schwalm said, "You saw the RT news report. Rahm received The Khaled Alkhatib International Memorial Award. He was in Moscow last month on the fourteenth for courageous reporting on the conflict in Syria."

"Nyet. I vork, not vatch TV."

"Not even the Russian network?" Rahm asked.

"RT wrong name," Danilov growled. "Should call PT, Putin Television, not Russian."

"There is great concern in Tel Aviv about the Iranian regime, too, after the Hamas debacle," the Israeli woman said. "Do you think the hostility goes beyond the traditional Muslim infighting? The Sunnis and Shias argue about who is the rightful successor to the Prophet Muhammad."

The Russian waved his hand and said to the reporter, "I cannot speak about!"

"Why not?" the woman persisted. "Do you have something you need to hide?"

The big man snorted, turned his face toward the side window, and settled into stony silence.

"It's not about religion," Rahm said over his shoulder. "It's about politics and governments that don't deliver services to their citizens. So, leaders look to blame someone else."

Adi Ovitz leaned forward, "I think you're right about the governance issue, but there it is an old religious element that won't go away. Who is the rightful successor to the Prophet Muhammad? That ancient divide runs deep."

"True, but let's not forget the elephant in the room. As the world's surviving superpower, the US needs oil, and US foreign aid drives a lot of what is wrong in the region. Three billion dollars a year props up your country. So maybe it's a trio of issues. The corrupting influence of dollars. Inept governance, and old hostilities—all mixing into a deadly cocktail."

"Vun moment. Please forgive," Danilov spoke over his shoulder. "You say name vas Rahm Khalidi? Rahm is Hebrew, yes?"

"That's right. It's Hebrew for 'devoted.' It was my mother's grandfather's name. He was Jewish."

"But vhy. . ."

"I get this question from tourists," Rahm said, his tone tinged with weariness. "Khalidi is a Palestinian name. A famous Palestinian name, Arabic, really."

"I find hard to believe," the Israeli man in the back said with a slight accent, "dat Palestinian vould give son Jewish name."

Danilov turned to speak to Chaim, "Vy russkiy? You Russian?"

Chaim said, "Yes, I am born in St. Petersburg. But I speak lettle Russian, we move here vhen I was boy." Then to Rahm he said, "I not understand you family."

"Listen," Rahm said, "those were different times. If you must know, my mother's Jewish grandfather was the one family member who would take my mother in when she was pregnant with me and still not married."

Danilov said, "Vis dos two names, your school years must haff been eenteresting."

"Not when I was a kid," Rahm said. "In our neighborhood, we all got along. Jews and Arabs called each other 'cousin.' My great-grandfather had married a Palestinian. It was unusual, but it happened. Things were not as polarized then, as they are now."

Rahm fell silent, his hand absently reaching inside his shirt and fingering the key hanging around his neck. *What was that man in the lobby doing with his phone?*

"Rahm," Schwalm pointed at his iPad again and said, "Could I please show you that website about that pillar?"

"About what?"

"About Solomon's Red Sea Crossing marker."

"Still chasing that fairy tale?" Rahm smirked. The Professor was relentless once an idea gripped his mind. He never let go.

"Curiosity killed the cat, I always say."

"I know, Professor. Like you always told me, 'Curiosity killed the cat, but satisfaction brought him back.' "

Schwalm flipped open the black cover on his iPad and handed it over. "You decide."

"Pillar on Egypt side. Gulf of Aqaba," Rahm read the caption. "I see a picture of a man standing against a pillar. Who knows where the picture was taken? By whom? Or did someone doctor it? And even if it's authentic, what's so important about it?"

"I do not know if the photo is original or doctored. Please, just scroll down and read the text." Schwalm pointed a shaky finger at the screen.

Rahm frowned at the quivering hand, then read aloud, "A red granite column marking the Exodus crossing site. King Solomon had these columns erected 400 years after the miracle of crossing the Red Sea on dry land. Solomon's seaport was at the northern tip of the Gulf of Aqaba at Eilat (I Kings 9:26), and he was very familiar with the Red Sea crossing site, as it was in his neighborhood." After a brief silence, he looked at his mentor. He saw the older man's expectant expression. He said, "So you're suggesting that this pillar commemorates Israel's crossing the Red Sea at Nuweiba?"

"With the available data," Schwalm said, turning toward the Gulf and shaking his head, "I cannot be sure. There have been high-level heated debates about where the crossing took place. Some, the minority to be sure, suggest that the Exodus story is merely a fanciful myth."

He turned back toward Rahm, with eyes bright, and said, "However, the pillar's plaque says Israel crossed here and that Solomon placed the pillar. I remember seeing a map of the Sinai in my old Bible. Next to the name Mt. Sinai, there was a big question mark. Scholars can't agree on Sinai's location. That's intriguing. The giving of the Law was perhaps one of the most crucial religious events in history, and it's shocking that we can't pinpoint where it took place. If this pillar marks the actual crossing place, then we may find surprises when we get to St. Catherine's. But Rahm, here is a great rule to live by. Do not fear the unknown, but dread ignorance."

"Inshallah!" Rahm handed the iPad back to Schwalm, "But I've told you before that I'm not sure I believe your Bible. I have trouble believing the Quranic teachings I was raised with. So, how can I also accept your book?"

"Rahm, I have read your book. The Quran tells the faithful to 'read the book.' I'm sure that means the Bible."

"Here's my problem," Rahm said, his tone growing sharp. "My great-grandfather on my mother's side was a Jew. My mother told me he believed in the Torah and that God was kind and benevolent. Do you know what his faith got him? It got him killed. My father was a Muslim. He believed the Quran—that Allah is 'most merciful.' Israeli settlers gunned him down. Where was God's great mercy that day? And you, you told me you believe God has been a loving Father to you?"

"Quite earnestly," Schwalm said, his voice warm.

Rahm realized he was becoming caustic. He didn't care, "If there is a merciful God somewhere up there, where was he when Zionists butchered my father? Where was God when my mother later died of a broken heart? Tell me, where was God then?"

Schwalm sighed, "Those were awful experiences, tragedies."

"Yes. And your God did nothing to stop them."

"God belongs to the world, not to me. But how can you be sure he did nothing?" Schwalm studied Rahm's face. "Are you so naïve to think that if God does not do what you ask, he is not responding?"

"They died, Professor," Rahm shook his head. "They were murdered. God let it happen. End of story. If your God exists, he is either absent, preoccupied, heartless, or weak."

"Do you think God should be more heavy-handed and interfere with a person's freedom of choice?"

"No! But I've concluded," Rahm said, staring out the window as they rolled past the Nuweiba's big orange GO Bus terminal. He then turned back and said flatly, "that it doesn't matter much which of those things God is. If he exists, he's a heartless recluse. For me, he's irrelevant."

"I see." Schwalm looked away. Then, looking back intently at Rahm said, "But whether he exists or not, he is at fault."

"Exactly."

CHAPTER ELEVEN
THE WRAITH

"When the wicked dies, his hope will perish,
and the expectation of wealth perishes too."
Solomon

Aden Colony, South Yemen
1952

When the British patrol had passed, Jamil Ahmed emerged from the inky shadows. He flagged down a weathered camel cart, its two wheels creaking in protest as he climbed aboard. Murad watched with a cynical smirk as the big Egyptian struggled to clamber into the back of the cart and smiled. He's still weak.

Murad trailed behind. Watching for any opportunity to lighten Jamil's burden, he jogged along at a discreet distance.

As he jogged along in the dark, the previous night's covert meeting weighed heavy on his mind. He'd had an ominous feeling about seeing King Hamid arrive from Sana'a to Taiz, accompanied by only a driver. Murad's brow furrowed. He found His Majesty sitting alone in the back seat behind the tinted windows of his new Rolls Royce Silver Wraith.

When Murad opened the front door, he hesitated, noticing that it wasn't the King's regular chauffeur either. The two men studied each other. Murad had never seen the man before. As he slid into the front seat, all his senses were on high alert. His Majesty went nowhere without an entourage. Never. Too many people wanted him dead. Apprehensive, Murad noted the driver exuded an aura of formidable strength. Unmistakably a bodyguard.

"Murad Buckshan," the King's voice, soft yet commanding, pierced the tense air, "meet Borak al Ali. He has recently joined the palace security team after training abroad for the past three years in France."

An uneasy feeling clawed at Murad. The intrigue of the Yemeni court was a venomous serpent. Its coils tightened around him.

"Your Highness," Murad asked. "Am I being replaced?"

"Of course not," the King insisted. "You are too valuable to me."

When Borak reached inside his jacket, Murad tensed and slid his hand to his jambiya's handle, gripping it tightly, ready for action. As Borak pulled out a package of cigarettes, he made a conspicuous display of the gun protruding from his left armpit. What game was the king playing?

"Borak," the King said, "please leave us while I talk to Murad about his mission."

When Borak opened his door and stepped out of the right side of the car, Murad relaxed a little, then watched him light up and turn his back.

Murad closed his eyes and exhaled deeply. He kept his eye on the stranger but lowered his guard enough to run his hands across the tawny leather seat—then inhaled. The aroma of European wealth filled his nostrils. Everything about the car reeked of it. Only the rich could afford such a magnificent machine. He ran his fingers across its tiger maple dash. The contented purring of twelve cylinders under the hood promised a smooth ride. Then he shook off the allure of luxury.

He willed himself to focus on the business at hand. When he reported the discovery of the ring to the King, he surprised Murad by saying, "Under no circumstances are you to bring it to the palace or anywhere near me."

That made no sense. The King loved extravagance and surrounded himself with expensive toys. Murad had always assumed the habit came from the King's insecurity about being such a pathetic human being. Why refuse the ring? Murad flashed back to his discovery of it.

When he had pulled the tiny bag from between the foundation stones of the temple, he had been careful. He looked around and made sure no one was watching. He found the bag contained a ring with an enormous center stone when he opened it. Despite being layered in dust, the stone shone too brightly to be anything but a diamond. The gem would choke a camel. He wondered about the origins of the magnificent jewel. Probably South Africa, but who knows? The ring itself had looked to be made of old gold and tarnished silver. Around the diamond were a dozen smaller jewels that appeared to be emeralds. Their dull green color hinted that they might be emeralds.

It must be worth a fortune. Once he cleaned it properly, Murad was sure the King would reward him handsomely for bringing him such a marvelous object.

The ring was why the King had summoned him to this covert rendezvous in Taiz. Murad jerked back to attention when His Majesty spoke.

"Hawk, the King said, "from your description, our sources believe the ring you discovered could be Solomon's Seal. You must be very careful with it. We have heard fearful things about it. It has great power. You will be the Seal's guardian."

The coward. So, you're willing to risk my life for this treasure, but not your own? Murad's jaws tightened. King Yahya was the one man who had mocked Murad's prominent nose by calling him "Hawk"—at least the only one still alive. You fat swine. I hate that name. He pasted on a warm expression before turning to look at his highness.

"My grandfather told me," Murad said over his right shoulder, "that Solomon gave Queen Aliya the ring. She used the wisdom gained from it to design the world's first dam and her magnificent temple. The Seal has done our people much good."

"This is true," the King acknowledged. "But I believe I am unworthy of possessing an object of such rich history and significance. The old ones say that Solomon used the ring's power to design and build his temple in Jerusalem."

Murad was growing alarmed. You don't have a humble bone in your whole body. You're afraid.

Murad felt his stomach churning. "Highness, is there no one else who can take this thing wherever you direct it to go?"

The King continued, “But there have been great blessings for those who wear the Seal. It promises unimaginable wealth and success, like that experienced by Aliya.”

“Excellency, why then should I not bring it to you? It is truly a magnificent thing to behold.”

“The royal archives say that after Queen Aliya’s reign, the Seal fell into the wrong hands, the rains came early, and the dam burst, leading to the fall of the empire. They quote ancient sources that declare that this ring is either guidance or confusion—wisdom or madness, depending on who wears it. You must put a guard over your heart, or its power will bring you to an early grave. I have read fearful words about the Seal’s ominous curses. There are horrible diseases and unexplainable misfortunes threatened.”

“How,” Murad asked, “could a piece of jewelry—”

The King raised his voice. “One story tells of a man who was King Watta’s aide. Dazzled by the ring’s beauty, the man stole it. He not only caused the destruction of the dam, but the worms devoured his insides, then he died!”

Murad shuddered.

“But the old ones warn that if a man’s heart turns away from Allah, then great evil pursues them as it did Watta’s aide.”

“Excellency,” Murad turned toward the King, his face ashen, “how can an object made of metal and stone discern a man’s motives? What am I to do with such a fearsome thing?”

"What you *will* do is get rid of it as soon as possible," the King replied. "It sounds much too dangerous to keep around and too mysterious to fully understand. I wish Solomon were here to explain how to use it and reap its benefits without experiencing disastrous consequences."

The King bit his lip and was quite emphatic. "You will be cautious this time. Do not seize it in a casual or reckless way again. I must insist that you not bring it to me."

"Then what shall I do with it? I do not possess Solomon's wisdom." Murad said, his mouth dry.

"You will be the Seal's guardian."

Murad's stomach churned. Not only was the King willing to risk his life, but he had such low expectations about his survival that he had already lined up Murad's replacement. The armed man standing outside might be assigned to terminate Murad's career.. He dared not reject the King's command. "Highness, I fear that it does not need protection from me, but I from it."

"You may be right. But I am convinced that you are the man most capable of handling this mission. I would prefer to keep you by my side. But I must insist. Your mission is to gain custody of the Seal and protect it from falling into the hands of the American infidels, then see that it is returned to its place."

Lines formed between Murad's eyebrows, "Where is that?"

"That is a problem. I'm not certain. It makes the most sense that it be with Queen Aliya. Solomon gave it to her. So, perhaps it belongs where you found it, in Ma'rib. But maybe it should go back to Jerusalem, where Solomon created it. You must ask Allah for wisdom, the same kind of wisdom he gave Solomon. But you will handle this issue yourself. Understood?"

"I fear that if it is as you have said, then my loyal service to you will cost me my life," Scrambling mentally, Murad said over his shoulder, "Excellency, if Solomon created the ring and used it to build the Jewish temple, and if the shrine called the Dome of the Rock stands on the site where Solomon built his temple, then I could take it there."

"See! I knew you were the right man for this job, Hawk. Stop worrying. That is a brilliant plan. It appears that Allah has already given you wisdom. Only I think that it should not be taken to the shrine. It was built two thousand years after Solomon. I think it is better to return it to the Well of Souls. It will be closer to its source there."

Murad scratched his temple and grimaced. "Excellency, I do not know this place. Is it in Jerusalem?"

"The Well is beneath the shrine. As a young man, I visited Jerusalem. I was shown a small room accessed by climbing down sixteen steps and directly below the spot where the Jewish holiest place was."

"Can the faithful visit this place?" Murad asked.

"Of course, Allah has seen fit to make sure that most of the holiest places in the world are owned or controlled by Muslims. Mecca and Medina, of course, but even places that Jews and Christians consider holy. Many of the holy places in Jerusalem, like the Temple Mount and the church, built where Jesus is said to be buried. But many other places as well. Mt. Sinai, Jacob's Well, Damascus, Hebron, Bethlehem, Nazareth, and even Mount Ararat have all been entrusted to us by Allah for their protection and preservation."

"How do I find this well?"

"It is not a well. It is an underground cave. The name is symbolic. You enter the cave beside the southeast pier of the Dome of the Rock shrine. In one of the four prayer niches, there was a crack in the stone. I dropped a coin in the crack during my visit. I heard the coin clinking as it fell. The crack is deep. If you can find that place, you will, in a way, be returning it to where it belongs."

"Yes, Excellency."

"Now that Jamil has the Seal," the King added, "it is no longer in immediate danger of discovery by the infidels. But who knows what that Egyptian dog might try to do with it? It's late. Return to Aden." The King gestured for him to leave as if he were a peasant. "Tell Borak I am ready to go. Remember, do not bring it to me."

He took one last look around the plush interior of the car. Then when he closed the door and heard the solid thunk, he smiled, and his eyes sparkled. *If all goes well, I will have one of these myself someday. Soon!*

Murad resolved to never touch the Seal but always keep it in its pouch.

As the purr of the departing Wraith faded into the night, Murad swore an oath to himself. He would be the guardian, the arbiter of the Seal's fate, even if it meant betraying the king. The spark of defiance lit his eyes, casting a gleam that betrayed his inner resolve. One day, he vowed, the Seal would be his ticket to a life of unimaginable luxury, a reward for the risks he had endured.

CHAPTER TWELVE
NO CONFIDENCE?

"No change can there be in the Words of Allah."
Quran 10:64

Road to St. Catherine's Monastery
Present

"Absolutely, Professor," Rahm said, his voice laced with skepticism. "I don't doubt that the Quran references reading the Bible in the surah you quoted,

Rahm leaned back in his seat, eyes fixed on Abdullah, the driver, who was navigating the coastal road. Abdullah's driving was as unnerving as the conversation they were having.

"But I was taught that because your book has been so heavily edited, I should not read it. I was also told biased translators corrupted it. As copies and translations were passed down from one generation to another, accuracy suffered. I mean no disrespect, but you are intelligent and well-educated—two doctorates—after all. Given the issues, how can you possibly believe it?"

"Our sheik say zhat Bible have 50,000 mistake. Is true?" Distracted by Rahm's question, Abdullah had drifted into the oncoming lane. He jerked the wheel to the right, narrowly avoiding a collision with a massive, multi-colored bus. Rahm's heart raced.

"Is there any air conditioning for back here?" the Israeli man asked.

Abdullah pushed a button and then said, "Sorry, Chaim. Better?"

"Yes. Thank you."

"Our knowledge of the biblical text is constantly being refined," Schwalm continued. "The science of textual criticism is practiced both by those who believe and those who do not. As our understanding of the manuscripts grows, so does my confidence. You need to understand that faith and scholarship are not antithetical."

Abdullah frowned into the mirror. "What zhat? Antizhetical?"

"Mutanaqid," Rahm said. "They do not conflict."

"Shukran."

"You're welcome, Abdullah. But Professor, how—"

Schwalm interjected, "The transmission of the Bible from one generation to another is not like the old parlor game called Telephone. In it, one person would whisper a message in their neighbor's ear, then that person repeats whatever they think they heard. By the time the message circled the room, it would be unrecognizable. Those copying errors, once discovered, do not get included in published copies. Still, perhaps your sheik meant copying errors made by scribes. The 5,300 ancient manuscripts were hand-copied before the invention of the printing press."

Abdullah's hands released the steering wheel and gestured widely. "I read zhe Quran. Glancing into the mirror again with the same worried expression Rahm had seen in the lobby. "Zhe blessed Quran say, 'Zhe difference between guidance and error is clear.' Abdullah not read anysing zhat is lie."

"Good. But have you ever wondered how we know about those errors?" Schwalm asked with raised eyebrows.

"No," Abdullah shook his head. "Not ask such question."

Rahm tapped the Professor on the arm, "I'll play your little game," he said with a wink. "How do we know about all those errors in your book?"

"Over the centuries, scholars have spent millions of hours studying the manuscripts of the Bible and related ancient documents. They examine things like sermons and teaching materials that quote the Bible," Schwalm said. "By comparing what those ancient documents say, we know with a very high certainty what the original manuscripts said. Once they discover an error, they remove it. Of course, we do not include them. Furthermore, even skeptical scholars agree. None of the variations affect the Christian faith's essential beliefs."

"My thesis advisor at the university," Rahm said, shaking his head in the negative, "spoke of the copying errors and pointed to contradictions."

"I am Muslim," Abdullah stated, raising his voice. The fingers of his right hand bunched together at their tips as he waved his hand over his head. "I believe zhe blessed Quran and zhe Prophet, peace be upon him."

"Abdullah," Schwalm said with a smile, "I agree with your sheik about there being a large number of copying errors. In fact, there may be ten times as many copying errors in the manuscripts. However, we are aware of these variant readings because of the work of people like the monks at St. Catherine's."

"Half a million mistakes?" Rahm turned toward Schwalm. "What about the Gospel of Thomas and other books that Constantine banned?"

"Mounce is right when he states that the books that were included in the Bible, what we call the canon, were recognized as authoritative rather than winners of a popularity contest."

"You're not claiming there was no selection process, are you?"

"What I am saying is that Constantine had nothing to do with the books included in the New Testament. The church did not struggle for hundreds of years before recognizing the authoritative books."

"A church council didn't take a vote?"

"They did not discuss the canon at Nicaea. And Constantine's primary concern was political unity. In fact, the first Council to focus on settling the issue of the canon was the Council of Trent in the middle of the 16th Century. And even then, the discussion was about whether to include the Apocrypha in the Roman Catholic Bible."

"My advisor said that human beings wrote the Bible, not by the finger of God like the Quran."

"True, human authors wrote it ," Schwalm conceded, "but the Bible claims for itself that God inspired every word. From day one in Eden, everything God envisioned benefiting humanity would be a partnership between himself and humankind."

Rahm raised his hands in supplication. "Enough sermonizing. Why do you always have to talk about religion? Is that all there is to you? Just you and God?" Without saying another word, he turned his attention back to the argument Abdullah had with the man in the lobby. Then scribbled some thoughts in his notebook and chewed his lower lip while scowling out his window at the rugged mountains. Their ruddy faces scowled back like lurking thugs. The only living thing he could see was a vulture scanning for signs of death as it soared high above, then disappeared inland.

Seeing the vulture reminded him of the Israelis. He flipped open his notebook again, skimmed his sparse notes, and added, *Why sit in the rear? They're trapped. Would Mossad agents do that?*

He fingered the chain around his neck and closed his eyes, pretending to sleep. But once a question wormed its way from his reptilian brain to the frontal cortex, he had no hope of dislodging it. If Mossad, why here? Would a Kabalist work for Mossad? He thought about that for a moment, then scribbled. *Why not?*

After a few moments of silence, Rahm heard Schwalm close the cover on his iPad. He jumped when Schwalm tapped his shoulder. "My main point is that I came on this trip to see the monastery. I came because it has been a place where so many biblical manuscripts have been preserved. They built the monastery here because the builders thought they were at Mt. Sinai. If the Red Sea crossing took place at Nuweiba, then the real Mt. Sinai and the Split Rock of Horeb must be in Saudi Arabia."

"Then why are we still going to the monastery?" Rahm asked.

"Because—"

"Just kidding," Rahm said without smiling. "By the way, that's the second time you've mentioned a split rock, as if I should know about it. What is it?" He didn't believe in coincidence. "Saudi Arabia keeps coming up."

"This may sound absurd to you. But this is history. Moses was told by God to strike a rock with his staff, and water would pour out."

"An old man hears God talking to him, and that's not absurd?"

"That's what both the Bible and the Quran state," Schwalm said. "Do you believe that reality only consists of what you can perceive with the five senses? What about personality or character?"

"Zhe rock? Yes!" Abdullah brightened. "At madrasah, imam say zhat zhe Prophet Moses, he strike zhe rock and zhen water for zhe people."

"Okay. So, everybody knows about this but me. But Professor, what does the rock have to do with Sinai? And what does any of this have to do with us?"

"God gave Moses the Ten Commandments at Mt. Sinai *after* the Red Sea crossing. Not before," Schwalm said, as if stating the obvious. "If the Red Sea crossing took place at Nuweiba, then Mt. Sinai must be in Saudi Arabia."

"You think Mt. Sinai is in Arabia?" Rahm asked.

Schwalm sat straight up and grabbed his iPad. "Arabia. Arabia. Paul mentions Arabia, but where?"

"There you go again, Professor. What are you talking about?" Rahm watched Schwalm scan his screen.

"I found it!" Schwalm said in triumph. "Galatians 4:25, 'Mt. Sinai in Arabia.' "

"I'm sorry, I forgot to introduce myself," the woman said from the van's back seat. "My name is Adi Ovitz. I was raised hearing the Torah read. What Dr. Schwalm says is true."

"What is true?" Rahm half-turned in her direction.

She brushed a strand of blonde hair away from her face. "The Red Sea crossing came before the giving of the Law. But Professor, I've heard that in antiquity, the Egyptian border was at al Qantara near the modern Suez Canal."

"The Galon Fortress was twenty miles southwest of Jerusalem and dates back to the 12th century before the common era. It suggests otherwise."

"Adi, is it?" Rahm asked. "Do you always butt into other people's conversations?"

She waved his question aside. “I can’t say that I’ve done very well living up to it. But I believe what the Hebrew scriptures say. I am stunned that you Muslims have so little confidence in Allah’s power. You don’t seem to think that he can protect his word from infidels or meddling friends.”

CHAPTER THIRTEEN
HERE IT IS!

"Wisdom has built her house; she has hewn her seven pillars."
Solomon

Sinai, Egypt
Present

Abdullah slammed on the brakes. As the van slid onto the shoulder of the road in a spray of dust and gravel, he shouted, "Allahu akbar! God is great!" Then he turned and glared at the Israeli woman. "How can you say we have no confidence?"

"Well," Adi said, "how can you say in one breath that the Quran commands the faithful to read the holy books and then say that infidels have changed his book? Is your God so weak?"

Abdullah's anger boiled over and he stormed out, got out, slamming the door.

Rahm watched Abdullah stalking around the front of the van, waving his arms and shaking his head. He was about to spill his own belly full outrage, when Abdullah jerked open the van's sliding door. He pointed at the Gulf, "Abdullah tour guide and driver, not scholar. From here, good view. Maybe take picture?"

"I would love to get some pictures," Schwalm replied eagerly.

When Rahm exited, he helped Schwalm climb out. But when Adi moved toward the door, he turned away.

Everyone had a camera or phone out—everyone except Danilov. The enormous Russian exited the front seat, walked to the edge of the road, and lit a cigarette, his gaze fixed east.

Rahm, now with a few good images, lowered his phone and turned to Danilov. "What are those mountains called?"

Danilov shrugged, discarded his cigarette with a flick, and stalked back toward the van with purposeful strides.

Abdullah watching the fuming Russian march away, whisper to Rahm, "Those are the northern peaks of the Hejaz Mountains.' "

"I know," Rahm said, his eyes narrowed. "The range extends along the entire east coast of the Red Sea, from the southern tip of the Arabian Peninsula all the way north, almost to Aqaba. I was trying to start a conversation."

"Oh," Abdullah mumbled and walked toward the van, where he wiped the dust off the license plate and went around kicking tires.

Rahm followed Danilov. "Is that where you work? I heard about the Crown Prince working on his pet project The Line—the mega city that he claims will be the model for all future cities. Or maybe it's missiles. I think there used to be a missile installation in those mountains. That was before the King bought his newest missile system from China."

Danilov held up his massive hand with the palm out, silencing Rahm. He climbed back into the van and slammed the door so hard that the whole vehicle trembled.

Adi walked up, and said, “What makes you think he is working on the Saudi missile system?”

Without saying a word, Rahm turned and walked back toward the van himself. The seasoned reporter muttered, “There’s a story behind the fact that he won’t talk about his work.”

“Perhaps you’re jumping to conclusions,” she called after him.

“I apologize,” Rahm stopped, whirled toward the woman, and said, “I’m sure this misunderstanding is all my fault. I may have given you the impression that I was interested in your opinion. Please forgive me. I am not.”

Adi’s mouth was open for a moment, her shock evident before she snapped it shut. Her facial muscles tensed involuntarily.

Schwalm approached, addressing the geopolitical complexities around Saudi Arabia. “Powerful neighbors like Israel and Iran surround the Saudis,” his voice warm. “They get a lot of criticism because their human rights record has not even been close to scintillating, either. They have gotten high marks for improving the lot of women but unprecedented condemnation for the murder of that Saudi journalist a while back. Rahm’s point is that they are probably not granting many work visas to Russians, given Russia’s ties to Iran.”

Adi turned to Schwalm, her eyes meeting his weathered gaze. “Things have been shifting, especially with the prospect of a regime change. Lots of expatriates work in the Kingdom.

“Expatriates are welcome, especially those working on The Line smart city project. Saudi Arabia recently opened its doors to non-Muslim tourists too. There’s that, and Aramco will hire engineers from anywhere.” Still studying Schwalm’s face, Adi said, “Besides, the Kingdom has something the Russians are desperately hungry for right now.”

“Cash,” Schwalm offered.

“That’s right,”

“I hadn’t heard about the lifting of the ban on non-Muslim tourism. I wish I had known. I would have loved to visit.”

“Traveling there should be very inexpensive,” Adi said. “You should consider it. It’s never too late, you know.”

The money is the least of my--”

Something over Adi’s shoulder caught his attention, and Schwalm gasped, and his eyes widened.

Adi spun around. Her right hand instinctively reaching to the small of her back. When she saw no threat, her hand dropped, relief flooding her.

Schwalm touched her shoulder. Reacting unconsciously, she grabbed his hand and twisted hard, nearly throwing him to the ground. When she realized who it was, she let go. “So sorry,” she stammered, pulling her hands away.

Schwalm, looking apologetic, rubbed his wrist, “No, no. I’m sorry to startle you,” he said before turning and walking in the direction of his reporter friend. Pointing toward his discovery, he called over his shoulder, “Rahm! Rahm! Here it is! It’s here!”

Adi watched as Rahm’s surprise mirrored her own upon seeing the massive carved pillar Schwalm had found, reputedly built by Solomon. It stood nearly twenty feet tall, a historic artifact standing proud against the backdrop of the shoreline. “How did I miss that?” she murmured, her amazement evident.

Stirred by the significance of this discovery in relation to her mother’s faith, Adi quickly pulled out her phone and began capturing a series of images.

Meanwhile, Schwalm, his expression mystified, asked, “What’s it doing up here?”

Abdullah rushed over and said, “Yes, I tell you name of zhis beach,” his arm swept across the shoreline, “is Nuwayba al Muzayyinah. Zhis mean, zhe waters of Moses open.”

Rahm Khalidi shook his head in disbelief point toward the Gulf. “This is it? The crossing happened down there?”

CHAPTER FOURTEEN
IN THE GAP

"For the believer, God stands at the beginning of their speeches; for the physicist, at their end."
Max Planck

Nuweiba Road, Sinai
Present

"Is okay?" Danilov asked Abdullah as he pointed at the air conditioning controls.

Abdullah nodded.

"Excuse me," the Israeli man, Chaim, spoke up. "I think you turned off the air back here."

Danilov glanced at Abdullah, then pressed a button. "Okay now?"

"That's good," Chaim said. "Spaciba."

As they continued their journey, Danilov spoted a boy, maybe ten years old, leading a camel adorned in a tourist saddle. The boy wore blue shorts and a striped shirt walking along the shoulder of the road. Saudi camel saddles were typically strapped on behind the hump. The fact that this was for tourists was obvious from how ornate it was and that they cinched around the camel's middle. A bright red halter wrapped the beast's head. The diminutive handler held a red lead rope to guide his beast along the road's shoulder between the asphalt and the guardrail.

“Why is he here? So far from home?" Abdullah's puzzled voice broke the silence, drawing Danilov's attention.

“You know boy?” Danilov asked. His eyes fixed on the youngster in the mirror. The kid glanced up as they steered around him, and his eyes opened wide. A few seconds later, the kid pulled out a phone, and it looked like his thumbs danced across the tiny screen. Then he turned around and strained at the rope to persuade the stubborn beast to reverse directions.

“I see at hotel zhis day, early,” Abdullah said.

Danilov couldn’t shake the feeling that something was amiss. His unease grew, but he pushed the nagging thoughts to the back of his mind when they rounded the next bend and lost sight of the tug-of-war between the boy and the beast.

As the road wound through barren mountains, his thoughts drifted to his contract in Saudi Arabia, his daydreams of a luxurious villa in Sochi, and the immense wealth he envisioned.

He smirked at the idea that he was working on a missile system.

He wondered if he could ask for an advance to tie up the property before someone else bought it. Then he considered whether he should ask for payment in riyals or rubles. But then again, since the Saudis pegged their currency to the U.S., maybe he should ask for it in dollars. His contract with the Saudi National Cybersecurity Authority was for almost two million dollars. How big an advance can a contractor ask for? Lost in his fantasies, Danilov's reverie was abruptly shattered.

Ahead, he saw a figure emerge from behind a massive boulder, his face concealed by a black keffiyeh. Panic surged through Danilov as he recognized the rocket-propelled grenade launcher aimed at their van. "Stop!" he shouted at Abdullah, but it was too late.

He grabbed the wheel and tried to steer away from their attacker standing on the left shoulder of the road. Danilov saw the burst of smoke coming from the launcher and the exhaust trail that traced a lethal path toward them. “Nyet! Nyet!”

The RPG hit. Glass and metal exploded in a deafening roar. Thick smoke surrounded Danilov as he began to cough and curse.

The deafening explosion pushed the back of the van to the right as the front spun left. They crashed into the roadside boulder. The impact crushed the left front fender and shoved the engine against Abdullah. Danilov lurched forward and slammed back his nose bloodied by the deploying airbag,. Glancing to his left, he saw Abdullah's lifeless form, a cruel testament to the attack's brutality.

Automatic gunfire raked the van's side, and Danilov felt a searing pain in his neck. The shooting ceased, leaving behind an eerie silence. Through the smoke, he heard Adi's distant voice, urgency lacing her words. "Hurry. Everybody out!”

When the attack ended, panic set in. Where did the attackers go? He could not see through the smoke. His eyes were stinging, and he started coughing uncontrollably. When the shooting was over, he heard Adi shouting, her voice sounding far away. “Hurry. Everybody out!”

“What happened?” Schwalm's voice trembled.

"We're under attack. Get out!" Adi's command was sharp and urgent. "Danilov. Move!"

Desperation seized him as he attempted to exit the van, but his legs refused to respond. Despite the desert heat, he felt an icy chill creeping over him. His trembling fingers explored his neck, finding a wet, sticky warmth—blood. He moaned, fear and disbelief mingling in his voice. "Am I dying? I cannot to die. I must r-r-retire to villa on Black Sea."

ৡ ৡ ৡ

"Chaim?" Adi's voice was raw, filled with desperation. But there was no response. She looked around. Her ears were ringing. Where her partner had been seated, there was only emptiness. Where is he? Her mind raced, struggling to comprehend the sudden void beside her.

The aftermath was eerie silence. There were no attackers in sight. The world was a haze, her ears ringing, and her head throbbed in agony. Fueled by adrenaline and training, she reached for the small of her back, fingers closing around the grip of her 9mm pistol, just in case.

The acrid stench of burning rubber and nitric acid was overwhelming. "Chaim?" She called out again, her voice tight. Her nostrils flared at the scent of burning plastic, the metallic tang of blood lingering beneath it all. Perhaps it was Chaim's blood, and the thought was almost unbearable. But she couldn't afford to break down. She had to push forward, to act.

She forced herself to focus and yelled to the others, "Get out!" Her words choked out the words and peered out the yawning wound that moments ago had been the van's rear doors.

Rahm's voice cut through the chaos, "I'm okay, I think. But Abdullah is not moving. Professor? How are you?"

"What? I can't hear you!" Schwalm shouted. His voice barely above a whisper in her ears.

"Are you hurt?" Rahm's concern etched on his face.

Schwalm groaned. His grip on his shoulder tight. "My shoulder is bleeding. But I'm fine." His determination reflected in his set jaw.

Adi flicked to Schwalm's left shoulder, where blood oozed between his fingers. Her assessment was that his bleeding, while painful, was not serious.

She yelled, at Rahm, "Grab your friend and get him out of here!" Her command cut through the smoky air as she rolled out through the gaping hole at the rear of the van, her movements urgent. She strode to the shoulder of the road, glad to be upwind from the stink of the toxic dioxin and furan fumes released by the burning plastics.

The scene was a nightmarish vision, with the rear doors and the seat with the luggage were gone. The bench where she and Chaim had been riding was nowhere in sight. How she had not been eliminated as well was a mystery. She saw only torn metal, broken glass, and shredded upholstery. She looked herself over for any sign of blood. Nothing obvious. There were a couple of places where she expected to have bruises later. But as far as she could tell after a quick check, she had somehow, inconceivably, escaped serious injury.

When she tried to put her fingers in her ears to clear the ringing sound, she let out a yelp. Her left shoulder felt like it was on fire. She probed her deltoid, felt a damp spot, and found her fingers sticky with blood. No time for that now. She turned her attention to a quick scan of their surroundings. The canyon narrowed at a bend in the road, and its steep walls reached toward the sky. “Perfect spot for an ambush,” she muttered.

The van looked like a busted piñata. Billowing smoke pushed by the wind obscuring her view of the bend in the road around which their attackers had disappeared. The fight was far from over.

CHAPTER FIFTEEN
DAUGHTER OF SHEBA

"If at first, an idea is not absurd, then there is no hope for it."
Albert Einstein

Ma'rib
1952

An alluring rumor came to Lenard Jones' attention during his African expedition three years earlier. It hooked his imagination. The notion that the Queen of Sheba might be from the Ancient Yemeni Ma'rib kept him awake at night.

So, last year, he did an aerial survey of the ancient city and its surroundings. Photos showed the tantalizing remains of the Temple of the Moon, poked up through the sand. Those photos transformed that possibility into a driving ambition. If he could raise the funding, he would organize a dig at Ma'rib.

Now, a year later, his diverse team of archaeologists, photographers, epigraphers, and physicians, had hit pay dirt. They'd barely scratched the surface but had already uncovered tombs, thousands of remarkable inscriptions, alabaster statues, bronze figurines, and an 8th-century BCE statue of a Sabaean Queen. She ruled 200 years too late to be the object of his search. But confirmed that from time to time, a woman indeed ruled Ma'rib. With permission from the Yemeni King, his American Trust For the Study of Man funded the excavation. As the expedition's leader, Jones hoped their efforts would unearth irrefutable proof that the local legends and his theory were right. Ma'rib was undeniably the Queen of Sheba's fabled capital.

Despite all their remarkable discoveries, Jones had seen no solid evidence confirming the legends about the Temple of the Moon. So far, the real prize had eluded him.

At the day's work concluded, Lenard Jones walked between the eight limestone columns that guarded the temple's entrance. The pillars cast their evening shadows into the ovoid pit within the temple's sixteen-foot walls. Setting his 16-mm camera on its tripod in this elevated position, he aimed it down into the excavation, and started filming, panning across the ruin and back again. He stopped the camera, hoping this footage would be the key to raising more funding for future seasons of excavation.

Influenced by the Quran, the locals called the temple Mahram Bilqis—Queen of Sheba's Sanctuary. Jones knew these rumors were not enough. There were competing legends about the Queen being from Ethiopia. He hungered for irrefutable verification—something linking her to Ma'rib. A document, inscription, or artifact would calm his doubts and satisfy his detractors. Despite recently turning thirty, many viewed him as just another grave robber. But if they had enough time to find proof that the Queen once ruled here. He could establish his reputation as a legitimate archaeologist.. Lacking proof, his status in the field teetered on a fragile edge.

Wrapped in his red and white keffiyeh, Jones pondered the uncertain future. The classic Arab headdress flapped in the breeze and obscured his view. After adjusting it, he tried to imagine how long it might take to find the evidence required. He rested his hands on the pair of pearl-handled Colt 45s that were slung low on his hips. At that moment, it hit him it might never happen. But his bit of confidence rested on the hope that they'd found enough to fund digging deeper. He smiled, imagining the responses when he made his presentation scheduled that fall in Washington, D.C.

People told him that the mix of gear he wore at the dig made him look like a combination of Lawrence of Arabia and a gunslinger from an old Western movie. His Ray-Ban Aviators and crisp white shirt completed the eclectic outfit. He decided that the next time he visited the President, he would dress for work while showing the film rather than wearing a suit.

As he climbed down the stairs to the entrance, he thought how every day was the same: streams of Yemeni workers carried away tons of sand. Then every evening, the malicious winds picked up some of the sand and dumped it right back on their excavation. It seemed bent on blotting out their progress. It was as if the belligerent desert intended to keep Ma'rib's greatest secrets shrouded in mystery.

Jones rubbed his cheek, resolved that he and his team would be more relentless than the wind. But worry about the report he had gotten that morning eroded hope. The Yemeni King's nephew, Nabeel Ibn Khaldun, was the tribal chief and doing his worst to obstruct the dig. He didn't seem to see any benefit in learning his people's history unless there was a treasure to be found or some other financial angle. Jones curled his lip in disgust at a man who could see no further than his own self-interests.

Jones had to admit that he had made a mistake snubbing the man when he and his team first arrived. Being the King's nephew carried a lot of weight in this culture.

Added to his concerns about the King's nephew was his fear that the inter-tribal hostilities. These swirled around him, and might break out into a full-fledged war. That would end their opportunity to dig. He shook his head, trying to shed the nagging feeling that a disaster was approaching.

Engaged in conversation with his colleague, Dr. Fallbright, Jones explored a daring theory. He said, "That statue we uncovered of that Sabaean Queen has me thinking. Were you aware that King David may have had an Arabian wife?"

"Which of his wives are you talking about? He had eight. I suppose one of them could have been Arabic."

"Think about it, Frank. What was the name of Uriah's wife? Uriah the Hittite, the soldier King David had killed."

"Bathsheba?"

"Exactly!" He turned and pointed across the wadi at the ruins of the ancient city of Ma'rib with its five-story buildings. "What if her name means just what it sounds like? 'Bath' means 'daughter' and—"

"Yes! And Sheba means 'of an oath' or 'of a promise'?"

"There you go again, defaulting to the majority view," Jones shook his head. "In Hebrew, it means 'promise' or 'oath.' But what if it's an Arabic place name? This place?"

"That's crazy! You can't be serious." Fallbright arched one eyebrow. "The consensus is against you. She was Hebrew."

"That's so typical. How can you call yourself a serious scholar if you always side with conventional wisdom? All major breakthroughs in history and science started with ideas that most people considered heretical.. The earth is round? Heresy! Until it wasn't. The earth is the center of the universe? Blasphemy! Until Copernicus went against scientific orthodoxy."

"Yes, but now the majority opinion is that the earth is a sphere. Sometimes orthodoxy is what it appears to be, a fact."

"What if we could establish that Bathsheba and the Queen of Sheba are connected? Perhaps both trace their roots to Ma'rib. Here's my theory. Everybody says Bathsheba was a Jew. The biblical record states that her grandfather Ahithophel was one of King David's chief advisors. But all we know about his origins is that he was from Giloh. That makes his son, Bathsheba's father, Eliam, a Gilonite. The Bible never says that he was Hebrew. Everybody says he was a Jew. But it's an assumption."

Fallbright snorted, "You're arguing from silence."

"Besides that, you have to . . ."

"Everybody says it," Fallbright poked his finger in Jones's chest, "because there is no evidence to the contrary."

"No evidence yet. True. But look at the facts. Number one, we don't have a clear genealogy for Eliam that unequivocally establishes his ethnicity. Two, Bathsheba married a Hittite."

"What does that prove?"

"Nothing. But it makes me wonder if she was rebellious. Even if Eliam was Hebrew, that doesn't mean he couldn't marry an Arab. Perhaps by marrying Uriah, Bathsheba was just following her father's example of interethnic marriage. I don't know, but when the nation of Israel was new, wouldn't lineage be less important than it currently is in Great Britain? And three, the woman's name and its meaning are subject to interpretation."

"By you, maybe," Fallbright said. "But the consensus—"

"When you add that to our discovery of the bronze statue of Ma'dikarib, which we unearthed three days ago, we have a potential solution to all the questions. It's thin, I admit. But his statue shows Ma'dikarib wearing a large ring on his left hand. What if it's a 6th-century B.C. representation of him wearing Solomon's Seal? It's a considerable leap, but what if Bathsheba's mother was from right here?"

Fallbright looked skeptical. "By imagining a connection, I think you're spinning cloth out of spider webs."

"Cloth as smooth as water but strong as steel. I could be wrong, but Bathsheba was Solomon's mother. What if the Queen of Sheba—Yemen's Queen Aliya—heard about Solomon because she and Bathsheba were related or connected somehow?"

"You're reaching, Jones. Your hypothesis rests on a series of flimsy suppositions. However, I will grant that if you could uncover evidence of such a connection, that would rival the discovery of Tut's tomb. In fact, if there were a connection between Bathsheba and Aliya, that would be even more spectacular—a bombshell. But I know that look. Don't get your hopes too high."

CHAPTER SIXTEEN
SURVIVORS

"I am not what happened to me. I am what I choose to become."
Carl Jung

Nuweiba Road
Present

Adi's heart pounded in her chest as she slipped her gun into her waistband, walked to the front passenger door, and jerked it open. She yelled at Danilov, "Get your bag and get out! Now!" Her eyes darted around, searching frantically. Where is Chaim? He couldn't have just vanished. But there was no trace of him amidst the turmoil.

She glanced up and nervously scanned the left side of the road. The smoke was clearing, but she couldn't see any sign of their attackers as she looked down the stretch of the road they had just traveled; nothing suspicious there either. It still didn't make any sense. Why did they stop in the middle of the operation? Especially since the van had been immobilized and half the passengers neutralized. She knew what they were after. What she didn't know was who did the shooting.

Her mind replayed the violent attack. After Danilov shouted, she'd looked up just in time to see the smoke trail as the RPG traced its lethal path. It impacted the van just as Danilov jerked the wheel right toward the guardrail while Abdullah seemed oblivious. The deafening explosion followed as the vehicle's rear end was blown away. Chaim must have been taken out with it. One moment, he was there. The next, he was gone.

A faint moan pulled her back to the present. She yawned twice to relieve the pressure in her ears but the ringing persisted, drowning out most sounds.

She had an idea and stepped to the front of the van, where some expended brass was scattered on the pavement. She picked up one casing and studied it. The caliber was 7.62×39mm. Definitely Russian. But that could be anybody. Maybe Russians, North Koreans, Chinese, even the Iranians. She slipped the evidence into her pocket and hustled back to the front door. Danilov hadn't moved. He said something, but she couldn't hear it over the incessant tinnitus in her ears.

Danilov took his left hand away from the back of his neck and showing it to her. It was covered in blood. His eyes pled for help.

She leaned in, "What?"

"My neck," Danilov yelled. "I am bleeding. Cannot feel legs. Am I dying? I cannot to die!"

His breath was foul. She gestured for him to stay put, her own pain shooting through her arm.

With a harsh pound on the window, she demanded Rahm and the Professor to exit the van. When they didn't move, she reached to open the van's sliding door with her left hand, nearly passing out from the pain. She pointed at the two men, and shouted, "Get out!"

Rahm hesitated, consumed by something hidden under his shirt. Instead of getting out, he shouted, “The chain’s not here! Where is it?” He continued frisking himself and looking around in the wreckage.

"Forget it! Help your friend and get out. Now!” He still didn’t move.

Adi grabbed his shirt and screamed, “Those guys will come back. Do you want to die in this wreck?”

Rahm reluctantly climbed out and gent helped the Professor. But as soon as the older man was clear, he climbed back in and returned to rummaging, “I can’t lose it! I promised!”

Looking around, Adi scanned the rocks again. She was unsure which direction she should head to avoid danger but concluded that her best bet was to move right since the attack had come from the left. Scanning that slope, Adi barked instructions in Rahm’s face. “We are being attacked! Forget it, whatever it is. Get out!”

“I’m not taking orders from you! Back off! I promised. I’m not leaving without—"

Just then, Rahm stopped searching, reached under the front seat, and scooped up something in his hand. A silver chain dangled from his fist. He stuffed it in his pocket and grabbed two backpacks.

As Rahm climbed out of the wreck, Adi heard moaning. It was Danilov, “Pahzalsta! Please! I cannot die now. They paid me so much.”

Adi turned to Rahm, “Danilov’s too weak to move on his own and too big for me to handle.” She pointed at the Russian. “See if you can help him. I’ll help your friend.”

Rahm glared at her but moved toward the front door.

Danilov muttered, “Cannot die. Not now.”

Danilov held out his enormous right hand as he tried in vain to stop the blood flowing from the wound above his collar. Adi gasped when she saw Rahm reach out to take the drive! It looked like one of those multi-bladed pocket knives. He’d had it on him all along.

Danilov clutched the front of Rahm’s shirt and pulled him close. He choked out a few unintelligible words. Then released his grip. His whole body sagged.

Adi stepped forward, reaching in, and placed two fingers on Danilov’s right carotid artery searching for a pulse. Nothing. She stepped back. “He’s gone.”

Rahm looked bewildered, struggling to comprehend the loss. “What?”

He obviously couldn’t hear well, either. She shouted, “Leave him. Let’s go!” Adi's voice cut through the confusion, her determination unwavering. Death loomed close, but she refused to succumb. "Stay focused. Hurry! Bring your friend. Head up there, away from the direction of the attack." She pointed towards the rocky hillside. Her eyes fixed on Rahm, a suspicion creeping in. Why was he unharmed while others had fallen? But survival was her immediate concern. "But keep your eyes open. There may be more of them

Rahm looked at the dead man and turned pale.

Adi considered seizing the drive on the spot—but figured there was plenty of time to take it later—if they survived. A chilling reality made her shudder. Death was stalking her. With that certainty jangling in her head, Adi's attention returned to survival. "Stay focused, Ovitz," she muttered. She started shouting instructions again, "Hurry! Bring your friend. Head up there, away from the direction of the attack." She pointed to the rocky hillside to their right. These civilians will die right here if I let them. She had no intention of becoming a statistic in someone's incident report. "But keep your eyes open. There may be more of them."

The three survivors scrambled from the wreckage—away from the pretzels of metal that reached out for them like the talons of a greedy grave. She shuffled toward the sloping canyon walls. Her determination to survive roared louder than the gunfire that had silenced her fallen comrade.

CHAPTER SEVENTEEN
KEEP MOVING

"Whoever destroys a single life is considered by Scripture to have destroyed the whole world, and whoever saves a single life is considered by Scripture to have saved the whole world."
The Mishnah

Nuweiba Road
Present

After the attack, Rahm Khalidi helped Professor Schwalm escape from the wreckage. They cautiously worked their way up the hill, leaving the chilling sight of the van's wreckage behind. Rahm stared back down and felt the horror of it all. The van lay dead, its wounds evident and recent, smoldering like the aftermath of a riot.

The acrid stench of burning plastic and debris brought back the chaos of that day. The university was roiling with political turmoil after Prime Minister Rafiq Hariri's assassination. He'd been heading toward McDonald's exit when the building rocked. A kilometer away, a ton of TNT exploded. He never made it to his English Lit class that day or the rest of February. The university roiled with political turmoil. The Prime Minister Hariri's death staggered the entire country. When he arrived at the St. George Hotel, he found an enormous crater in the street. Buildings were in shambles. Every window for blocks gaped at him, blown open by the blast, and eviscerated vehicles smoldered in the street. Funny how a smell could resurrect the past with such intensity.

Beside him, the Professor leaned against a boulder, rubbing his knee. Shaking off the haunting memories, Rahm said, "Let's keep going."

The Professor hesitated, his voice edged with pain. "I'm not sure I can do it, Rahm. My knee is swelling up."

"Okay," Rahm said. Climbing around his mentor, he suggested, "How about I get up here and pull you up." Climbing around his mentor, he said, "Take my hand. I see a flat spot I can see from her. You can rest there?"

The Professor said, "I think I would rather be shot than take another step."

"Please. A little more." Rahm reached out. The Professor sighed but complied, taking the offered hand. Rahm pulled him up gently, his heart aching to see this man, the only father figure left in his life, in pain.

At each tough spot, Rahm pulled him up to the next level as carefully as possible.

Meanwhile, Adi Ovitz dragged herself up the hillside with her right hand while gingerly favoring her left shoulder. Her face contorted with pain. Every movement seemed to cause her agony. She groaned every time it shifted or she bumped it. After several of those complaints, she stopped and unbuttoned her blouse's left sleeve. She lifted her injured arm, held it to her chest, and after fumbling with it twice, buttoned the cuff to the front of her blouse. Her arm was immobilized in this way, and she continued to climb.

Rahm raised an eyebrow at her cleverness. He wasn't sure how long that button could support the dead weight of her injured arm, but he couldn't help admiring her tenacity. She's a tough one, like a velvet-covered brick. And attractive, too.

While the Professor rested, Rahm looked back at the wreckage again. The van once pristine, lay ruins. It's white paint smudged and blackened. The right rear side of the vehicle twisted forward as if a giant hand had ripped it open from the left. Clothes, shattered glass, and shrapnel littered the road.

Seeing the wreckage, Rahm's mind buzzed with questions. Who were their attackers? Why did they try to kill them all. Why did the rocket hit the rear of the van where the? Was the attack aimed at them? Was it because they were Israelis or Mossad, as he suspected? And what was the connection with Danilov?

Pulling Rahm out of thoughts, Adi called down, "Let's keep moving." She climbed with caution and often stopped, surveying the road and the opposite slope.

Rahm pulled the Professor to his feet to continue their retreat. When he saw Adi looking around again, he hollered up, "Why were they shooting at us? Where did they go?"

"Keep your voice down," she said in a low, irritated tone. "I don't know why. And it makes little sense for them to break off the attack when they did. Very unprofessional."

"Unprofessional?" Rahm said. "So, you don't know who they are. But you have suspicions?"

She ignored his question. Instead, she pointed to a large boulder above her. "That looks like a good spot to regroup."

The way she looked at him made him suspicious. What is she hiding?

They arrived under a quartz-peppered granite outcropping. Adi looked around and said, "This is not nearly enough cover to protect us from further attack, but it will do."

Rahm sized up the spot. With the sun near its zenith, the sparse strip of shade offered little relief from scorching heat. But she was right. It would have to do. He wasn't sure the Professor could climb much higher with his knee swelling up like a cantaloup.

A labyrinth of jagged desolation surrounded them. Mountain peaks combed the sky. He'd never imagined that beige came in so many cheerless shades. Every hill was naked, no a bit of green visible anywhere. Below their perch, a two-lane ribbon of asphalt meandered into the distance. No cool Red Sea breezes here. The sun was not yet straight overhead, but their refuge was already hot and stuffy. Ghost-quiet ruled.

Rahm rechecked himself, noticing bloodstains on the front of his shirt, and the pocket had a tear. But the blood must have belonged to the Russian, because Rahm felt no pain and could find no evidence of a wound. He could escape such a brutal attack with nothing more than ringing ears and a persistent headache.

Sweat traced damp crescents on Rahm's beige shirt under his armpits. A wet sheen covered his face, and salty drops stinging his eyes. The aroma of his sweat was well on its way to being rancid. I smell like that homeless guy who sells flowers in Ramallah.

Both the Professor and Adi needed immediate medical attention. The bleeding in the Professor's shoulder had stopped with pressure and an improvised bandage. But shrapnel protruded from the wound but Rahm didn't want to start more bleeding. The Professor's left knee, already an issue before the blast, had swollen to twice its normal size, aggravated by their climb. Rahm felt helpless. There was nothing he could do about either injury. He wondered how long they could hold out regretting his failure to pursue better first-aid training.

Rahm sat and positioned himself, keeping the Professor between him and Adi. He dug into his backpack and fashioned a makeshift sling for Adi's useless left arm. He thought it would be a little better than her shirt sleeve trick. When it was finished, he stood, walked over to where she sat and cautiously offered to help her put it on.

"Thanks. I'll do it!" Adi took the sling and started to slip it over her left arm.

When she struggled, he bent to help.

"Don't touch me!" she snarled and pulled away, grimacing at the sudden movement.

"I was trying to help." Rahm stepped back and surveyed her efforts. Noting to himself that the velvet veneer was thin in places, revealing the hardness beneath it. Her wound was deep enough that blood kept oozing through her shirt sleeve. Rahm feared she would bleed out if they didn't get help soon.

She wouldn't allow him to touch her hip, either. He couldn't tell if she was touchy from pain, or was it a lot of religious modesty, racism, or maybe bravado? He was convinced she needed attention, whether she liked it.

Rahm realized the van seat separating him and the Professor from the Israelis had spared the Professor from more severe injuries. He felt guilty that his reflexive act of pulling the Professor toward him may have shielded his own body from damage. Was I protecting the Professor or myself?

They settled in the shade to rest, gather their wits, and consider their next steps.

"Professor," Rahm said to distract the older man, "isn't it strange the things you think about when your life is dangling by a thread? I remember an assignment you gave us. It changed my life. You know?

Schwalm tried to flex his knee and winced. "What assignment was that?"

"It was when we were discussing pre-history." Rahm found a place to sit near his mentor and adjusted the Professor's bandage again. "You told us to read Ray Bradbury's short story, 'A Sound of Thunder,' and write a paper asking us to either defend or debunk Bradbury's thesis."

"Yes, of course, a great story. It first appeared in Collier's magazine back in the 1950s. A man went back into the prehistoric past, stepped on a butterfly, and changed the entire course of history."

Rahm flinched when a long-legged lizard with a blue head and neck scurried past like a scalded cat. He saw Adi curl her lip when he reacted to the lizard. Why does she despise me?

Regaining his composure, continued, "I concluded Bradbury was right. Our choices matter, not just for ourselves, but they have rippling effects outward to the rest of the world and into the future. It was right after that I became a journalist. That's why I wanted to thank you."

"And why now?" Schwalm stared at the scavengers circling in the sky.

Rahm pointed at the ground. "We're sitting here with our lives hanging in the balance, all because of choices made by people we don't even know."

Adi looked away.

Rahm watched her. He pulled out his notebook and wrote, Does Adi know attackers? Or who they are?

CHAPTER EIGHTEEN
POOR LITTLE PALESTINIAN!

"The land cannot be sold permanently because the land is mine, and you are foreigners—you're my tenants. You must provide for the right of redemption for any of the land that you own."
Leviticus 25:23

Road to St. Catherine's
Present

Adi Ovitz, Rahm Khalidi, and his mentor, Kaarl Schwalm, found a moment to rest after their harrowing escape. With Rahm's sliver of shade rapidly shrinking, he squinted at the Professor under the blinding mid-day sun. His voice laced with the glaring light, Rahm spoke. "Writing about Bradbury's butterfly effect convinced me that choices matter. That led me to join the environmental cause."

The Professor leaned against the granite face with his eyes closed. A smile played across his lips. "I remember. During your senior year, you wrote with grand passion about saving whales."

"It was as if someone drove that lesson home. A couple of years later, I saw a photo of a Holocaust survivor with his five children, thirty-four grandchildren, and nine great-grandchildren. It shook me up. If stepping on a butterfly would change the course of history, it didn't take long for me to wonder what impact the death of a single human has on the future. One day, I woke up and realized that I didn't believe in capital punishment. I concluded that if every whale matters, then every human matters too."

"Maybe Allah it was making the point," the Professor said with a wink. "I did not realize your career choice had anything to do with the story. But in retrospect, it makes sense. I read the article you wrote about that holocaust survivor. It occurred to me you might be the person I came to Ramallah looking for."

Rahm poked his mentor. "I'm trying to give your assignment some credit. Thank you."

Adi grimaced at them, struggling to adjust the sling that was still didn't fit right. "I hate to interrupt this mutual ego-stroking, but somebody had better come up with a plan to get us out of here."

"You came here looking for someone? You mean Ramallah?" Rahm asked.

"Exactly," Schwalm said. "Jesus taught that whenever one of his followers went to a new town, they should look for a person of peace."

Adi shook her head. "Could you two focus, please? Our attackers are not men of peace, and they're coming back. We need a plan to get out of here, or we're dead."

Rahm snorted. "Getting you two out of here will be a major operation. If an ambulance pulled up on the road right now," he pointed at the lone section of the two-lane highway, "it would take four able-bodied men forever to carry the two of you down the hill. I don't see that happening anytime soon."

"You people are always such optimists, aren't you?"

"You people?" Rahm jerked his head around and glared at her. "I am sick of Israeli racism!"

"Racism?" Adi looked confused. Then her eyebrows arched. "You thought. Wow! I am not a racist! I'm talking about 'If it bleeds, it leads.' Journalists always sensationalize the negative. I was talking about you journalists, not your people."

"Okay, maybe that's too strong." Rahm put his open hand under his chin. "But I have had it up to here with Israeli put-downs and attacks." He held up his hand, showing its back to her. A jagged scar ran across three knuckles. "This is a gift from some Israeli settlers that put my friend and me in the hospital. I was lucky. Only sixteen stitches. It laid my friend up for three months."

Adi mocked, "Poor little victim. I've heard enough whining from Arabs too. If you didn't go around throwing rocks and rioting, you wouldn't get hurt."

"We were just hiking on a trail near their settlement, and they jumped us. We did nothing. You want me to believe that it's okay for Israel to steal the land where my great-grandfather's great-grandfather planted our olive grove? If it's evil for a German madman to kill Jews, how is it okay for you to kill our people, occupy our land, and destroy our homes?"

Adi tried to blow the wisp of blonde hair that had slipped down in front of her left eye. "This has nothing to do with Hitler. This land is ours because God gave it to us four thousand years ago. And when Mark Twain visited Palestine he said it was an empty desolation."

"God?" Rahm countered. "You think God gave Israelis our land so they could build illegal settlements? And you're justified in taking it from us at gunpoint because of a quote written over 160 years ago?"

"My lit professor quoted him. Why wouldn't I take it seriously?"

"Because an American humorist wrote it whose stock in trade was ironic satire. That's why! Besides, a few years later, a Jewish man, a Jew named Cyrus Adler, wrote, '(It) impressed me with the idea that this little country is one of the prettiest on earth.' "

The Professor spoke, "I think both men were playing to an audience. Twain was writing to people wanting to hear evidence of biblical prophecies against the land had confirmed."

"And he was trying to sell books," Rahn interjected.

"Perhaps," the Professor replied. "While Adler was writing to his Jewish mother so he would naturally speak well of the Holy Land."

"Okay, maybe all that's true," Adi said. "I'm sorry about your home. But many of the demolitions happen because of security issues or code violations."

"The Israeli Committee Against House Demolitions says that nearly 50,000 Palestinian structures have been razed. If they were all considered security risks, then you people are paranoid."

"And ICAHD rebuilt a bunch of Palestinian homes, too."

The Professor interrupted. "You both must admit that you cannot lump any nationality together. Plenty of Israelis befriend and support their Palestinian neighbors."

"That's right," Adi said.

"And plenty of Palestinians treat their Israeli neighbors like family—calling them cousins," Schwalm added. "They don't all throw rocks and riot."

"Right," Adi said. "But don't forget, the Torah says that all the land, from the Negev to Syria, belongs to Israel."

"Did God give you a deed showing legal ownership? Because I have a deed to 68 hectares in Safa, signed over to us by Sultan Ahmed III in 1709."

Adi lowered her voice. "The Torah is four thousand years old."

"The Torah? Any court that would recognize the Bible as a legal land contract would have to be run by Jewish lawyers and judges."

"Now, who's the racist?" Exasperated, Adi wiped the sweat from her forehead. "The United Nations recognized Israel's right to a homeland. We didn't dream that up."

Rahm's fists clenched, and the muscles in his jaw flexed, "Does Israel have a deed to our land in Safa from the United Nations? Or not?"

Adi rolled her eyes and looked away.

"I didn't think so. Israel has no right to build a wall on my land. No right!" Rahm stopped pacing and noticed the Professor, whose eyes looked moist. Rahm opened his mouth to say something, closed it, and continued shuffling back and forth. Look at me. The Professor's man of peace? What a joke! Venting his pain couldn't help their situation. But he had a belly full. He needed to vomit it on somebody. I need to man up. Especially if the guys who shot up the van were coming back. But trying to de-escalate, he said, "I didn't vote for Hamas."

"Good for you." Adi reached behind her and produced her 9mm pistol, motioning at the ground with it. "But you need to sit down. Do you want to get shot?"

Rahm cocked his head. "Are you threatening me?"

Adi waved her gun toward the road. "No. I'm trying to be ready when they come back. I am not the enemy. So, unless the man of peace wants to rest in peace, he had better sit down."

CHAPTER NINETEEN
SINAITICUS

"Codex Sinaiticus is a priceless treasure. Copied around the middle of the fourth century in the south-eastern Mediterranean, it is the earliest extant manuscript to contain the complete New Testament and the oldest and best witness for some of the books of the ancient Greek version of the Old Testament, the Septuagint."
The British Museum

Ma'rib, North Yemen
1952

Lenard Jones stood on the stairs, nestled in the cool shade between two ancient limestone pillars that marked the entrance to the Temple. His eyes scanned the chaotic jumble of rocks and artifacts their excavation had unearthed. It was a treasure trove of history waiting for his team to decipher and share the story with the world.

“Frank, could you take a break from translating those inscriptions?” Jones’ gaze lingered on the rubble, his mind racing with possibilities.

“Gladly. This is making my brain itch.” Replied Dr. Frank Fallbright, the dig’s principal archaeologist, his voice laced with frustration.

Jones looked his colleague in the eye. “You should have been with us when we landed in Aden. King Hamid told me about Queen Aliya’s purpose for going to meet Solomon. He said it was a mission to open new trading opportunities. Solomon had just completed the construction of the temple. Is that right?"

Fallbright closed his field book and nodded an affirmative. "Absolutely."

Jones furrowed his brow, grappling with the intricacies of the story. "I wish I knew the region's history a little better. I gathered that there would have been an increased market for the frankincense produced here."

"Want me to give you a little background?"

"I know the biblical story about the exchange of gifts. But there are lots of gaps in my mind about the rest of the history."

Fallbright began, "The Quran says that one of Solomon's birds, the hoopoe, reported that the Queen worshipped the sun. So, he wrote and asked her to worship God. She responded by sending gifts. When he rejected them, she came with a caravan." A grin broke out thinking about the tales he would tell in D.C.

Jones asked, "Her motive doesn't matter as much as Solomon's response, does it? If he sent gifts back with the Queen, a trade agreement would make a lot of sense. If we could prove that Solomon sent Jewish merchants and ambassadors here to Ma'rib, that might connect with the later developments in Yemen. The King mentioned the Himyarite Kingdom."

"It's a surprise to most people to learn that Jews ruled Yemen for 600 hundred years," Fallbright enjoyed. Sharing some of what he'd dug up. He also found pleasure from provoking Jones. "But that doesn't prove your point."

"It sure supports it."

"Maybe," Fallbright replied mysteriously, "The Himyarite Kingdom started in the 2nd Century BC and lasted until 525 AD. For Jews to take over, they had to have been in the country for some time. Maybe we could establish a link between their presence and Solomon's trade delegation."

"Excellent!" Jones grinned.

"Hold on." Fallbright held up a cautionary hand. "Two plus two don't make five. Connecting her to Ma'rib is problematic. Himyarites had their capital in Sana'a. That's sixty miles away."

"Capitals move," Jones said, shrugging. "Our own moved from New York to Philadelphia and didn't wind up in D.C. until 1801."

"I will grant that the list of gifts the Queen gave Solomon sounds much like the list of Ma'rib's chief exports: gemstones, incense, and gold."

"If the Jerusalem Temple was a major trading partner." Jones lifted his chin. "Then there would have been a strong connection between the monarchy in Jerusalem and the one here."

"Well, Jones, all that you have is pure speculation. You can't confirm, beyond any doubt, the Yemeni belief that Queen Aliya lived here. But when I landed at the airport in Aden, I saw a poster. It said, 'Land of the Queen of Sheba.' The locals are convinced that Queen Aliya was the Queen of Sheba that the Bible speaks of and the Queen mentioned in the Quran. The British ambassador told me that the locals give her credit for building the ancient Ma'rib dam and praying at this temple. You have that going for your theory."

"Those details only support my theory," Jones said. "What I need is proof people can hold in their hands. I hope to find it right here! The problem is that too many layers of this site show evidence that the best artifacts have already been stolen."

"Until the discovery of Tut's tomb in 1922," Fallbright said, "people thought Egypt was completely picked clean. Let's not give up too soon."

"Finding Solomon's ring would seal the deal."

"Pun intended, right? Is that what this trip is all about? You led me to believe that this was a scientific expedition. You're here on a massive treasure hunt? I can't believe you!"

Jones swelled with pride. "It's exactly like I said the first time I called. We're here to conduct systematic scientific research. With an emphasis on archaeological research." Jones shrugged. "But if we find the Seal, it would be such a tremendous discovery that we could count on funding to continue our research. If nothing else, we could sell it for a fortune."

"Listen," Fallbright warned, "there is no evidence that the ring is anything more than a fantasy. None. We can be open-minded, but let's not be naïve. Besides that, I've heard that the legends claim that there are blessings and curses attached to the Seal. So, even if it exists, are you sure you want to be anywhere near it?"

"Good point, Frank. There might be nothing to the stories." Jones stared down a digger who'd stopped working and was watching them through squinted eyes. Jones wondered if the man might be a spy working for the King's cousin.

When the man saw Jones squinting, he scurried off.

"If we're ever going to find out anything about the Queen of Sheba," Jones added, "we had better get it done. Studying the suspected spy, he said, "Trouble's brewing. So, before we get run out of here, we need to get impressions of those inscriptions on the granite blocks, like the Egyptian team did last season."

"I'll have someone take care of it." Frank Fallbright's fingers traced over a line of Sabaean characters etched in stone.

"What does it say?" Jones asked.

"I haven't worked it all out yet. But here's mention of a queen. What follows appears to be something about pilgrimage and sacrifice. But with no vowels, the grammar is a challenge. I need more time. It would be nice to find another Rosetta Stone."

"Speaking of Egypt, what's the status of our manuscript cataloging a project\ at St. Catherine's?"

Fallbright turned to follow Jones as his boss strode up the stairs. To the upper level of the dig, "The messenger said the team estimates nearly 3,000 manuscripts in the monastery's collection. It will take time to catalog it all."

"Amazing. If we're going to stay on, we need to make sure we keep the funding that's been promised. I don't want to lose it. We need as much time as possible at St. Catherine's, seeing if we can't find the missing pieces of Sinaiticus."

"The good news is that we can have staff on-site year-round despite it being in the Sinai. Our season here is over at the end of March?"

"Yes. After that, it's insufferably hot. But doesn't that happen in Egypt too?"

"St. Cat's is in the mountains, same elevation as Denver. It rarely gets over 80 degrees, even in July."

Jones' head tilted. "This is a tremendous opportunity. Thank God for the grant from Truman's National Science Foundation.

"You believe the missing pages are there?"

"I don't know, Frank. But when Count Tischendorf hijacked Sinaiticus and took it back to the Tsar in St. Petersburg, he was not aware that he'd missed some pages. It's the most logical place to look. It really miffs the monks that Tischendorf told them the Tsar only wanted to borrow it. So if we could help them find those pages, it would guarantee us access."

"It wouldn't hurt your standing in the academic community, either."

"That thought did occur to me," Jones said, a glimmer of excitement in his eyes.

"When the Soviets sold most of their holdings to the British Museum, ownership got really complicated." Fallbright looked back down into the excavation.

"It is complicated. With pages scattered from London, to St. Petersburg, and Leipzig, but the monks believe they are the sole owners of the entire collection. Finding those missing pages at the monastery would help their claim. They want the whole thing back. All of it." Jones started walking away, , his determination clear.

"Sinaiticus is the most complete ancient manuscript of the New Testament. Even without those pages," Fallbright said emphatically. "It is one of the most important books ever written. Sinaiticus belongs to the world."

Jones whirled around and barked, his passion inflamed. "Never talk about Sinaiticus like that!" His tone then softened, his ambition seeping through.. "At least not in public. I agree. But the monks are so touchy about the Tischendorf episode that every time they hear Tischendorf's name, they get huffy. If anyone at the monastery ever heard us say that there was any question about their right to Sinaiticus, they would cut us off. We wouldn't be allowed near the place. With the project here looking precarious, we need to make sure we don't lose that one."

CHAPTER TWENTY
OPPRESSION OLYMPICS

"An eye for an eye only ends up making the whole world blind."
Mahatma Gandhi

Wadi Watir
Present

Rahm Khalidi stalked back and forth, keeping his eye on Adi, who continued waving her gun around to punctuate her conversation.

"Don't be paranoid," she said as she jabbed her gun toward the road. "You don't need to worry about me shooting you. But if you insist on making yourself a target, our attackers will be glad to oblige. It's basic tactics. If you can't be seen, you can't be shot."

Rahm Khalidi rolled his eyes, averted his gaze toward the road, and remained standing, arms folded.

"Please sit," Schwalm smiled and patted the ground near him.

Rahm kept his distance and plopped down, stirring up a puff of dust. His eyes prosecuting Schwalm for siding with the woman.

Adi probed her wounded shoulder with her finger and winced. "We know there are at least two of them. And they're heavily armed. We have just one sidearm. They will be coming for us."

"Too bad we don't have a nice Israeli wall to hide behind," Rahm said.

“Everybody knows that the security fence protects Israelis from terror attacks,” Adi snapped.

“We’re terrorists?” Rahm snorted, “In 1946, was Menachem Begin a terrorist when he blew up the King David Hotel? Palestinians say they learned their tactics from him.”

“They blame Begin?” Adi’s eyes flashed angry. “Ridiculous. Let’s focus here. Someone needs to watch the hill we just climbed.” She tried to stand.

“Stay!” Rahm stood and walked a few steps and looked down the hill. “I can see clearly from here. There’s no one anywhere.”

Adi’s eyes fluttered, then closed. “Okay,” she said, her voice weakening. “We need to maintain our situational awareness and hope someone comes along.”

Rahm charged ahead. “Menachem certainly taught us the path to peace at Deir Yassin with the slaughter of innocent women and children,” Rahm’s voice dripping sarcasm. “And you call us terrorists? Incredible!”

“Prime Minister Begin was fighting for our land. And the Netanya Center bombing wasn’t what I would call Palestinians playing nice.” Adi’s voice trailed off.

“Although I disagree with their tactics,” Rahm said, “I think Palestinians who take up arms against Israeli theft of our land are not terrorists either.”

“You cannot. . . Wait,” Adi opened one eye, “You disagree with their tactics?”

"That's right," Rahm pointed at Schwalm. "The Professor is right. Violence isn't getting us anywhere. But what other options do we have?"

"Would you two stop?" Schwalm shifted his position and flinched from the effort. He waved his hand. "Just stop it! Your oppression Olympics exhaust me."

"That's easy for you to say," Adi gave Schwalm the laser look. "You're American."

"Americans are not immune to suffering. Fear and its greedy cousin affluenza abuse my entire nation."

It was Rahm's turn to sound incredulous. "Affluenza? Are we talking about capitalism?"

"I'm talking about the disease, not an economic theory," Schwalm took a breath. "I'm talking about greed—but the America's soul-sickness."

Rahm's jaws tightened. "What does all this have to do with today?"

"An ancient dread drives the Israelis," Schwalm said. "And despair drags Palestinians down. How long will both sides allow fear to steer policy?" Schwalm sighed. "Listen, Rahm, I agree that Palestinians have suffered."

Adi said to Rahm, "Any movement now?"

"Nothing. The assault team is gone. Even the kid with the camel is nowhere to be seen."

Schwalm pointed at Adi. "Jews have a four-thousand-year history of suffering."

"Professor," Rahm complained, "I've heard you say, 'I am pro-Palestine, pro-Israel, pro-peace, and pro-Jesus.' But you can't possibly believe they are innocent. You know the situation too well."

"No one's innocent. Not Israel and not Palestine, and certainly not America. You both think that because you have suffered," he pointed at them both, "they should suffer." He winced but crossed his arms and pointing at them. "You are both badly mistaken."

"Meaning?" Adi said.

"What would happen if Palestinians stopped relying on violence? And instead spent their time and energy making sure their Israeli cousins felt safe?"

"Yes," Adi brightened.

"That damnable wall would come down in a heartbeat if Jews could stop living in fear," Schwalm said.

"The barrier stays," Adi insisted.

"Adi," Schwalm said, "what if Israelis honored the Beersheba Covenant and stopped blaming Arabs for everything?"

"And stopped building settlements," Rahm demanded.

Adi glared at Rahm. "We can't stop jihadists with platitudes." She then turned to Schwalm, puzzled, "What is the Beersheba

Covenant? Was that the agreement at the end of the Six-Day War?"

"No, it goes back a lot further. 4,000 years ago, Abraham swore to a Philistine king by the name of Abimelech that his descendants would always deal fairly with Abimelech's lineage. That's significant because the words 'Palestine' and 'Palestinian' derive from 'Philistine.'"

"Well, if these Philistines," Adi smirked, jerking her thumb in Rahm's direction. "If they would stop shooting rockets at us and stop blowing things up, then we would treat them better."

"And, if the Hebrew descendants of Abraham would treat the rest of the family fairly. If they would just stop stealing our land, and stop building settlements on it, then we would stop fighting."

"What if," Schwalm said, "both sides preemptively resolved that, regardless of what the other side did, they would stop the madness? Think about it. If you resolve this conflict with guns, wouldn't we see evidence of progress by now? Another thing, you both need to recognize that both alive. I believe that was an act of God's protection, and when he protects or preserves, it is always for some purpose. If you grant my premise, then you should consider that it may be meaningful that an Israeli and a Palestinian were both spared today and forced to talk to each other. Maybe there could be some actual conversation instead of just pontifications."

A chittering call overhead startled Rahm. His heart pounding, he gazed up and saw three vultures circling so close above them that Rahm could see their red heads. He jumped to his feet. "No more preaching." Pointing at Adi, he said, "She's right. Somebody has to go get help."

The birds squawked at Rahm's sudden movement and flapped to gain altitude.

"Any movement now?" Adi asked.

Rahm scanned the road that disappeared into desolation in both directions. All he could see were boulder-strewn mountains in a half-dozen shades of brown boredom. Searching the sky, he said, "Nothing. I don't even see those vultures anymore."

Adi struggled to stand. "I am going to see if I can get down to the road. We can't stay here."

"You're wounded and can hardly stand up. The Professor's no better off." Rahm stepped forward. "It's up to me. I'll go." He turned to leave.

"Wait." Adi offered her handgun. "You'll need this."

Rahm turned around and hesitated.

Adi gritted her teeth, "Take it. For God's sake, keep your eyes peeled and watch for tour buses or vans. Keep your ears open for our attackers. There is no limit to what they will do to get their hands on that drive the Russian gave you."

Rahm reached out to accept the 9mm, then paused. "What drive? The Russian gave me one thing. This knife." Rahm reached into his pocket and pulled out the red knife with the white Swiss flag emblem on the side.

She nodded. "It looks like a knife. But isn't it a little light for a knife? Look again. It's a high-capacity drive. That's the reason for the attack."

Rahm looked at the knife look-alike. Stunned, he opened it. It looked and worked like a pocket knife. But once opened, he could see that instead of a blade, there was a portable drive to plug into a USB port. It had a label in bold Cyrillic letters. His face turned red. "I thought I was going to protect us with this . . . knife . . . this thing," he said as he studied the drive. "What's on this thing? What's really going on? And who are you?"

Grimacing, Adi said, "We were following—" she gasped. Her eyelids fluttered then closed momentarily.

Rahm ran his fingers through his hair. ***I'm losing her.***

Her eyes popped open again. "I'm with Mossad."

"I told you they weren't newlyweds," Rahm said to the Professor.

"We were following Danilov. He was a cyber specialist—a high-priced code writer working for the Saudis. We suspected he was carrying information about his project. We had intel that suggested agents from Tehran, Cairo, or maybe even Beijing were pursuing him."

She started panting.

She's going into shock. I need to get help. Rahm turned to go.

But then she continued. "We wanted to make sure we got that drive before anyone else did." She pointed the gun at Rahm. "Give it to me." Her eyelids trembled. She leaned back against the granite surface that towered behind her and slid to a sitting position. Her gun hand suddenly went limp, and the gun slid across the rocks in Rahm's direction.

Before Rahm could react, her eyes reopened, and she recovered the gun. "Give me that drive!"

He looked at it. "I thought it was a weapon."

"It is. These days, the most powerful weapons involve bits and bytes, not bombs or bullets."

"I disagree," Schwalm said. "The most powerful thing in the world is love, and the most powerful kind of love is love for enemies."

"Love them? Ha!" Rahm snorted. "Most of the time, I don't even like them. Like now." He jammed the drive back into his pocket.

Adi took a deep breath and pointed her weapon at Schwalm. "You may not value your own life, but I know you care about Professor Schwalm. I've watched how you take care of him."

"So?"

"So, Israel's future is at stake." She cocked the gun. "I won't ask again."

Rahm glared in defiance. Then his shoulders slumped. He handed over the drive.

Adi looked at it, "This right here says 'Infectsiya.' Care to guess what that means in Russian?"

"Not really," Rahm feigned disinterest.

"Our techs believe it is a program that will immobilize a country's power grid. We suspect it targets Israel."

Rahm scrunched up his face. "I did a story a few months ago about the Palestine Power Generation Company. With all the security protocols in place, there is no way you could plug that thing into our system. I'm sure yours is even more advanced."

"That's what our technical section told me," Adi said. "But they also said that there are multiple ways a savvy agent could break in. We don't really care. I could just destroy it now, but I need to get it to our techs. They need to prepare for this type of attack. Besides, we don't know if Danilov delivered any part of the project yet. I have strict orders to secure it." She held up the drive. "Our attackers will be back. If this is in the wrong hands, our country is not safe. While it is in your hands, we're not safe." With that, she put the drive into a plastic evidence bag, sealed it, and put the bag in the pocket of her beige cargo shorts.

When Rahm heard a distant engine start, they all froze in place. No one breathed. None of them moved until they heard a vehicle engine fire up and then fade into the distance.

"Okay. I'm going," Rahm said.

Adi cocked her head to the left, held up the 9mm again, and said, "I assume you won't use it on me."

"I don't plan to use it all," Rahm said as he turned to go.

"Take the gun." Adi held out the 9mm. "You may need it to stay alive." Then she pulled it back. "On one condition."

"Yes. I know. You want to keep the drive. No problem." Rahm reached out, took the gun, looked at it, then handed it back to her.

Adi looked at his scarred hand. "I'm sorry about what those settlers did to you and your friend. Most of us aren't like that, you know?"

"Thanks. I know. Listen. I can at least run away if attacked. Neither of you can move. I think you should keep it."

Adi shook her head. "I feel like I could lose consciousness. And I don't think your pacifist friend will use it. No. You take it. If they are going to attack us, they will have to go through you."

Rahm stuck the weapon in his waistband in the small of his back and turned to go.

"Be careful. Move slowly and watch your surroundings. Stay out of sight as much as possible. We need to get the Professor out of here."

"I'm guessing that our attackers were in that vehicle we just heard drive away," Rahm shrugged, then added, sounding more confident than he felt. "Besides, I've been avoiding Israelis with guns my whole life. I think I can handle this." He eased his way down the rocky slope toward the road, his head on a swivel.

CHAPTER TWENTY-ONE
REVENGE

"The best revenge is to be unlike him who performed the injury."
Marcus Aurelius

Wadi Watir, Egypt

Present

In the desolation of the Sinai Coastal range, Rahm Khalidi descended back down to the site of the attack. The road approaching the scene had a view of the wreckage from both directions. I have to get those two some help soon. And this is a not a good spot to persuade someone to stop.

The burned-out remains of what ninety minutes ago had been a new van twisted against a rugged boulder. Wispy feathers of smoke wafted toward the Sinai's interior. Rahm scanned the horizon and listened for sounds of more attackers, but there were no signs of life except the vultures tracing circles in the sky.

Unsure how long Adi could hold on, she was clinging to life by a thread, and Rahm knew he needed help, and he needed it fast. He marched east, where people would be approaching from the coast.

Wiping the sweat rolling down his face, Rahm rounded the corner. When he arrived, he erched on the guardrail, Rahm's eyes darted anxiously, his senses tuned to the eerie silence that enveloped him. Suddenly, a rustle behind him snapped his attention. He spun, his hand instinctively reaching for the gun. It was nothing more than a lizard, fleeing from the harsh reality of the desertsat on the guardrail, panting in the meager shade of a large rock, hoping to catch a ride.

He had just plopped down again, when the distant hum of an approaching vehicle pricked his ears. When a van with a sign, Meridian Hotel, Dahab, approached. Rahm ran out into the road, waving his arms. Instead of slowing down, the van swerved and sped up. As it passed, Rahm could see that the Bedouin driver looked afraid, his face turning ashen.

Rahm yelled, "Help us! Please!"

But the van raced away. The tourists in the back of the van were wide-eyed.

Cursing his luck, Rahm surveyed his surroundings, his mind a whirlwind of tactics and desperation. He had strategically placed himself out of sight from the wreckage, ensuring no passing soul could spot the van's tragic remains. Glancing down, he discovered Danilov's blood staining his sleeve, a stark reminder of their dire situation. "Idiot!" he moaned.

Shaking his head at his carelessness, Rahm shed his outer shirt and threw it behind a nondescript rock along the road. Confident that his black T-shirt would conceal any bloodstains. With the passing minutes feeling like an eternity, another Meridian van approached. Rahm composed himself, mustering a smile as he flagged down the vehicle.

The van, packed with curious tourists, cautiously halted.

Rahm approached the driver's window, his voice steady but desperate.

The driver lowered his window a few inches

"My friends are up there, injured. I need your help to get them to the road as soon as possible."

The driver hesitated, citing the risk to his job. But three courageous tourists stepped forward, their accents revealing their diverse origins. Rahm noted the determination in their eyes, a spark of humanity amid the barren landscape.

Rahm crossed one lane of asphalt to step to the driver's window. He pointed at the hill. "My friends are up there and injured. I need help to get them to the road."

"I cannot leave the van. It will mean my job." The driver opened his hands and shrugged.

Three of the male tourists, a large blond man with an accent, sounded Scandinavian and two shorter but stocky Asians, said they would help. Rahm thought their accent sounded Korean.

The trio piled out.

He turned to leave, but then stepped back to the driver's door. The man lowered the window the rest of the way. Rahm held out his hand. "I'm sorry, but I can't have you driving away. Give me the keys, please," he said. The driver put the window up and started the van. Rahm pulled the 9mm out of the small of his back and jammed it into the driver's left ear to assist his hearing. He repeated his demand. "Keys! Now!"

Leaning away from the muzzle of the gun, the driver turned off the ignition and handed over the keys.

A Korean woman tourist in the back said, "You should be ashamed!"

Rahm turned to the blond guy. "Do you know anything about cars?"

A shake of the head.

An older Korean man said, "I know a little."

Rahm said, "Can you pull a wire or something to make sure he doesn't drive away and leave us stranded?"

The man told the driver to release the hood and removed a small fuse from a box mounted on the firewall. He handed it over.

"Thank you," Rahm said, and headed up the hill. "Come with me." With his makeshift team in tow, Rahm ascended the hill, his determination unwavering in the face of adversity.

~ ~ ~

In the slanting afternoon shadows of the Sinai desert, the atmosphere hung heavy with tension. Schwalm, the weary professor, strained to rise upon hearing the approach of footsteps, his frail form etched with exhaustion. "Hello?" he called out, his voice strained and weary

"It's me, Professor," Rahm called. "Don't worry. I brought help."

Schwalm sank back to the ground, his gaze falling upon Adi, her unconscious form a testament to the ordeal they had endured.

"Adi, she..." he stammered, pointing at her prone figure. "She passed out shortly after you left."

Rahm rushed to Adi's side, his concern palpable. He found himself captivated by her vulnerability, a strange mix of fear and admiration stirring within him. He wondered if she was still alive, his fingers trembling slightly as he checked her carotid for a pulse. To his surprise, her eyes fluttered open, her strength asserting itself even in the face of distress.

She swatted his hand away, her voice sharp. "Take your hands off of me."

Rahm stood and gestured toward the arriving tourists. "I brought help."

"I'm sorry. I—" Adi said. "I'm sorry. I worried. I—"

Rahm redirected his attention to the Dutchman and the others. "Can you two help her? While we assist my friend?" he urged, his focus unwavering.

What earlier took Rahm five minutes to travel by himself, took thirty minutes, but Rahm and the three tourists returned to the van with Adi and the Professor.

The younger Korean man helped Schwalm into the front seat.

"Thank you, sir," Schwalm said.

The man with mechanical skills reinstalled the fuse.

The big man squeezed into one of the rear seats.

Once he was in, Rahm helped Adi climb in next to the woman who had scolded him.

The woman said, “You poor lady.” She pointed at Adi’s shoulder. “Does it hurt?”

Adi managed a nod as she fumbled with her seat belt.

Rahm stood by the driver’s door, holding the keys hostage until the driver met his determined gaze. “Take us back to Nuweiba

When the driver reached for them, Rahm pulled them back. “To Nuweiba, right?”

“I will do anything you say. I have no wish to die here. But—”

“Turn this van around.” Rahm handed over the keys. “Take us to Nuweiba.”

The driver hesitated, his gaze flickering with uncertainty. “I will. But the medical care in St. Catherine City is closer,” he interjected.

“That’s near the monastery, right?” Schwalm inquired, his voice laced with.

“Yes,” The driver said. “Just four kilometers. There is a small hospital in the city and an airport. Mostly the military uses it. But if there is an emergency, you can arrange a charter flight.”

“Okay, but hurry.” Rahm urged, his eyes fixed on Adi, slid in next to her, then closed the door. “She’s in shock.”

With a screech of tires, the driver’s resolve solidified. He flipped the van’s AC back on, the cold air filling the vehicle as they sped away. Adi slumped against the Korean woman, her eyes fluttering shut as they turned the corner.

Adi slumped against the Korean woman. Her eyes fluttered shut as they rounded the corner.

In the fading light, the wreckage of their van came into view, a grim reminder of the peril they had narrowly escaped. The Korean woman gasped, her hand flying to her mouth, her eyes accusing Rahm. "Did you do that? There's a person in there!"

"Did you do that?" Her eyes prosecuted Rahm. "There's a person in there!"

Rahm met her gaze, his expression hardened with determination. "What's left of three people," Schwalm stated grimly, his voice heavy with sorrow.

Everyone stared with morbid fascination.

The driver's eyes met Rahm's, a silent understanding passing between them. "We need to alert the authorities," he declared, his tone grave.

"We will notify the authorities *after* my friends receive medical attention." Rahm asserted firmly, his resolve unshakable.

"There is an army outpost in St. Catherine City," the Meridian Bay driver informed him. "We can alert them on our way to the hospital."

"After we get medical attention, but not before," Rahm affirmed, his tone resolute.

The driver nodded, his eyes reflecting the gravity of their situation. He sped onward, carrying them away from the wreckage and deeper into the heart of the Sinai.

Rahm studied Adi with concern. Reflecting on what the Professor had said. Was there a purpose in thrusting the three of them together into this perilous odyssey? He pulled out his notebook and jotted a few words.

CHAPTER TWENTY-TWO
NO SURVIVORS!

"Never doubt that a small group of thoughtful, concerned citizens can change the world. Indeed, it is the only thing that ever has."
Margaret Mead

Nuweiba Hilton
Present

In the dim-lit recesses of the Hilton's opulent lobby, Saeed Qatal's steely eyes blazed with intensity. He spat his words in Farsi, a language that dripped like molten metal from his lips. "No excuses!" His voice, despite its harshness, was a mere whisper, meant only for the ears of his subordinates. A menacing mustache, sharp and black as obsidian, curled downward at the edges, emphasizing the severity of his expression.

"You let them escape? Incompetent! Why did you retreat?" The rebuke hung heavy in the air, punctuated by the defiant stance of the crew leader, arms folded across his chest.

"We had only that one RPG round left, and the old Kalashnikov you gave us jammed. Is that our fault?The crew leader's retort, tinged with defiance, crumbled beneath the weight of Qatal's fury.

"Silence!" Qatal's bark cut through the air like a gunshot. "VAJA has supplied all you need."

The desk clerk, a mere spectator to the clandestine drama unfolding before him, wore a mask of worry as he glanced up from his duties.

Qatal's voice lowered to a venomous hiss. "Kalashnikovs are the most reliable automatic weapons ever built. If you weren't so incompetent, the supplies I issued should have been sufficient. You should've charged the van and taken out any resistance with your sidearms."

"But Colonel," the driver dared to interject, his voice quivering, "you told us to keep a low profile. I saw the flash of a reflection from a scope or binoculars on the hill above us. We feared the military was in the area."

"Cowards! I don't know what made me think you could handle this simple assignment." Qatal's disappointment hung in the air, thick as smog, suffocating his underlings.

The crew leader's arms dropped to his side, and he looked down.

On his best days, Saeed Qatal exuded a fearsome aura. But this was not one of his best days. At six foot three inches tall, he towered over his subordinates. His slender frame disguising the ruthless reputation he held within the secretive corridors of VAJA. The fear reflected in their eyes brought a cruel satisfaction to Qatal; to him, it was as good as respect.

Removing his mirrored Cartier sunglasses, Qatal leaned closer, his eyes aflame with determination. "I want that thumb drive in my hands today. Do you understand? Today! Stop sniveling and trying to blame others for your failure.

Complete the assignment. Do the job with what you have, and quit complaining!"

The trio of men exchanged nervous glances, their resolve flickering amidst the intensity of Qatal's gaze. Then, with a collective gulp, they nodded and hastily retreated.

"Come back here!" Qatal's command sliced through the air like a dagger. He glanced around, ensuring no prying ears lurked nearby. "No survivors this time."

Three heads nodded in unison.

"While you work for me, you are VAJA. We get things done. We do not make excuses!"

Once the men had vanished, Qatal stood tall, his posture unwavering. He replaced his sunglasses, smoothed the front of his suit jacket with a practiced hand, and stepped out into the world.

In the reflective surface of the Hilton's lobby window, he scrutinized his own image with meticulous care. A thin smile tugged at the corners of his lips as he straightened his tie, a symbol of his unwavering confidence.

With a swift motion, he pulled out his phone, dialing a number with deliberate precision. "Danilov and the hotel driver are dead," he intoned coldly. "The team found their bodies in the van's wreckage. The male Mossad agent's remains littered the road. We could not locate the drive."

Qatal's jaw clenched as he listened to the voice on the other end. "What? No, sir, they found no evidence of the drive in the wreckage. One of the three survivors must have it. Two are tourists, a Palestinian and an American. The third, a female agent, Ovitz, is with them. Two of them left blood trails. We will have all three in hand soon."

Silence fell, and Qatal's face contorted with a mixture of frustration and determination. He absentmindedly pulled on the end of his mustache, his mind whirring with plans and contingencies. "I understand. Yes, sir. I know. Have I ever failed? Ever?"

The voice on the phone responded, and Qatal's resolve hardened. "That's right. Not once. I will get the job done. I always do." With a decisive click, he ended the call, jutted out his chin defiantly, and strode away, a force of nature bound to accomplish his mission, no matter the cost.

CHAPTER TWENTY-THREE
THE JACKAL

"There is no greater danger than underestimating your opponent."
Lao Tzu

Port Aden, Yemen
1952

Weakness clung to Jamil Ahmed like a stubborn shadow, a bitter reminder of his recent battle with dysentery as he left the Republic Hospital in Aden. Evening descended, casting elongated shadows over the hospital's parking lot. His fever had subsided, but its traces lingered, gnawing at his bones. The gentle breeze from the Gulf of Aden offered a momentary respite, but as he ambled towards Main Street, the sunset chilled him to the core.

A passing camel cart became his reluctant chariot, the effort to hoist his massive frame onto its back a Herculean task. Aden's potholed roads tortured him with every jolt, his feet occasionally dragging along the ground. "The Westerners always seize the glory for my toil," he grumbled, his voice lost in the wind.

The diminutive driver looked back. "Did you say something?"

"It was nothing," Jamil replied, his voice barely audible. Beneath his apparent calmness, a storm raged. He dreamed of an end to British occupation in Egypt and across the Muslim world, along with a hope that justice might finally grace the field of archaeology. The disparity between Western accolades and the obscurity that shrouded him and his Egyptian colleagues rankled him. Jamil couldn't ignore the bitter truth: the fruits of his labor fattened the pockets of foreign interlopers.

The road smoothed as they neared Aden's British-controlled harbor. Jamil's thoughts wrestled with conflicting desires. "I want them out," he mused internally. "But I love their hotels." He made adjustments. Like trading traditional Egyptian attire for Western shirts and trousers. These marked his attempts to blend in with his British overlords. The facade of conformity alienated him from his neighbors, yet he remained unflinching in his resolve. Hypocrite or not, he did what he had to do.

Initially, Jamil had accepted Western dominance. Believing it a fair trade for their guidance in his archaeological pursuits. Yet, as his expertise grew, resentment festered. His hard work became a beacon, leading others to fame and fortune while he toiled in obscurity. It was an injustice he could no longer stomach.

Now, holding Solomon's Seal in his pocket, he envisioned recognition and wealth within his grasp. His fingers caressed the precious artifact in its protective pouch. Contemplating how to claim credit for its discovery and maximize his financial gain. The British Museum in London beckoned with its deep pockets, but trust lay with the Egyptian Museum of Antiquities in Cairo.

Fantasies of fame and unimaginable wealth flooded his mind. Then a chilling thought pierced his reverie. Murad Buckshan, if he spoke of what he knew, it would allow Jones to snatch the acclaim away. Anxiety clenched Jamil's stomach. Murad had to be silenced. But first, he needed rest. A low groan escaped his lips.

The cart driver asked, "Are you in pain?"

"In here." Jamil tapped his fevered head. "Only in here."

Now, holding Solomon's Seal, he envisioned recognition and wealth within his grasp. His fingers caressed the precious pouch, contemplating how to claim credit for its discovery and maximize his financial gain. The British Museum in London beckoned with its deep pockets, but trust lay with the Egyptian Museum of Antiquities in Cairo.

After realizing that Jones could try to grab all the glory, Jamil made up his mind. He would take the Seal to the Egyptian Museum after delivering Jones' message to St. Catherine's Monastery.

The following day, revitalized by a night's reprieve and a hearty lunch, Jamil set out on his mission. Shopping for his journey, including a stop at a pharmacy for seasickness remedies, filled his day. Anticipation coursed through him as he contemplated the path ahead. First, he would deliver Jones' message to St. Catherine's Monastery. Then, he would secure his rightful place in history and wealth.

As twilight settled over the harbor district, Jamil emerged once more into the labyrinth of bustling activity. The dimming light painted a canvas reminiscent of Cairo, yet his senses remained sharp, attuned to the slightest hint of danger. His eyes darted like a hawk, scanning the labyrinthine alleys, vigilant for threats veiled in shadows. Tension swelled, reaching its crescendo with a sudden epiphany. Murad Buckshan, his relentless pursuer, would not stop.

Before he could double back to Ma'rib and confront Murad, he needed to secure passage on a boat destined for the Sinai. The nocturnal harbor, usually a deserted realm, now buzzed like an anthill in daylight. Walking along the waterfront, he inhaled the salty tang of the sea; the sun dipping low, casting long shadows over the quay. The billowing sails of feluccas stirred memories of Cairo. While water taxis weaved like agile serpents, ferrying supplies and souls to the SS Uganda, poised for its voyage to India.

At the ticket booth, Jamil scanned the schedules for the journey to Sharm el-Sheikh. The bustling port on the Gulf of Aqaba. He recounted a fictitious tale of visiting his cousin in St. Catherine City to the ticket agent. With his keen peripheral vision, he caught a flicker of movement reflected in the ticket window. Fixated, he scrutinized the reflection, uncertainty gnawing at him. Pedestrians, trucks, bicycles—a mundane parade. But paranoia had never been his style. There, amidst the mundane, a balding head and a hooked nose. Murad, attempting to slither out of sight. Adrenaline surged. "I see you, vermin!"

"Sir? May I help you?" The impatient ticket agent interrupted his thoughts.

"I'm sorry. Yes. When's the next departure?" Jamil asked, feigning composure, while his senses remained on high alert.

"At high tide, at 8:00 p.m."

"Tonight? One ticket, please." He handed over the required sum, met with disdain for not using British pounds.

Jamil scowled, resolving that such condescension would end with the British occupation. After the currency exchange, he pocketed his ticket and change, all the while aware of Murad's lurking presence. The pursuit intensified; Murad hungered for the Seal, a feeling Jamil knew all too well.

With purposeful steps, he entered a dimly lit restaurant, eyes darting like a caged animal assessing threats. Seated in the farthest corner, he pretended to study the menu, all the while discreetly observing every patron and the fading daylight outside. Detecting nothing amiss, he ordered a plate of lamb mandi with basmati rice.

"Our specialty," the waiter declared.

"My stomach prefers the sea on a full tank," Jamil quipped, his smile belying the turmoil within. He ate, savoring every bite, yet thoughts of Murad eclipsed his appetite. The waiter, clearing his plate, eyed the uneaten portion.

"The big man has a small appetite," he remarked.

Jamil smiled thinly. "I've been sick," he replied, the half-truth disguising his inner turmoil: his unease stemmed from the jackal trailing him. "But the Seal is mine." His fingers reached into the pouch in his pocket, finding solace in its familiar shape. Inspiration struck like a bolt of lightning. Leaving a generous tip behind, he strode into the growing darkness, his smile now a mask for the storm brewing within.

A showdown loomed, and Jamil was ready. The taste of betrayal soured his mouth, but determination set his jaw. His mission was clear: protect his discovery, silence the traitor, and claim his rightful place in history.

With every step, Jamil felt the weight of destiny on his shoulders. The Seal in his pocket pulsed with ancient power, a reminder of the stakes at hand. As he disappeared into the gathering darkness, a steely resolve glinted in his eyes. Fate had dealt him a hand, and he was prepared to play his cards. The game was afoot, and Jamil Ahmed was ready to seize his place in the annals of history.

CHAPTER TWENTY-FOUR
WE'RE A MESS!

"He is most free from danger, who, even when safe, is on his guard." Publilius Syrus

St. Catherine City, Egypt
Present

They emerged from the sterile confines of the hospital. Rahm Khalidi halted at the entrance, his eyes scanning the surroundings with a mix of caution and anticipation. Beside him stood Adi Ovitz, her determination cutting through the air like a blade. “Well, I guess this is goodbye,” Rahm said, his voice edged with concern. “We’re heading to the monastery. I still think you should stay here, as the doctor suggested.”

A flicker of defiance crossed Adi’s eyes. “Actually,” she replied, her tone unwavering, “I’m going with you

Schwalm, the older man in the group, chimed in. “Really?” he asked, his surprise mingled with amusement. “I’m delighted, although I tend to agree with Rahm.”

“But you’ve recovered the drive. That was your mission, wasn’t it?” Rahm questioned, trying to grasp the depth of Adi’s resolve.

Adi brushed off the query, her gaze fixed on a distant horizon. “While they were tending to you, Professor,” she said, her voice tinged with urgency, “I contacted headquarters. The techs are eager to get their hands on the drive immediately. But the

General hopes to resolve matters at the embassy level. Either way, he assured me an extraction team will be here within 36 hours."

"You're going to take that thing to the monastery?" Rahm interjected, his concern etched across his face. "Is that safe?"

Adi met Rahm's gaze with unwavering determination, her silence more eloquent than any words she could have spoken. As she turned her attention back to Professor Schwalm, Rahm shook his head in exasperation. She was, he thought, remarkably impudent.

"Dr. Schwalm," she addressed the professor, her voice steady, "I need to take the drive to a secure location. I understand the monastery is like a fortress. Would it be alright if I accompanied you?"

Schwalm's broad smile spoke volumes. "It's settled then. Let's be on our way."

They stepped out of the entryway into the slanting sunlight of late afternoon. The temperature was already dropping. The light breeze that drifted down from the El Tor Mountains caressed Rahm's face.

~ ~ ~

Meanwhile, Habib, an observant taxi driver, waited patiently for a fare near the hospital's entrance. His eyes sharpened as he spotted two men and a striking blonde woman emerging from the hospital doors. He put aside his book, curiosity piqued. "Taxi?" he offered, gesturing towards his cab.

The woman, her left arm in a sling, nodded in agreement. Habib noticed her uncovered blonde hair and couldn't help but wonder if she was not a Muslim. His observations, however, swiftly shifted to the state of their clothes – bloodied and torn, indicating some sort of violence.

"What happened?" Habib inquired as he loaded their backpacks into the trunk, concern etched on his face.

"There was an issue with our van," the woman explained cryptically

She opened the car's rear door and urged the older man to get in. He complied and moved to the center.

Zhey do what woman say. She boss?

"My name Habib. Where to, please?" he asked the woman over the roof. He looked into her stunning brown eyes. "Hotel? Or maybe monastery?"

"The monastery, please." the woman did not return his gaze but looked nervously over her shoulder and got in.

Habib slid behind the wheel and sized up his passengers in the rearview mirror. *In accident?*

The young man, who looked like he might be an Arab, got in behind the driver's seat. "You should have stayed, Adi," he said. "The doctor thought you should recuperate for two days longer."

Adi shook her head resolutely. "You saw how they acted when I showed them my passport. I'll take my chances at the monastery."

"Rahm's right," the older man said. "You don't look too good. You need rest."

Habib turned the cab toward the monastery. *Adi Israeli? Old man American?* His mouth went dry.

Zhey spies? His suspicions deepened as he listened to their conversation.

"I can rest at St. Catherine's," Adi insisted. "I trust the monks at the monastery more than those people at the hospital."

Habib maneuvered the cab towards the shrine, his mind racing with possibilities. The atmosphere in the car grew tense. He couldn't shake the feeling that he had unwittingly become part of something far more complicated than a simple taxi ride. He glanced over his shoulder. "What happen?"

"There was an issue with our van," Adi repeated.

"Yes, there was an unfortunate incident," the older man said. "Thank you for asking. But the people at the hospital did a great job. The doctor said that I might have a permanent limp, but I'll be fine. Your English is good. Did you study it in school?"

"Many tourist here. Habib talk."

"That is very clever."

"Sank you." Habib slowed as he approached the open-air tourist market strategically placed on the only road to the monastery. A dozen stone stalls lined the right side. They were built with the same brown rocks that formed the mountains that towered above them. Scarves, handbags, and backpacks draped their arched facades. Racks of postcards stood in front of several. Most also displayed stuffed camel dolls. One upscale stall specialized in religious art.

"Sis is suq." Habib said, then he glanced up in the mirror and asked, "Would you like stop and shop? You take home Bedouin gift? Habib, wait." *Distance plus time. How Habib make a dime.*

The older man sitting in the middle said, "No. No shopping. Please." Then he said to the young man, "You've been worrying about us. But what about you, Rahm? How are you doing?"

Old man American.

Habib navigated the car through the bustling market, his eyes darting between the road and his rearview mirror.

Adi craned her neck and looked out the back window.

"I banged my head during the attack," Rahm said. "While I was waiting for you two, I had a stabbing pain behind my eyes. I wonder what's wrong?"

In the mirror, Habib saw the woman give her head a slight shake and a disapproving look.

Attack? Not tell Habib? Why at hospital?.

Rahm held his hand to his forehead. “I have a raging headache. It feels like there’s pressure right behind my eyes.”

Is he a Palestinian? Wait. The American called him Rahm. Is he a Jew? His accent is Arab. The conversation inside the cab was laced with mystery and tension, and he couldn’t shake the feeling that he had stumbled upon something far more significant than a simple fare

“Any dizziness or nausea?” Adi asked. Concern in her voice.

“Old guy is American, woman Israeli, and he Arab?”

“No nausea, but a little dizziness,” Rahm said.

“Sounds like a concussion. Look at me. Let me see your eyes.”

Rahm leaned away from her.

She wife?

“We’re all a mess,” the old man chuckled.

Habib snaked his way through the market, where a few tourists wandered into the road.

He honked his horn at one man standing in the middle of the street, taking photos. “Look before walk in street!” He shouted out the window. When the man looked startled, Habib extended his hand, palm down, then flipped it over quickly to show his irritation and said, “Crazy people!” In the mirror, he noticed the

Israeli woman looking from side to side, studying every person as if she were a cop or a fugitive.

There was something more going on inside his taxi than he had bargained for. Habib felt it in his bones and hoped it would be over soon. It was very short drive.

CHAPTER TWENTY-FIVE
NAPOLEON'S WALL

"Denial ain't just a river."
Mark Twain

St. Catherine's Monastery
Present

As they rounded a corner and drove up Wadi el Deir, the ancient monastery materialized on the horizon like a relic from a forgotten era.

“Look at that place,” Rahm pointed.

Habib glanced at the meter and slowed again. Mindful of the delicate balance between distance and time.

“What did you expect, Rahm?” the old man asked.

Rahm hesitated, his eyes still locked onto the distant citadel. “I’m not sure. I’ve seen the pyramids and Petra in Jordan. But I just didn’t realize what was here. Look. It’s a fortress.”

“Zhis monastery small and not so nice as St. Anthony Monastery.” Habib sniffed.

“My name is Kaarl, Kaarl Schwalm,” the American interjected. “Where exactly is St. Anthony’s?”

“So nice to meet you, Mr. Schwalm—”

"Its Dr. Schwalm," Rahm said. "We usually refer to him as 'Professor."

Habib nodded and asked, "You Rahm?"

Rahm lifted his chin.

"Just 160 kilometers to St. Anthony, Professor," Habib pointed northwest, "Forgive please, you American?"

"Yes, indeed," Schwalm nodded.

"About 100 miles zhat way," Habib pointed again. "Across Red Sea, half zhe way Cairo. I can take. Much nice. Everybody like. Habib make deal."

Rahm asked, "Does St. Anthony's boast a wall like this?"

"St. Anthony wall fifteen meter," he said. "Fifty feet. Zhis only eleven meter. And St. Anthony have two tower. But zhis wall look big because is more short and stand by mountains. Was build in 6th Century."

"Remarkable and shows its age." Schwalm pointed. "What kinds of stones are those?"

"Wall?"

"Yes," Schwalm said. "In the photos, I saw online, they looked like they might be granite."

"Bottom granite. Justinian pay for build."

“I heard someone at the Hilton say something about Napoleon’s involvement in building a wall.” Schwalm frowned. “Is there another?”

“Only zhis wall, Doctor.” Habib shook his head. “After big flood, Napoleon commander build again in 1801. When closer, you see small stone at top.”

““You certainly possess an impressive knowledge of history.” Schwalm looked ahead and squinted.

“Habib read while wait. Like Middle East history. Help when people ask question.”

“Indeed,” Schwalm continued, “I’ve noticed, throughout my studies, the gaps in history. Just as with ancient walls, there are cracks, openings, and voids. I’m constantly endeavoring to fill in those missing pieces.”

“Yes,” Habib said, “If believe scientist, everysing is empty space, sings like rocks and mountain look solid. In books, history look same with good explains. But gaps is everywhere.”

“The Professor here is a history teacher,” Rahm said.

“Really?” Habib grinned. “Wonderful. Zhen you know gaps.”

“I am very familiar,” Schwalm said.

“I sink,” Habib said, shifting in his seat, “as time pass, mystery grow more.” As he navigated around a pothole, he pointed at the peak looming ahead. “We call mountain Jabal al Musa, Mountain of Moses.”

Out of the corner of his eye, Habib saw the woman looking over her shoulder out the rear window. *Why she worry? She sink another attack, maybe?*

“We came because of al Musa and the monastery,” Schwalm said.

“Many come for zhis,” Habib said. “But you see more. Painted Canyon. Dahab. Sharm el-Sheik. Habib drive you. You like.”

“The continuing existence of St. Catherine’s Monastery baffles me,” Schwalm said.

“And why here? Archaeology guys riding in Habib taxi say no proves Jews pass zhis way.”

“I told you we should have stayed at the beach,” Rahm said, grinning.

Schwalm leaned forward. “I heard they built a chapel at what they believed was the site of the Burning Bush. If this mountain,” Schwalm pointed through the window, “was designated as al Musa, I suppose they would consider any nearby shrub a candidate for the flaming bush, wouldn’t they?”

“Yes. But why monastery here long time easy.”

“How so?” Adi said. “How in the world can a Christian community continue to survive in such a harsh desert? Especially given the often-hostile nature of relations between Islam and Christianity?”

“St. Catherine’s oldest Christian monastery in world where peoples is always living.” Habib sounded like he was quoting from one of his books. “Was build between 548 and 565. For one zhousand five hundred year, priests get help from Bedouin neighbor. We help do work of saving artwork and papers. Muslim good neighbor, right?" Habib beamed.

"That's right, brother," Rahm said.

Adi, her eyebrows arched, expressed skepticism. "My personal experiences don't always align with that sentiment."

Schwalm, gazing at the ancient wall, remarked, "Looking at this wall, it's clear that it has not always been the experience of these monks either."

"Wall build before Islam come," Habib said over his shoulder.

"Yes, but weren't there hostilities during the Fatimid Caliphate?" Schwalm asked.

"Sad days." Habib nodded gravely. "But caliph make truce and monk change chapel to mosque."

"But they kept the wall," Schwalm said as they approached the monastery.

"Yes. Monks keep Order of Protection, too. Prophet Muhammad, peace be upon him, sign," Habib added. "Ask monk, zhey show."

Rahm turned to Schwalm and asked, "So what makes St. Catherine's so important?"

Habib interrupted, signaling their arrival. "Excuse, please. We stop here. You walk to room. Habib carry bag."

Adi insisted, "We don't have much to carry. We can manage," and was the first to disembark from the vehicle. Habib noticed her startle at the sound of a nearby van door slamming shut.

As he exited the taxi, Rahm handed Habib their fare and a generous tip and said, "Shukran. A little extra for you, brother."

Habib's eyes widened in appreciation. "Shukran. Habib give more ride. You call." He gave Rahm his business card. The printed number was crossed out. Hand-written numerals replaced it. "Remember. Ask about Order. Muslim good neighbor," Habib said.

The elderly man struggled to exit the taxi, and Habib rushed to assist. Schwalm waved him off, saying, "I'm fine, thank you very much, Habib. I enjoyed our conversation." With a grimace, Schwalm hobbled toward the guesthouse, while Rahm shouldered two backpacks.

"You tough guy, like Rambo, Professor," Habib called after Schwalm.

"The wound in his shoulder won't result in any long-term damage," Rahm said, "but the piece of shrapnel they removed was good-sized. The painkiller must still be working."

In a hushed voice, Habib said, "Please tell Habib attack happen."

Rahm looked at Adi and said, "Can't talk now. But right after the Nuweiba road merges with the Dahab road."

"Shukran, broser. Habib careful in zhere."

Rahm looked up at the wall, muttering to himself, "I hope they're still expecting us. They expected our arrival this morning."

Schwalm turned to wait for his young friend, "Rahm, you worry too much. Remember what Habib said. Tourists are becoming scarce. Why don't you run ahead and see what you can learn? I'll sit on this wall and wait here."

"Are you sure? I want nothing else to happen to you while I'm not looking. I would not forgive myself."

"Go ahead. Don't nag. I'll be fine," Schwalm reassured him, settling onto the ancient wall to await Rahm's return.

CHAPTER TWENTY-SIX
TISCHENDORF

"Essential Christian beliefs are not affected by textual variants in the manuscript tradition of the New Testament."
Bart Ehrman

St. Catherine's Monastery, South Sinai Governate, Egypt
Present

When his phone chirped and he saw Nabeel, his head security man's name, on the screen, Stephanos answered. "Yes, Nabeel?" He listened as Nabeel explained that one of their guesthouse boarders wanted to speak with him.

"The party involved in the attack?" Stephanos asked. After Nabeel confirmed that, he said, "Trouble seems to follow some people. Will he pose a threat?" Despite receiving assurances from Nabeel, Stephanos remained skeptical. "Send him up. But have security keep a sharp eye."

With a flick of his wrist, Stephanos ended the call, a curtain of secrecy descending upon his office. He methodically closed his laptop and tidied the documents strewn across his desk. Finally, he adjusted the ebony hat that identified him as a guardian of the Greek Orthodox faith. His keen eyes scanned the room, ensuring that all was in perfect order. Time slipped by imperceptibly, an interminable wait, until a series of raps reverberated through the silence. Come in."

A tall man stepped through the door. Stephanos guessed he was in his late sixties or early seventies. Pausing before entering, the man leaned on a single crutch. No wonder he was so slow coming up the stairs.

Stephanos noted the unease that clung to the man's every movement, though he appeared as innocuous as a lamb. Stephanos could only attribute this apprehension to the grandiose title displayed on his office door. Abbot Stephanos Climacus, Sacred Monastery of the God-Trodden Mount Sinai. *I hate that pretentious sign.* Stephanos stood and smoothed his black cassock.

"Your excellency, my name is Kaarl, Kaarl Schwalm. I have . . ."

Stephanos raised a calming hand to halt the unfolding introduction. "Stephanos, please," he humbly insisted. "I am only the Abbot. Come in. Have a seat." He motioned toward the ornate wooden chair. After shaking hands, he sat down.

Schwalm eased himself into the chair and elaborated on his purpose. "Yes, Reverend Father. I have been eager to visit your monastery for many years. Despite my aches and pains, I wanted to come to see you." He laid his crutch on the floor.

"Please, Kaarl, just call me Stephanos." He gazed into Schwalm's eyes, his own hiding a sea of questions: *Why the attack?* The man seemed harmless. But two people were dead. When his guest offered nothing further, he said, "I heard about the attack on your tour. I'm afraid this kind of thing is becoming all too common in the Sinai. Are you okay?"

"The doctors said that given enough time, all my wounds will heal."

That's an odd way to put it. Stephanos kept that thought to himself and instead asked, "What interests you about St. Catherine's? Our collection of manuscripts? Or perhaps it's our Crusader art?"

Schwalm, a shadow of pain crossing his face, replied, "Your manuscripts, sir. The legend of Count Tischendorf's discovery of the Sinaiticus here at St. Catherine's has beckoned to me for years. I yearn to lay eyes on those remaining pages." He winced and reached for his aching shoulder.

"Are you alright?" Stephanos half stood, his own unease dancing beneath the surface

Schwalm motioned for him to sit.

Stephanos eased back in his chair but remained vigilant. One heart attack symptom was pain on the left side of the upper torso.

"I will be fine, thank you. I never expected someone to blow up our van."

"Yes. I'm so sorry to hear about your troubles. I heard they recovered two bodies."

Schwalm held up three fingers. "Actually, three died, and we three survivors got banged up pretty good. Two of us had to be patched up at the hospital, and my young Palestinian friend may have a concussion."

"We weren't sure you would keep your reservation. We thought doctors might detain you at the hospital. What was the reason for the attack? Was it just a random thing? We've had more than our share of these kinds of things in the Sinai in recent years."

"I'm afraid I'm not at liberty to divulge the details of the assault," Schwalm admitted, his gaze unwavering. "But I can assure you, it was no random act. The intended target is no more. Yet, let us not dwell on my trials. I've heard that some pages of the Sinaiticus are still sheltered here. Is that the case?"

Stephanos, concerned for the safety of his sacred sanctum, pressed on. "I bear the responsibility of safeguarding those who live, labor, and visit here. I must understand if there is any lingering danger in accommodating you and your companions."

Schwalm stroked his beard before responding. "We were innocent bystanders. Just in the wrong place at the wrong time."

I'm not so sure about that. "I am sorry, Mr. Schwalm. Sadly, we do not allow the public to access our manuscript holdings."

Schwalm's lips formed a thin line, an undertone of disappointment coloring his expression. "I have journeyed great distances, investing both time and resources for this opportunity. I had hoped my academic credentials might influence your decision."

Stephanos, peering closely at the man, inquired, "You are a history teacher, are you not?"

"Yes," Schwalm confirmed. "I teach history at the Friends' High School in Ramallah. My initial doctorate was an exploration of the life of Osman I, the illustrious founder of the Ottoman Empire. Yet, I hoped my subsequent doctorate in biblical studies from the George Fox School of Theology might carry more weight."

"George Fox?" Stephanos interjected. "Is the Ramallah Friends' School affiliated with the Quakers?"

"Yes, operated under the auspices of the International Baccalaureate Organization."

"So, you are a visiting scholar," Stephanos remarked, inching his chair closer to the ancient desk. "That certainly alters the context." He harbored a fleeting suspicion about the validity of academic credentials, but such doubts remained unspoken. "Could you shed some light on your dissertation?"

"I focused on the variant readings at the end of the Gospel of Mark."

Good enough. "I'll see what I can arrange." Stephanos picked up his cell phone. "Do you have any special interests besides Mark's Gospel?"

Schwalm met his gaze unflinchingly. "Yes, your pages of Codex Sinaiticus."

"I still have concerns about the attack on your party. Until we have clarified those issues, I am afraid that will be quite impossible."

CHAPTER TWENTY-SEVEN
CONSTANTINE'S FIFTY

"I have thought it expedient to instruct your Prudence to order fifty copies of the sacred Scriptures, the provision and use of which you know to be most needful for the instruction of the Church, to be written on prepared parchment in a legible manner, and in a convenient, portable form, by professional transcribers thoroughly practiced in their art."
Emperor Constantine

St. Catherine's Monastery
Present

"That is quite disappointing. But I certainly understand the need for caution," Schwalm said.

He took that well. "Thank you for understanding. The pages of Codex Sinaiticus are our greatest treasure. But we can talk about the codex. Have you heard about Emperor Constantine ordering Eusebius of Caesarea to produce fifty Bibles for the churches in Rome?"

With an intrigued flicker in his eye, Schwalm leaned forward. "Yes, of course. How does that relate to St. Catherine's?"

Stephanos, however, wasn't about to reveal all his secrets just yet. He swiveled his chair with an air of mystery and retrieved an ancient, weathered tome from a towering bookshelf. Its pages carrying the weight of centuries. "This," he began, "is Eusebius' 'Life of Constantine.'" His fingers danced through the brittle pages as if caressing history itself. "Paragraph 4.36 contains the emperor's order. 'Fifty volumes with ornamental leather bindings, easily legible and portable for easy use. To be copied by skilled calligraphists well trained in the art, copies that are of the divine scriptures.' "

Schwalm leaned in, intrigue replacing his initial disappointment. "I've heard about Constantine's fifty," he said. "But again, how do you connect them to Sinaiticus?"

Stephanos, now brimming with anticipation, raised a single index finger and turned the page, tracing the lines of ancient wisdom. "Then again, in paragraph 4.37, Eusebius writes, 'These were the Emperor's instructions. Immediate action followed upon his word, as we sent him threes and fours in richly wrought bindings.' "

A furrow creased Schwalm's brow. "Threes and fours?"

As they talked, Stephanos could feel himself getting excited and letting his guard down. "There are at least a dozen theories about what that phrase means. Schwartz thought it might mean some copies had three gospels, and others had four. Kirsopp Lake believed they produced three or four copies at a time. But one theory was that Eusebius was sending Bibles in which they copied the text in three and four columns. Count Tischendorf proposed this after he got here in 1844 and saw Sinaiticus. They produced Sinaiticus about 325-350 CE, and its pages are in four columns."

Schwalm, now captivated by the enigma before him, nodded in understanding. "The timing is right, and they created Codex Vaticanus about that time, didn't they?"

A knowing smile played on Stephanos' lips. "Exactly! Both Sinaiticus and Vaticanus were copied at about the same time. And recalling the Eusebius puzzle about threes and fours caught Tischendorf's attention. That led to his theory. He had already been to Rome and had seen the Vaticanus manuscript."

"Three columns?" Schwalm inquired, his mind racing to connect the dots.

"Exactly! Sinaiticus was copied in four columns, but Vaticanus in three," Stephanos said.

Schwalm, now on the verge of an epiphany, posed the crucial question, "You're claiming Sinaiticus was one of the fifty?"

"We would like to think so," Stephanos said, "but we cannot say with certainty. We know Sinaiticus is the only Bible from that period copied in four columns—the only one in the world. Vaticanus is the only Bible on the planet in three columns. Sinaiticus and Vaticanus could be the last remains from Constantine's fifty. As Schwalm met his gaze, Stephanos felt a connection of kindred spirits. He let go of his suspicions and extended an unexpected offer. "I hope I'm not making a mistake. Dr. Schwalm, given your credentials and your interest in Sinaiticus, I am going to make a concession here because you've had an arduous journey.

"I hope I'm not making a mistake. Dr. Schwalm, given your credentials and your interest in Sinaiticus, I am going to make a concession here because you've had an arduous journey. Normally, granting library privileges to visitors is arranged months in advance. But I think we may accommodate your request. Let me check with our librarian."

Stephanos picked up his cell phone and tapped out a text to the head archivist. Then looking up at Schwalm and noticing how the man seemed nervous, he thought, *He's not telling me everything.* He sent a terse text to Nabeel. "Double the guards." He set his phone back on his desk and kept one eye on it while he waited for a response.

He explained the stringent security measures: "Before we can allow you to enter the library, you will be thoroughly searched. Some of our visiting scholars have complained about feeling physically violated. Let me apologize in advance."

Schwalm recoiled and looked pale.

"Please understand that we regard these documents as priceless. More valuable than our own lives. The pages will be brought to you one at a time. You will be required to wear gloves, which we will provide. An attendant will remain in the room with you, and an armed guard will be at the door."

A smile fissured Schwalm's white beard. "Thank you for your consideration. I will understand if your library cannot allow me this privilege. If I remember right, they found those pieces of Sinaiticus back in the 1970s, didn't they?"

Stephanos nodded. "I was a novice, straight out of university, when I found them in 1975. Extraordinary circumstances guided me to them. Some would call them 'coincidences.' One of my fellow monks calls them 'God-incidences.' We found over twelve hundred manuscripts. 108 pages of previously unknown Greek poems. A recipe attributed to the Greek physician Hippocrates. And manuscripts of a couple of dead languages. We're still sorting through it all."

Stephanos rubbed his bearded chin. *Finding Solomon's Seal led me straight to those manuscripts. I hope it is safe.*

CHAPTER TWENTY-EIGHT
TRASH OR TREASURE?

"And we revealed the Book to you with truth, confirming the part of the book in his possession and guarding it, so judge among them according to what Allah has revealed."
Quran 5:48

St. Catherine Monastery
1975

In the hushed labyrinth of St. Catherine's courtyard, Stephanos, a novice monk, stumbled upon an enigma that defied reason. A loose stone, an inconspicuous irregularity at the base of the tower, drew his attention.

Wondering if some men working on the remodeling project had disturbed it, Stephanos nudged it with his sandal, and it fell to the ground. He pulled up his cassock and knelt.

There was a small niche behind the stone. Peering into the shadows, he spied a wadded piece of yellowed newsprint. Unfolding it he discovered a cryptic time stamp 1952. Questions flooded his mind. Who put it there? Why? Wrapped inside the newspaper was a modest leather pouch and further mysteries. His fingers trembled as they unveiled a ring. Its golden band adorned with intricate silver filigree, crowned by a flawless diamond that sparkled with an eerie light. When he poured the ring into his hand, he felt a rush in his head. What in the world?

Driven by an inexplicable intuition, Stephanos found himself drawn toward the monastery's outer wall. An irresistible urge to dig consumed him, as if an ancient force guided his hands. Armed with a nearby shovel, he descended into the earth, unearthing a truth that had slumbered for ages

Driven by intuition, he moved towards the monastery's outer wall.

He grabbed a nearby shovel and started digging. An ancient force guided his hands as he dug, unearthing an age-old truth. The shovel struck the wall, resonating through the foundations. The ancient wall shuddered and groaned as the shovel point sank into the dirt.

The ground opened and swallowed a chunk out of the wall. The shovel slipped from Stephanos' hand. After a split-second of free fall, it clanged to the bottom of the void, yawning at his feet. He scrambled backward to avoid falling into it the pit. His black kalimavkion hat tumbled from his blond head into the three-foot-wide cavity. A cloud of dust billowed up.

As Milos left, Stephanos gazed at the chamber, its contents a hidden history etched in scrolls and parchments. His pulse quickened; he had become a conduit to a veiled past. Beneath the monastery's gaze, Stephanos stood on the edge, an unwitting pilgrim poised for a revelation.

Milos scurrying across St. Catherine's flagstone courtyard, muttered, "Who does Stephanos think he is, ordering me around? He's a novice."

Arriving at the abbot's upstairs office, Milos burst in, "Father, Father! There has been a collapse near the remodeling site. Brother Stephanos insists you come immediately."

In his mid-eighties, Abbot Ephraim gripped the arms of his chair and stood unsteadily. "A collapse? I thought I heard something."

"Yes, Stephanos was digging near the central tower's foundation. He caused a cave-in."

"Cave-in? We're remodeling the basilica. Why in heaven was he digging at the tower?"

Milos threw up his hands. "Who knows why Stephanos does anything."

"Was anyone hurt?"

"No, Father. The rest of the crew was still on their break. But when I gave Stephanos my flashlight, he examined the pit and got all excited. He refused to explain what he saw and started ordering me around."

Ephraim shook his head. "That's not at all like Stephanos."

"He demanded that you come immediately. You should probably see the mess he's made." Milos turned and held the door open.

They headed across the central courtyard. Abbot Ephraim called, "Milos, I will deal with Stephanos. Go alert a few of the brothers about what has happened. We may need their help."

Stephanos caught sight of Abbot Ephraim hurrying toward him. His unkempt grey-black beard streaming behind him like a ghostly banner. A quick nod passed between them before Stephanos descended the ladder he had propped against the hole. In his haste, another section of the crumbling wall gave way. A massive stone plummeted, shattering the wooden ladder and crashing heavily to the ground below. With a swift leap backward, Stephanos narrowly escaped being crushed beneath its weight.

"Look out!" Abbot Ephraim shouted. "What are you doing digging here? We're remodeling the basilica. That has nothing to do with the tower or the wall. You should not take matters into your own hands, young man."

"I'm sorry, Father. I dug here because when I started working on the basilica wall, I noticed a loose stone. When I kicked it, it fell out of place. So, I looked where the stone had been," he pulled a piece of crumpled newsprint from his pocket, "and I found this newspaper dated 1952."

"Curious." Ephraim pursed his lips.

"Yes, what's odd is that the paper is from Aden. What's a Yemeni newspaper doing here?" He didn't mention the ancient antelope skin bag wrapped inside the paper. Or the exquisite gold and silver ring. He considered saying something. But then had a thought. What was the tingling about?

Stephanos caught sight of Abbot Ephraim hurrying toward him. His unkempt grey-black beard streaming behind him like a ghostly banner. A quick nod passed between them before Stephanos descended the ladder he had propped against the hole. In his haste, another section of the crumbling wall gave way. A massive stone plummeted, shattering the wooden ladder and crashing heavily to the ground below. With a swift leap backward, Stephanos narrowly escaped being crushed beneath its weight.

"Look out!" Abbot Ephraim shouted. "What are you doing digging here? We're remodeling the basilica. That has nothing to do with the tower or the wall. You should not take matters into your own hands, young man."

"I'm sorry, Father. I dug here because when I started working on the basilica wall, I noticed a loose stone. When I kicked it, it fell out of place. So, I looked where the stone had been," he pulled a piece of crumpled newsprint from his pocket, "and I found this newspaper dated 1952."

"Curious." Ephraim pursed his lips.

"Yes, what's odd is that the paper is from Aden. What's a Yemeni newspaper doing here?" He didn't mention the ancient antelope skin bag wrapped inside the paper. Or the exquisite gold and silver ring. He considered saying something. But then had a thought. What was the tingling about?

"Father, I got the idea that something more might be hidden here," Stephanos said, pointing at the scene. "I looked at the rest of the wall and saw no other loose stones. But I got a strong impression that I should dig right here. So, I grabbed a shovel and dug. That's when this happened. Look for yourself."

Ephraim took the flashlight and looked Stephanos in the eye, "Sometimes impressions are God's guidance."

When the Abbot stepped forward, they looked into the hole together. Stephanos felt a strange mix of awe and trepidation. The ring he had found, concealed in the antelope skin bag, seemed to pulse with an otherworldly energy. Was this discovery divinely ordained? Or was it the artifact itself guiding him? Perhaps, he thought, it was both. He pulled the bag partway out of his pocket and glanced at it. He raised his eyebrows and stuff the bag back into his pocket.

Ephraim aimed the light into the gaping hole and caught his breath. When he turned toward Stephanos, his eyes were large and moist. "Perhaps this was no mistake at all," he said. "Give orders to have the monastery cleared of all visitors and non-essential staff. We cannot allow what happened with Tischendorf to happen again."

"Yes, Father," Stephanos spun to go but turned back, looking puzzled. "What should I say?"

"Tell the truth," Ephraim said. "We must always tell the truth. There has been a collapse. Those documents are a major concern. But so is the well-being of our guests."

Stephanos nodded and headed toward the front gate.

Ephraim called after him, "Do not mention what you've seen to anyone. As the good book says, 'Only a fool tells all he knows.' Just say that we have safety concerns."

Stephanos waved and was gone.

Milos arrived, out of breath. He had two fellow monks with him. "Would someone please tell me—"

Ephraim held up his hand. "I gave the order to close the monastery. As for Stephanos' discovery of those documents," he pointed into the hole. "We must keep this in strictest confidence. Understood?"

"Yes, Father."

Milos' mouth gaped when he arrived at the crater, yawning at his feet. His brow furrowed. "What documents, Father?"

The Abbot frowned. "There is a room below, filled with debris and several baskets of documents. We must preserve them." Ephraim glanced at his watch. "Please assemble our brothers and our most trusted workmen. Have them here by 4:00."

Milos and the others scurried away. Ephraim overheard Milos mumbling as he went and sighed. If Milos could be at home with himself, he might be easier to live with.

Just then, Stephanos returned, gasping.

"Well, brother, you're back soon. Is everything okay?"

"Yes, Father. They heard the rock falling throughout the compound. It was easy to persuade the people to leave when I explained that a small section of the wall had collapsed."

"Well done," Ephraim smiled. "Now, we must stabilize the wall. Then we can start transferring these documents to the archives.

We must take our time with them. Some of our predecessors have made serious errors in judgment with priceless manuscripts. I do not wish to have someone in the future second-guess how I handled this situation." Then he winked at Stephanos. "Or take my name in vain." Bending down to peer into the hole again, the Abbot said, "I could see scrolls and parchments. Paper replaced parchment in the Middle Ages. And by the 4th century, scrolls were becoming obsolete. Some of those documents must be ancient. We assume that in all this trash and debris, there may be some treasures."

"How shall we proceed?"

Standing up and stroking his stringy beard, Ephraim was silent for a moment. "Someone must alert the tour companies that we are closed. Indefinitely. It won't help our financial shortfall any good. But it will take time to make these repairs and process those documents. I will take care of that matter." The Abbot headed toward his office. "Milos will be back with the others at 4:00. In the meantime, think about how to best stabilize the wall."

Stephanos examined the structural damage sustained by the ancient wall. A crack zigzagged upward across the surface of the spalled plaster for about nine feet. Good thing the wall is so thick right here.

The work crew arrived, and Stephanos saw their Bedouin supervisor, Dani. He felt relieved. If anyone can fix this damage, he can.

"Dani, please get your crew to stabilize the wall. I think we need to start wherever this crack begins, even if we have to go all the way down. What do you think?"

Milos jammed his fists on his hips. "Who do you think you are, giving orders like you run this place?"

Everyone stopped and watched the two monks.

Stephanos' voice was calm, "I simply passed on what the Abbot said." He stepped back.

Dani spoke into the awkward silence that followed. He was short and stocky and the most skilled builder in the entire South Sinai governorate.

"Like good dentist, we clear away zhe decay." Rubbing the wall near the edge of the crack, he laughed. "When finish, zhis wall more strong zhan new."

Stephanos felt himself calming. He looked at Milos, who was still glaring at him. What is his problem? Then he said to Dani, "Thank you."

"What zhose paper?" Dani asked.

Stephanos said, "They look like—"

Milos held up his hand. "We won't know what they are until we've examined them. Please be careful that your crew doesn't do more damage than ***he*** already has," Milos said, pointing at Stephanos.

"You did zhis?" Dani's eyes widened.

"It was an accident. But yes." Just then, his fingers found the leather bag again. "I will tell you more about that later. Right now, I have to take care of something." Stephanos spun on his heels and strode away with his pocketed hand, clutching the bag tightly. Heading toward his cell, Stephanos wondered about the significance of his find. What mysteries did those documents hold? One thought throbbed more incessantly in his head. I need to know more about the ring.

CHAPTER TWENTY-NINE
AT DEATH'S DOOR

"The best among you is the one who doesn't harm others with his tongue and hands."
Muhammad

December 2016
Aleppo, Syria

In the dim twilight of the desert evening, Farhad Ghorbani stood paralyzed, his eyes locked on the gruesome scene before him. Major Saeed Qatal, his VAJA overseer, loomed like a malevolent specter over Kazem's lifeless body. Farhad's heart pounded in his chest, echoing the dread that pulsed through his veins.

Qatal's sinister smile twisted the corners of his lips as he spoke, his voice a low, menacing murmur that sent chills down Farhad's spine. "Kazem, you should have listened. I am a reasonable man. We could have avoided this unpleasantness if you had followed orders." Qatal stood and pointed at the body. "Did you see that? One shot." He turned, looked toward the entrance, and then back again. "At about sixty feet. Right between the eyes."

Farhad's trembling fingers clenched into fists, his mind reeling with disbelief. How could this be the end for Kazem, a loyal comrade for six long years, all because of one act of insubordination?

"Amazing shot," Farhad managed to stammer, his voice barely audible amidst the suffocating tension that hung in the air like a storm cloud. The realization struck him like a lightning bolt – he was standing on the precipice of a bottomless abyss, with Qatal as the merciless guide.

Qatal's eyes bore into Farhad, their intensity like daggers cutting through his soul. "Captain, how do we report this unfortunate incident?" Qatal inquired, his tone deceptively calm, as if discussing the weather.

Farhad's mind scrambled for an answer that wouldn't get him killed, too. "Well, Major, you, I mean . . . he disobeyed a direct order. But perhaps we should start by stressing that the mission was accomplished."

"Yes. Start the report on a positive note. Good idea." Qatal stroked his mustache and straightened his starched fatigues. He took out a handkerchief and dusted off his spit-shined boots. "We could not allow these pigs to resist."

"No, sir," Farhad replied, his voice hollow, his eyes fixed on the blood-stained sand beneath his boots.

"Why do you suppose he refused my order?"

"To shoot the children?" Farhad's voice faltered, the words catching in his throat.

"They were Syrians," Qatal snarled. "We are VAJA. We follow orders. We do not hesitate in doing our duty."

Farhad's voice trailed off, the weight of guilt settling upon him like an insurmountable burden. He hung his head, unable to bear the weight of the atrocities committed in the name of duty.

"Farhad! Listen to me," Qatal walked to the captain's side and patted him on the back. "You followed orders. You deserve a medal."

Farhad shuddered involuntarily at Qatal's touch, his mind consumed by a chilling realization. With this unhinged madman in command, any moment of hesitation could lead to his own demise. He realized with dread that the only medal he would receive would be one made of cold, unyielding lead.

St. Catherine Monastery
Present

Kaarl Schwalm read the brochure's description of one of the monastery's unique features:

Over the centuries, thousands of monks have lived and died at St. Catherine's. Because the monastery's cemetery is too small to accommodate all their remains, the monks are exhumed after three years. Their bones are placed in the Charnel House. There is no better way to grasp the legacy of the monks than to visit the crypt and see the piled host of skulls staring back through the eons in silence.

His recent visit to an oncologist had cast a stark light on his own mortality. Limping through the garden, he descended to the cemetery below. Each grave, outlined by fist-sized stones painted white, held a simple wooden cross, devoid of grass or flowers, embodying a sense of impermanence. Yet, amid the temporal nature of existence, Schwalm found solace in the promise of resurrection. Their friends were not buried; they were merely sown, awaiting a future reunion.

His injured hip protested the climb back up the stairs, his knee grinding with every step. He paused three times on the ascent, pain etched across his face. The looming specter of mortality clung to him like a shroud. Inside, the Charnel House revealed its eerie contents. He could see why some called it the "Bone Room." Stacks of human skulls reached chest high, their hollow sockets casting a disconcerting gaze. There must have been hundreds, maybe thousands.

Adjacent to the chamber, in a wooden cabinet behind glass, sat Saint Stephen, a 6th-century monk. Clad in black vestments and a white cross on a gold chain, the skeletal figure seemed frozen in prayer. Schwalm pondered the peculiar honor bestowed on Stephen when a reflection in the glass door drew his attention. A familiar face entered, shattering the monastery's silence.

The man was tall, with dark hair and mustache. Impeccably groomed, he wore an expensive beige suit, white shirt, and red and gold paisley tie. The man strode toward Schwalm, removed his aviator sunglasses with his left hand, and offered his right, smiling warmly. "Hello, my name is Saeed Qatal. I hope you can help me."

Schwalm reached out and shook his hand. "Kaarl Schwalm. Have we met?"

Keeping his grip on Schwalm's hand, Saeed said, "You were in the van, weren't you?"

The color drained from Schwalm's face. He tried to pull away, but the grip squeezed like a vise. He watched the smile disappear from Qatal's face, replaced by a stern scowl. Then Schwalm remembered where he'd seen the man before. The Hilton lobby!

"Dr. Schwalm, I believe you or one of your companions have something that belongs to me."

Schwalm jerked his hand away and said, "I don't have it."

Qatal's smile returned. "But you ***do*** know what I'm talking about." Qatal drew his pistol and chambered a round. "Hold up your hands."

Schwalm complied, and Qatal patted him down.

"Kaarl, I am a reasonable man. We can dispense with a lot of unpleasantness if you would just tell me who has it. Is it the man or the woman?"

Schwalm looked for an escape, but Qatal stood between him and the exit.

"I'm sorry," Schwalm said. "I can't help you."

CHAPTER THIRTY
THE PRICE OF MERCY

"For if you forgive other people when they sin against you, your heavenly Father will also forgive you."
Matthew 6:14

St. Catherine's Charnel House

Present

Rahm found the cryptic message left by the Professor, hidden cunningly within the door jamb of his room. It was succinct yet laden with intrigue: "Rahm, please meet me at the Charnel House. I have something for you."

Navigating the twisting corridors of St. Catherine's, Rahm's journey to the Charnel House was fraught with confusion. Anxious moments passed, forcing him to seek guidance from the vigilant security personnel. At last, he stood at the base of the steep stairs that ascended to the enigmatic Charnel House, drawn by an eerie sound echoing from within. "Professor?" he called out as he ascended with haste.

As he crested the stairwell, his eyes fell on a man in a distinguished beige suit, hastily retreating towards the distant parking lot. Rahm was on the verge of addressing the vaguely familiar figure when the sound of anguished groaning grabbed his attention. "Professor?" he exclaimed, his voice trembling. Intrigued, he ventured inside.

Schwalm lay prostrate on the unforgiving stone floor, his countenance contorted in pain as he gasped for precious breath. Rahm rushed to his side, beseeching answers. “What happened, Professor?”

Schwalm strained to lift his head, his voice raspy and strained, “Rahm, you must forgive . . .”

The raspy breath echoed off the limestone walls. That doesn’t sound good. Rahm had heard too many similar sounds in his coverage of war zones.

Desperation etched across Schwalm’s face, “You must forgive.”

“Forgive?” Rahm inquired, his mind a tumult of confusion and fear. “Who did this?”

“Man in the suit . . .” Schwalm’s voice trailed off, his strength waning. “Qatal. He . . . wanted the drive. I didn’t tell . . .”

Tears welled in Rahm’s eyes his chin trembling as he surveyed the morbid surroundings of the Bone Room, then fixed his gaze on the fallen scholar. “I should have been here with you. Qatal will die for this!”

Schwalm fell back. His voice visibly weaker. “For your own sake,” he whispered. “For mine. You must forgive.”

Through tear-streaked eyes, Rahm’s voice quivered as he bellowed, “Help! Someone help us!”

With a final, trembling effort, Schwalm issued an extraordinary proposition: “Forgiving is not easy or cheap. I want to buy yours.”

"Buy?" Rahm's head was spinning. "What are you talking about?"

"Here is my payment for your forgiveness," Schwalm smiled. His trembling hand pulled a folded envelope from his shirt pocket and presented it to Rahm. his eyes gleaming with an enigmatic smile. "Here is my payment for your forgiveness. Please, take it. I am paying you to forgive Qatal."

Two raspy coughs escaped Schwalm's weakened form. His hand slipped to the floor, his eyes closed, and he passed from this world, leaving behind an inexplicable aura of serenity. Kaarl Schwalm left the world the way he'd lived in it—quietly with a smile on his face.

Rahm, gripped by profound grief, bowed before his fallen mentor, tears flowing freely. More than a teacher,The Professor had filled the void left by Rahm's father, a void that grew ever more cavernous with each passing day. Rahm bowed with grief, his forehead on the cool flagstone floor, weeping. A wound opened in his soul, and the crushing chill of loss flooded in. It was a festering wound—a massive stone at the bottom of his heart, like a shadow that grows longer as daylight fades. The longer Rahm lived, the more significant that loss loomed. He groaned, "You took my father, then mother. Now the Professor?"

He felt a hand on his back and flinched. As he turned to see who it was, his eyes flitted past a gap between the threshold of the enclosure holding the skulls and the floor. In that gap, he saw a braided leather cord. It was visible from his angle on the floor and from no other. He glanced over his shoulder. It was Adi. "Leave us alone."

She stepped back.

Rahm saw that his tone had landed hard.

"What happened?" she asked.

"The Professor says—uh, said it was Qatal. I think I saw him leaving."

She nodded. "Should have known." She pivoted and headed for the door. "I'll get a doctor."

"Too late."

Adi stepped forward, bent, and put two fingers on the Professor's carotid artery. Then nodded. "I'll alert security."

Softer than before, "Okay?"

When Adi had gone, Rahm looked around to ensure no one else was there, then peeked again at the dangling cord. Cautiously, he reached under the threshold and pulled out a small leather pouch. It contained something about the size and weight of a large marble. He was about to open the pouch when he heard the gate creak behind him. He jumped to his feet and stuffed the pouch in his pocket, turning to see who had entered.

The Korean woman from the van screamed. "What did you do?" she pointed at Schwalm, lying on the floor a bloody mess.

It wasn't until that moment that Rahm realized that, once again, someone else's blood covered him.

She dropped her camera and fled, screaming, "Murder!"

Seconds later, Adi returned with two unarmed Bedouin security guards. They took one look at the scene and rushed at Rahm.

"No!" Adi yelled. "He's the victim's friend. The attacker is gone."

Undeterred by her words, they grabbed Rahm and put him in flex cuffs.

"Release him. It was an Iranian agent!" Adi shouted.

"Turn around and put your hands behind your back," the guard with two green stripes on his khaki uniform said.

Instead, Adi hauled out her blue and white Mossad identity card. "I'm Mossad. This man is innocent. I insist that you release him immediately."

The guards looked at each other. Then the corporal shrugged, and the other one pulled out a pocketknife and cut Rahm free but maintained a suspicious watch. The corporal took out his phone and tapped out a text. While he wrote the message, he looked up at Rahm several times. Then he snapped a photo, then one of Schwalm's body. After a few more strokes with his left thumb and right index finger, he put the phone in his shirt pocket.

Moments later, the bell in the tower rang steadily, a signal for all outsiders to leave the holy precincts of St. Catherine's.

Rahm dusted himself off and wiped at the blood on his hands with his handkerchief. But the blood would not come off.

"The police have been called," the corporal said. "Tell me what happened."

Rahm repeated what the Professor had said.

"Why don't you go clean up in your room?" the corporal said. "There's no telling how long before they get here."

Looking at Schwalm's body, Rahm said, "I don't want to leave him like this."

Adi touched his arm. "Rahm, he's not here. He's gone. I will stay with the body. I'll make sure he's not disturbed."

"But what about the killer? He might come back."

"Trust me," Adi said. "The last thing he wants is to attract attention. He'll be back. But not before things have settled down. Besides, I have these men with me."

The corporal pointed at Adi. "We will wait with your friend. Go. Come back here in fifteen minutes. This officer will go with you."

His accusatory finger pointed at the lifeless form of his beloved mentor, Professor Schwalm. His voice reverberating with a vow that echoed in the ancient walls of St. Catherine's. "When I find Qatal," he declared, his words seething with righteous anger, "I'm sending him to the lowest ring of hell."

He retreated, a vigilant security guard in his wake, their steps echoing in the monastery's silence.

Inside his room, Rahm turned and faced the unyielding guard, his eyes pleading for a moment of solitude. "I'm going to change my clothes. Could I have some privacy?" The guard's stern facade wavered under Rahm's plea. "Please?" Rahm implored, his voice edged with desperation.

Reluctantly, the guard nodded, stepping outside but not without a stern warning. "Do not lock. I wait."

"I'm not going anywhere," Rahm assured, closing the door with a firm hand. His breaths came in ragged gasps, tears blurring his vision. "Gone. He's gone," he muttered, his sobs consuming him like a tempest.

Once the storm subsided, Rahm pulled himself up, his fingers brushing against an unexpected bulge in his pocket. His trembling hand retrieved the pouch and the envelope, artifacts of a mystery that had swallowed them whole. The envelope bore a single word: "Rahm." Puzzled, he placed it within his passport, hiding it away. "I'll read it later," he mumbled. He couldn't bear to think more about the Professor.

With meticulous care, he unfolded the shriveled leather pouch. Its ancient surface whispering secrets of centuries past. A peculiar brand seared into the leather, caught his eye—a cryptic line drawing another riddle. Rahm turned the pouch, scrutinizing the symbol, but its meaning eluded him.

Intrigued, he dared to peer inside; the contents revealing themselves under the dim light of the room. A magnificent ring, adorned with gold and silver, lay nestled within the folds of the pouch, its glimmering surface reflecting the enigma of the moment. Rahm held it aloft, the weight of the ring heavy with history and purpose, its significance hidden like the buried truths of St. Catherine's itself.

CHAPTER THIRTY-ONE
SHOTS FIRED

"Unexplained, obscure matters are regarded as more important than explained, clear ones."
Friedrich Nietzsche

St. Catherine Monastery, Egypt
Present

Stephanos heard the tower bell reverberating in the hallowed courtyard of St. Catherine's Monastery. His pulse quickened, the rhythm of uncertainty. What now? He grabbed his phone and called down to the guard at the gate. From his second-story office window, his view limited to the basilica and the northeast courtyard. "Nabeel, what is happening?"

"Security reports there was a shooting in the Bone Room. Uh, excuse me. I mean the Charnel House. All the commotion is outside the gate."

"Close the gate! Immediately!" Stephanos ended the call and hurried down the stairs, stumbled, and nearly fell. When he reached out to steady himself, he skinned his palm against the stone wall. His thoughts raced, consumed by a bone-chilling realization. He had hidden something deeply significant within the enigmatic Charnel House, something he hoped would never see the light of day again.

Despite his advancing years, he made good time. He scurried along the flagstone passageway on the south side of the basilica until he reached the small courtyard in front of the church. Panicked tourists and staff clogged the passageway, pushing and shoving in their anxiety to get to the exit.

"Stop!" Stephanos shouted. "The gate is closed!"

The crowd quivered, their frantic energy quelled, like a herd sensing a lurking predator.

One brawny British man in a well-worn rugby jersey with a large number eight on it snarled, "Cor, why ya stoppin' us?" He arched his right eyebrow. It had a wicked scar above it, bristled with defiance. "Leave it out, mate, ya bang outta ordah!"

The crowd swayed, teetering between deference and rebellion. Their gazes darting between Stephanos and the imposing Brit. Stephanos hesitated momentarily, maneuvering through the crowd toward the formidable Englishman. He spoke in a hushed tone, a flicker of camaraderie illuminating his eyes. "My name is Stephanos Climacus. I am the Abbot of St. Catherine's. Someone fired shots outside the wall of the Charnel House, and I ordered the gate closed. I was concerned about your safety. But, my friend," Stephanos' voice dropped in volume as he approached the big Brit, "But if you insist, I can order that the gate opened again."

Although shouting and screaming could be heard from the direction of the gate, the nearby throng, though restive, held their collective breath.

The rugby player spoke for them all, "No, be'ah keep it closed, right?"

"As you wish," Stephanos said. I thought so. "Now, please excuse me. I need to get to the gate to speak to the guards."

At this, the British man yelled in a booming voice, "You 'eard dah padre! Move ya, Khyber, let 'im by!" Then he bulldozed through the crowd to clear the way for Stephanos. The big Brit's rugby experience made him especially effective in the close quarters of the monastery's narrow passageways.

Although he did not appreciate the Brit's pushing and shoving, Stephanos tolerated it; no, he was grateful for the man's help to get to the exit and, hopefully, to the Charnel House.

When they pushed past the fenced-off tree known as the Burning Bush, Stephanos wondered. Since frightened crowds are mindless and amoral, is this the only way? He worried he was compromising. But driven by the urgency of the situation, he would have to resolve that question later.

Upon reaching the gate, the clamor around the entrance had settled into an uneasy silence. Yet, the collective agitation still lurked beneath the surface, the scent of fear clinging to the air like a shadow.

"Nabeel," Stephanos leaned close to the guard at the gate, "where are the police?"

"I do not know, Father. We have not needed them here often. When that heavy Swiss woman had a heart attack years ago, the ambulance took almost an hour to arrive. The police never came."

"I don't remember that."

"Because you were not here, Father." Nabeel winked.

"Where was I?"

Nabeel winked. "You were in Jerusalem, being consecrated as Abbot."

"Why didn't you tell me about—" The wailing of approaching sirens interrupted.

The crowd grumbled and renewed their pushing toward the gate. A woman cried plaintively, "Let us out!"

Stephanos held up his hands. "Please. You can hear that the police are coming. Let's wait for them to arrive and confirm that it's safe for you to leave. I don't want anyone hurt today."

That seemed to calm everyone. Recalling the Brit's usefulness, he motioned the man closer. In a lowered voice, he said, "I need to keep the crowd calm, but I also need to visit the Charnel House to see that everything is okay. Could I ask for your help?"

The man looked like he was having trouble seeing why Stephanos should leave if he couldn't.

The Brit had addressed him with respect, so before any awkward questions were asked, Stephanos said, "What is your name, please?"

"Oliver. Oliver Edwards," he said, drawing back half a step. "Why?"

"I wanted to thank you, Oliver. You have been a big help to me. Thank you very much."

The big man beamed, "Mum called me Ollie."

"Ollie, I need to watch out for everyone in my care."

"Anyfing ya need, Padre."

Stephanos replied, "I want you to stand with Nabeel while I open the gate. Please help him hold the crowd back."

Ollie puffed up his chest and stood tall, then said loud enough for bystanders to hear, "Ya can coun' on me! I'll bust the 'ead o' any bloke dat tries ta foller ya."

Stephanos leaned close and spoke in a hushed voice, "Ollie, I want you to restrain them. Do not harm anyone."

Although he looked disappointed, Ollie said, "Okay, padre, yor the bleedin' boss."

Before Stephanos could slip out of the gate, Nabeel's phone rang. He stopped and waited to hear what that was about.

"Yes?" Nabeel said. "Are you sure? All of them? Yes, yes, Captain. We will start when you give us the word."

He ended the call, leaned in, and spoke over the cacophony of the crowd in Stephanos' ear, "That was the police, Captain Abasi. He wants us to send out our visitors one at a time. His men need to search them to make sure the shooter or shooters didn't come in here. But Father, I know this didn't happen. I stood right here when I heard the shots. No one came in or out."

Stephanos patted Nabeel's shoulder. "I know, old friend. The police are just taking extra precautions. We must cooperate."

Nabeel's shoulders slumped, but he nodded in agreement, "One more thing, Father. Abasi wants us to wait until he tells us to proceed."

Stephanos nodded and turned toward the crowd. He motioned for the Brit to come and stand next to him.

The Brit stood tall and folded his thick arms across his chest.

Then Stephanos raised his hands for quiet. The crowd ignored him.

CHAPTER THIRTY-TWO
CAPTAIN ABASI

"Because power corrupts, society's demands for moral authority and character increase as the importance of the position increases."
John Adams

St. Catherine Monastery, Egypt
Present

"Pipe down, ya lot!" the rugby player bellowed.

Amidst the charged atmosphere, the rugby player's booming voice sliced through the air. Like a battle cry, it commanded immediate silence from the agitated crowd. Their eyes widened in response.

In the ensuing calm, Stephanos, his demeanor a mix of authority and concern, addressed the assembled throng. "The police insist we allow you to leave one at a time and not as a group. For your safety, they are taking extra precautions."

Nervous murmurs rippled through the crowd, suspicion etching lines on their faces. Stephanos gestured toward his head of security, emphasizing his trust in the man's judgment. "Nabeel here assures me that no one came in or out of the gate after he heard the shots. Do not worry. Be patient. The police have ordered us to wait until they signal it is safe for you to come out to them. The Captain knows me. So, I will go speak to him and arrange for you to leave safely. I suggest you cooperate with the police," he continued, his voice firm. "Captain Abasi is a fair but stern man. If you do not comply with his demands, he will not hesitate to arrest you. I've seen our local jail. I promise you will not like it."

The crowd that had pressed forward now stepped back, hesitating.

Nabeel opened the gate while Ollie faced the crowd with his fists on his hips.

Satisfied things were under control. Stephanos slipped through the gate and rushed along the flagstone path toward the Charnel House. He reached the bottom of the stairs leading to the entrance when he heard approaching voices. The Police! He hurried up the stairs, hoping to get inside. His heart drummed in his chest, each step echoing the urgency of the moment.

Halfway up the stairs, a voice shouted, "Halt!"

Stephanos' stomach clenched. . . I should have acted sooner. He was about to identify himself to the officer when Captain Abasi interrupted.

"As you were, Corporal." Abasi gave a slight bow to Stephanos. "I apologize, Abbot. The Corporal is new to our unit." Turning to his subordinate, the Captain said, "This is the man I told everyone about at our briefing last week. He oversees this holy place."

The corporal, eyes wide with realization, snapped to attention, acknowledging the gravity of the situation.

"Captain Abasi, thank you so much for coming. May I inspect our facilities," Stephanos said, pointing at the Charnel House, "just to make sure everything is in order?"

"Is that where the shooting happened?" Abasi inquired, his gaze fixed on the ominous building.

Stephanos nodded. "We think so."

"Sorry, Father. But we must maintain security for our investigation. My officers will check out the building and then secure it if it is the crime scene. Then we will interview witnesses. Your inspection must wait. We will be very thorough. This may take some time."

"I understand, Captain," Stephanos replied, his disappointment masked by a facade of cooperation. "I must go back inside. Could you please have someone notify me as soon as you have finished?"

"Yes, of course. Thank you for understanding. We will make sure that we leave the place the way we find it." Abasi assured him.

"Thank you again." Stephanos put his right hand over his heart and gave a fake nod of appreciation. I hope they are not too thorough. The Seal must not fall into the wrong hands.

Meanwhile, sent to his room by security, Rahm cleaned up as best he could with moist towelettes. He then picked up the pouch and opened it. When he saw the striking gold and silver ring at the bottom of the bag, it amazed him. Stunning! He tilted the large ring from the pouch onto the palm of his hand. An intricate blend of gold and silver it sparked an inexplicable surge of energy as he touched it, filling him with both awe and trepidation. It felt like he had swallowed a massive jolt of caffeine. Alarmed, he dropped the ring on the bed. His pulse quickened. Upon reflection, he realized the jolt hadn't been painful, just unexpected.

As he pondered these mysteries, the ring's power seemed to awaken something within him. Sharpening his mind and banishing the fog of uncertainty that had clouded his thoughts since the attack. A sense of clarity washed over him, juxtaposed against the adrenaline-fueled fear that had gripped him moments before.

As had often happened, the Professor's words came back to mind, "Do not fear the unknown, but be terrified of ignorance."

Using his handkerchief, he cautiously touched the ring. No tingle. He picked it up and looked at it more carefully. A geometric design formed the ring's gold face, like a sunburst or multi-pointed star. The ring's band was silver and as wide as his finger. There were smaller jewels at the sunrays' points. He counted twelve smaller stones and one large stone in the center of the setting. A diamond? Twelve points. That's when he recognized what the design was. One Star of David superimposed over, another forming a twelve-pointed star. Twelve points. Twelve stones. Twelve tribes. A Jewish artifact? Why would it be hidden at a Christian shrine?

Rahm puzzled over that as he picked up the leather pouch. He studied the branded design again and traced the outline with his fingers. But still could not make out the design. He sniffed the bag and decided, at one point, it had belonged to or been in possession of someone who smoked. The inside smelled woody, almost sweet.

He picked up a pencil and paper and tried to duplicate the line drawing burned into the leather, thinking that he might see it more clearly that way.

It still wasn't clear to him what he was looking at. He gave up trying to figure it out.

He wondered if he had imagined the tingle. Putting the pouch down, he shifted the ring to his left hand, still wrapped in the handkerchief. He carefully reached out to touch it again and felt the same sensation.

What is that? He slipped the ring on the little finger of his right hand. As soon as he did, it felt as if his brain had shifted into a higher gear. His brain revved.

Haunted by the lingering presence of the Professor. Rahm wrestled with the inexplicable connection between the ring and the location of the Professor's death. The gates of death, dead monks as witnesses—was this mere coincidence, or was some profound cosmic force at play.

Rahm pulled the ring off and returned it to the pouch. Although the racing sensation slowed, it remained. He frowned and put it back on, and his brain sped up again. He took it off. The raging ache that had pounded in his head since the attack was suddenly gone. His sense of foreboding apprehension was gone, too. His facial muscles had relaxed. A sense of optimism washed over him.

As the distant wail of sirens reached his ears, Rahm's newfound clarity collided with a surge of urgency. He pocketed the ring and stowed away the pouch. His mind abuzz with questions, his heart racing with the possibility of providence weaving its intricate threads around his fate.

CHAPTER THIRTY-THREE
LEGACY

"Out of suffering have emerged the strongest souls; the most massive characters are seared with scars."
Khalil Gibran

St. Catherine Monastery
Present

Rahm strode toward the Charnel House through terraced walks that buzzed with curious onlookers. The security guard scuttled after him, trying to keep up.

A couple, evidently in their mid-sixties, broke into laughter as they posed against the backdrop of the Charnel House. They exuded a distinctly Northern European aura, complete with a Dutch accent.

Four police officers in khaki uniforms frisked the tourists as they exited the monastery gate. They worked quickly, but sometimes they got familiar with younger women, and got rough with one young man protesting the groping. Two did the actual pat-downs while the others watched with sly grins at their comrade's antics—but kept their assault rifles at the ready.

At the bottom of the stairs leading up to the Charnel House, two others stood guard.

Adi's forceful voice echoed from inside. "The security guard told him to go clean up. That's why. He'll be right back!"

"I'm here," Rahm shouted up the stairs.

An officer moved to hold him back. But a man in a worn grey suit stepped onto the Charnel House landing and shouted, "Bring him here."

The closest cops brusquely grabbed him to steer him up the steps, almost lifting him off his feet.

The suit produced a leather wallet. Flipping it open to reveal a photo ID and badge adorned with three stars, signifying his rank in the Egyptian National Police. He identified himself as Captain Abasi and turned his gaze upon Rahm. "Why did you leave the crime scene?"

Adi braced her hands on her hips and attempted to intervene. "I already told you. The security guard told him—"

The captain silenced her with a stern gesture. "Silence, woman! I was speaking to him."

"It's like she said," Rahm shook himself free from the rough grasp of his two new friends. "The Professor's blood covered my hands and clothes and—"

Abasi dismissed Rahm's explanation. "This is an irrational excuse. No one in their right mind would ever leave the scene of a crime until we had released them."

Adi's nostrils flared. "Would you be in your right mind if the man who had been like a father to you died in your arms?"

Rahm, his emotions in turmoil, listened in astonishment. She's defending me? A surge of warmth swept through him, mingling with the sadness he felt over the Professor's death.

Abasi held up his hand, nearly in Adi's face, and turned back to Rahm. "Let's start with your name and your identity papers."

Rahm said, "The security guy told me I should clean up."

"He should have known better."

Rahm provided his information, declaring, "My name is Rahm Khalidi. I'm a reporter for The Breaking News Digest." He displayed his press pass and handed over his passport, sensing that it felt unusually thick. Glancing down, he noticed the edges of the envelope the Professor had given him. He attempted to reclaim it, but Abasi snatched it away, thumbing through the passport to reveal the envelope. "What do we have here?"

Rahm said, "I don't know. The Professor gave it to me after he was shot. I haven't—"

"Open it," the captain ordered.

Rahm took the envelope and tore it open. He was about to remove the contents when the captain reached over and seized its content.

For a few moments, Abasi studied both pages, then handed them back to Rahm. "What is this?"

Rahm scanned them, and his mouth fell open. He spoke in a quavering voice,, "It's the deed to his house in Oregon."

"Where is Oregon?"

"In the United States."

Abasi snatched the deed back and frowned. "Why would this man," he pointed at Schwalm's body, "why give you the deed to a house in America?" Abasi's eyes narrowed to slits. "What was he paying you for?"

Rahm couldn't offer a satisfying response. "I don't know."

"Do not test my patience. Tell me why."

"He was my teacher at the Friends' School in Ramallah." Rahm's voice trailed off.

"What have you done?"

"I'm telling you the truth. I did nothing wrong.

Abasi shook the deed in Rahm's face. "Answer the question. What did you do to receive this kind of payment? Nobody just gives away a house."

"The Professor knows—he knew that while my mother was dying of a broken heart, I promised to return to our family's estate. That's why I wear this." He pulled out the key hanging around his neck. "After Israel built a wall through our land, he knew it would be next to impossible for me to keep my promise." Rahm brushed moisture from his eyes.

"Why would he pay you?" Abasi demanded.

"I said I would take revenge on whoever did this." Rahm motioned vaguely.

"He paid you to avenge his death?"

"No!" Rahm breathed through his nose, trying to maintain some composure. "He . . . He said he was buying forgiveness."

"For what?" The captain's browed creased. "You make no sense."

"He said he wanted to pay me, so I would forgive his attacker."

Captain Abasi snorted. "You expect me to believe this fairy tale? Who would do such a thing? And he had these documents on his person when he was shot? None of this makes any sense."

"Or to me," Rahm replied, his attention drawn to the documents in his hands, his emotions overwhelming him. He wiped his tears on his sleeve and pointed to the top right corner of the cover letter. "Did you notice this date?" Gazing upward, he averted his eyes from Schwalm's lifeless form, which displayed the harrowing signs of death.

"Two months ago?" Abasi shifted his position and searched Rahm's eyes. "How do you explain that? Were you supposed to protect him? Perhaps he was paying you to keep him safe, and you failed?"

Rahm sought to explain. "I can't explain it. What I can tell you is that it was exactly two months ago when the Professor invited me on this trip. He said he wanted to come here to research some manuscripts."

Abasi probed further, "What did he mean when he called you the man of peace?"

Startled, Rahm looked back down at the letter. There it was in the Professor's handwriting; "You are the man of peace I was searching for." Rahm shrugged, bewildered.

Rahm stood there, shaking his head. He must have been confused. Then he read on, "But you must first make peace with God before anything else will change." Rahm shrugged.

The captain whirled and barked at the two officers and waved them off. "Go back downstairs and keep this area secure."

"Yes sir," one said. They did an about-face.

"Wait!" the captain barked.

He stabbed his finger at Adi. "Where were you when the shooting took place?"

"I was in my room—"

"You were not here?" he motioned her toward the stairs. "You must leave with these men."

Adi didn't budge. "I was in my room when I heard the two shots and footsteps running away. I was on my way to find security when I heard a woman's voice screaming about murder."

For the first time, Abasi wavered. "So, you ***are*** a witness?"

"Yes! What I heard corroborates his statement."

"Okay," Abasi said, "Our forensic expert is a surgeon from the local hospital. He will be here shortly and will examine the body. Let's move downstairs." Abasi led the way.

Rahm looked again at the papers. He reread the letter, confusion clouding his face.

CHAPTER THIRTY-FOUR
DO SOMETHING!

"Do not wait for a change of environment before you act; get a change of environment by action."
Wallace Wattles

St. Catherine Monastery
Present

Rahm nervously shuffled the pages from the envelope as he exited the Charnel House, following Abasi. When he headed down the stairs, a slip of paper fell onto the second step. Adi thought he might notice, but he kept moving. She opened her mouth to say something, but hesitated. Instead. she bent and picked up the paper, glancing to see what it was. She did a double-take and caught her breath. An oncologist had written the letter to the Professor. The diagnosis was grim. Schwalm was dying. That must have been why he had the deed with him. Was he going to give it to Rahm all along? A deep well of sympathy opened inside.

The two officers stepped aside as she reached the bottom of the stairs.

Abasi said, "Mr. Khalidi, I assume they will bury your friend here?"

Uncertainty flooded Rahm's face. "I don't know. I hadn't thought about that."

Boom. Boom. Two loud explosions rocked the parking lot. She turned to see two Egyptian police units in flames.

People screamed and scurried back through the monastery gate.

"Take cover!" Abasi shouted.

Dust, smoke, and the sulfurous smell of gunpowder floated across the gardens.

An amplified voice blasted through the smoke. "Good afternoon. Captain Abasi. Please do not call for reinforcements. I am a reasonable man. My colleague, with a rocket launcher, is not. And he's guarding the road. But I have not harmed you or your men. Not yet. However, you should know that I have the firepower to wipe you out if you do not cooperate."

Sound carried very well in the canyon. However, the contours of its walls scrambled Adi's ability to tell from which direction the sound was coming. But she knew it was Qatal.

They punctuated the claim about firepower with a bullet. It ricocheted off the flagstone paving, ten feet away from an officer who had pulled out his gun. The captain flinched and motioned for the man to put away his weapon.

The man holstered his gun and retreated to a safer location.

The voice continued, "A stubborn tourist has died for refusing my demands. There is no need for further bloodshed. The reporter Khalidi has something that belongs to me. You have two minutes. Bring me the flash drive he took from my Russian friend's body. If you do not do exactly as I have instructed, I will start killing your troops. Move Captain. One hundred and twenty seconds starts now."

Captain Abasi, desperation etched on his face, held out his hand to Rahm. "Give it to me!"

"I don't have it," Rahm said with a belligerent set to his jaw. "Even if I did, there's too much at stake. You can't give them the drive. There is no telling what kind of devastation they will unleash on Israel or the rest of the world."

"He's right," Adi said.

Abasi grabbed Rahm by the front of his shirt. "I don't care. Give me that drive. Now!"

"Ninety seconds left," the voice boomed. "Do something, Abasi."

The captain produced a pistol from inside his jacket. Adi recognized it as a Czech-made CZ 75 compact. Perfect for concealed carry.

Abasi put it to Rahm's head. Through clenched teeth, he said, "Unless you want to die, hand me that drive!"

"I told you, I don't have it!"

Abasi brought the butt of the gun down on Rahm's head with such force that Adi heard Rahm's teeth clack together before he collapsed into an unconscious heap.

The Captain fished through Rahm's pockets.

"Sixty seconds!" the voice said.

"He said he doesn't have it," Adi said as she grabbed Abasi's arm to stop the search.

Abasi's resolve wavered, Over his shoulder, he said, "They say he does. Step away!" He pushed her away and went back to frisking Rahm. Not finding it, he stopped and whirled in Adi's direction. "Where is it?"

Adi defiantly snapped, "If I knew, would I tell you?"

Abasi glared. "I have to save my men."

"Thirty seconds!" the sinister voice insisted.

Abasi started frisking Rahm's limp body again.

Time ticked away mercilessly, the countdown echoing like a death knell. Adi's grip tightened on Abasi's arm, her voice determined, "You can't give it away!"

He pushed her off and barked at his minions, "Keep her back!"

The two closest officers grabbed Adi and dragged her away.

She tried to shake herself free, but they held on.

"Time's up," the voice said. A single shot echoed through the canyon.

Amid the disturbance, Adi noticed Rahm stirring and looking around.

ꝸ ꝸ ꝸ

The echoes from the sniper's shot faded into eerie silence. Rahm saw the soldier who had earlier pulled his service weapon lying on the pavement with a bloody exit wound where his ear used to be.

Breaking the silence, Abasi shouted, "He's up there!" He pointed at the mountainside behind the Charnel House. "Take cover!"

While everyone scattered, Rahm jumped to his feet. With a burst of adrenaline-fueled agility, he dashed through the monastery gate, seeking sanctuary within St. Catherine's massive walls.

Safely inside, Rahm headed toward Abbot's office. He had gone only a few steps when a voice behind him shouted, "Stop!"

Rahm spun around to see a Bedouin man in a security guard's uniform. He had a barrel chest and thick arms and was pointing at him. "Come here!"

Rahm held out his hands to each side, palms up. "What?"

"I am security. Come here. Now!"

Rahm obeyed.

"Wait!" The man hurried to the gate and slid a heavy bar into a sturdy slot, flipped a lock, then walked toward Rahm. "What you do?"

Rahm pointed toward the gate. "Looking for cover. They just shot a policeman out there. I barely escaped."

"You bleed. You shot?"

Rahm shook his head and wished he hadn't. It continued to throb where Abasi had hit him.

"I must search. Put up hands."

Instead, Rahm pulled out his wallet and showed his press pass. "I am staying at the guest house. I wanted to speak to the Abbot about my friend's death."

After looking him over again, the man said as he pointed to the left, "Okay, go there. Take stairs by the basilica door."

"Thank you."

As he climbed the stairs to the Abbot's office, Rahm thought about how to ask for permission to bury the Professor's body at the monastery. He recalled advice from his internship at the Lebanon Star in Beirut and smiled. Establish rapport.

When he knocked at the office door, a voice invited him to come in. He took a deep breath and stepped through the door.

CHAPTER THIRTY-FIVE
PROTECTED

"Understanding grows at a snail's pace."
Yiddish Proverb

St. Catherine Monastery
Present

Rahm stepped into the office, his eyes scanning the room. It was far more modest than he had expected for someone of the Abbot's stature. A distinguished figure, whose white beard cascaded down his chest, stood by a window. His attention divided between a cell phone and the unfolding scene outside. His face, etched with concern, belied the tranquility of the monastery.

"Good morning." Rahm offered, attempting to mask the urgency in his voice.

"Good morning. What happened to you?" the man asked.

"Excuse me?"

"I heard two shots. You're unsteady and out of breath, and there's a gash on your forehead." He pointed at Rahm's face.

Rahm hesitated briefly, his hand instinctively reaching for the wound. "A terrorist threatened to kill Abasi's men if we didn't meet his demands."

The man offered him a tissue. "My window is open. I heard those threats clearly. That's why I was trying to call the captain. The attacker must have been using a megaphone. Did he shoot you?"

"No." Rahm replied, pressing the tissue to his forehead. "This was a gift from Captain Abasi when I didn't comply with one of his orders. The terrorists killed one of Abasi's men. In the scuffle, I escaped. Do I call you Reverend or something else?"

"Please, call me Stephanos." the older man said, extending a hand.

Rahm smiled and offered his business card. "Let me introduce myself. My name is Rahm Khalidi. I'm a reporter for the The Breaking News Network."

Examining Rahm's business card, his eyes alighting with recognition, Stephanos said, "Nabeel called and told me you were coming. So, you're Dr. Schwalm's friend?"

"Yes," his voice softening with the memory of his mentor. "A very close friend. He was my mentor. I met him while attending the Ramallah Friends School. He taught history and was the faculty advisor for our yearbook club. He and I worked closely together during my senior year. We kept in touch, and he reconnected when I moved back from Beirut. He was like a father to me, so I came to ask a favor."

Stephanos gestured for Rahm to sit, his eyes filled with empathy. "I'm so sorry about your loss. How can I help Mr. Khalidi?".

"During our drive from the hospital, our taxi driver told us that Prophet Muhammad, peace be upon him, wrote an order of protection. Is that it?" Rahm nodded at a document hanging on the wall in an elegant frame.

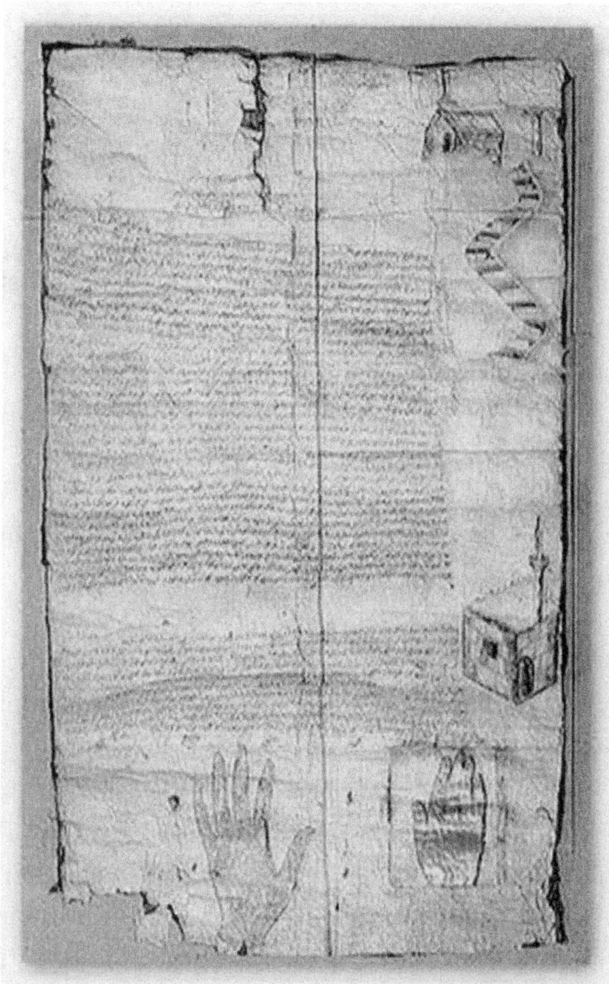

Stephanos followed Rahm's gaze, his eyes lingering on the framed document that had graced the walls of St. Catherine's for centuries. He extended an inviting gesture toward the piece of history that had stood as a testament to interfaith harmony. "You noticed our gift from the Prophet?" His voice held a note of pride as he led Rahm closer.

Rahm's brow furrowed in disbelief. "Why haven't I ever heard of this?"

Stephanos shrugged. "The Prophet granted our request and dictated this letter. His handprint was his official signature. It has been very helpful when we have needed his protection. And it has paved the way for peaceful and cooperative relations between Christians and Muslims. We have thrived during the fourteen centuries of Islamic rule here. Our continued existence shows the respect given to the Order and the principles of peace and cooperation that it represents."

Rahm got close and squinted at the document. "I'm having trouble reading the script. The classic Arabic is difficult."

"I understand." Stephanos picked up a book on a nearby shelf, opened it to a bookmarked place, and handed it to Rahm. "Try this English translation."

Rahm read aloud, "This is a message from Muhammad ibn Abdullah, as a covenant to those who adopt Christianity, near and far. We are with them." With a question in his eyes, Rahm looked at Stephanos with curiosity.

"I know," said Stephanos. "It surprises everyone who comes here. Sultan Selim, I confirmed our rights in 1517, but took the original copy to the royal treasury in Constantinople for safekeeping. It is in Istanbul to this day. He gave us this and two other certified copies. I especially like the line about monasteries and houses. Do you see it?"

Rahm nodded and read on,

"Neither are their judges to be removed from their jobs, nor their monks from their monasteries. No one is to destroy a house of their religion, damage it, or carry anything from it to the Muslims' houses. Should anyone take any of these, he would spoil God's covenant and disobey His Prophet. Verily, they are my allies and have my secure charter against all that they hate."

Rahm, mesmerized, handed the book back to Stephanos and examined the glass covering the document. His fingers brushed the yellow outline of Muhammad's handprint. "That's remarkable." "He had small hands," Rahm said. A distant gunshot shattered the tranquility of their conversation. Rahm jumped, his instincts on high alert.

Stephanos, too, flinched and glanced at his phone with a worried look. "Things are clearly not under control yet. But until they are, I think we need to stay put." He pointed at the document. "As I mentioned, this is a copy the Sultan had made. I haven't seen the original, so I can't be sure his scribe got the hand right. Despite some people questioning its authenticity, we have shown it to those rare groups hostile to our presence. They have honored his words. And as recently as 2019, the Prime Minister of Pakistan quoted it."

"Interesting." Rahm, intrigued by the richness of history, opened his notebook, looked up at the document again, and scribbled a few words. Turning to Stephanos, pen poised, he said, "I'm researching a piece about religious groups getting along. This is fascinating. So, let me get this straight. Is it accurate to say that some of the very best manuscripts of the Bible were preserved at St. Catherine's?"

"That's right. Sinaiticus is the oldest complete Greek New Testament in the world. We safeguarded it here for centuries."

Rahm wrote some details. "And St. Catherine's can trace its continued existence in the Sinai to Prophet Muhammad's Order of Protection. Peace be upon him."

Stephanos nodded, the weight of history and tradition in his eyes.

"Then I could safely say his protection has served you well," Rahm said. "You're still here."

"Yes. His protection has been our steadfast shield."

Rahm inquired further, "You mentioned that there are two stories about how this document came to be here?"

Stephanos leaned in, his voice tinged with storytelling charm. "Some say that Muhammad visited our monastery when he needed refuge after the citizens of Mecca drove him out."

"But—"

Stephanos held up his hand. "You're right. There is no evidence he was ever here." Stephanos conceded, "But the legend makes for a captivating tale."

Rahm jotted down a few more notes, intrigued by the allure of historical narratives

Stephanos, after a moment of silence, turned the conversation toward Rahm's own quest. "Now, you asked about Dr. Schwalm?"

Rahm nodded earnestly. "The Professor believed the work you and your coworkers are doing here is important. I was wondering, hoping, that since the founder of my religion, peace be upon him, showed you such great kindness that, perhaps, I could ask you for a favor. Would it be possible for the Professor's body to be buried here?"

Stephanos, reflecting on the practicalities of the request, hesitated. "Are you aware there is a cemetery in town?"

"I think the Professor would prefer a Christian burial site," Rahm said.

A pained expression clouded Stephanos' face. "We have limited space in our cemetery. That's why the Charnel House is necessary. We rarely allow outsiders."

Rahm's hope flickered, his chin dipped to his chest and his lips pressed tightly together.

Stephanos said, "However."

Rahm jolted to attention. "Yes?"

"There is some precedent. We have the remains of a visiting British scholar-in-residence who died here a hundred years ago. Perhaps we can accommodate your request."

"Thank you so much!"

"I'm not making any promises right now. Let me discuss this with my colleagues. Let me see what we can do."

"Yes, sir. Thank you."

"I'll see what can be—"

Bang! Bang! Stephanos's attention was suddenly drawn to the echoing of two shots from outside. He held up his finger and made a phone call to Nabeel, urgently seeking information. "What's happening? Where are you? Are you safe?" Stephanos listened, then said, "I understand. Thank you, my friend." He placed his phone on the desk.

"Nabeel says that Abasi's man just shot the sniper. The Captain told him that he hopes to have things under control soon."

"I sure hope so," Rahm said.

"So do I. This has been quite upsetting.

"Okay," Stephanos said, "we were talking about the Prophet's Order. We haven't needed the Order very often because we have excellent relations with our Muslim neighbors."

"Most of us make good neighbors." Rahm smiled. "As my cousin in Chicago describes our family, 'We are 7-Eleven, not 9/11.'"

Stephanos looked puzzled.

Rahm added, "7-Eleven is a chain of convenience stores in America, and 9/11—"

"9/11 was the date of the attack on the World Trade Center." Stephanos' head tilted to one side. "And?"

"My cousins own several 7-Eleven stores in Chicago and the western suburbs."

Stephanos said, "I get it. He was making a joke."

Rahm was about to express his thanks again when he heard a shot fired somewhere outside the monastery's high perimeter wall.

Stephanos grabbed his phone. "What's happening?"

CHAPTER THIRTY-SIX
THE DEVIL'S AFOOT

"the line dividing good and evil cuts through the heart of every human being."
Aleksandr Solzhenitsyn

Present

Adi had been taking cover between ancient buildings. Her heart pounded as she observed Rahm's escape through the weathered monastery gate.

Just then, Captain Abasi signaled his corporal to move into position. He stealthily worked his way up the jumble of rocks at Mt. Sinai's base. When he moved out of sight, Abasi, who had huddled with his four remaining men behind the Charnel House stairs, gestured toward the parking lot. Adi assumed Qatal and his other henchmen had taken defensive positions.

The sniper maintained his commanding perch, making it perilous for Adi to abandon her post. Though the high-capacity flash drive in her possession bore the weight of an entire nation's security.

Aware that Israel's fate hung precariously in the balance, she couldn't afford any blunders. The urgent need to safeguard her precious cargo propelled her into a whirlwind of speculation. Should she make a daring dash for the gate? But just as her thoughts edged toward a decision, the haunting echoes of two gunshots reverberated through the canyon's ancient stones.

Meanwhile, Captain Abasi orchestrated his men with tactical precision. Launching a classic pincer movement against their elusive adversaries. This development confirmed Adi's earlier speculation regarding the sniper's perilous presence. Emboldened by this revelation, she sprang into action, sprinting toward the fortified gate. The sharp report of a gunshot momentarily quelled her eagerness. She dove for cover when she saw the Egyptian police officer running ahead of her stumble and fall. The sudden bloom of a crimson stain on his trouser leg bore silent witness to the danger.

The soldier with him dove for cover behind the trunk of an ancient olive tree, poked his head up for a quick look at the parking lot, then dragged his partner to safety.

With pistol gripped tightly in hand, Captain Abasi hurried to a vantage point that afforded him a glimpse of the monastery's parking lot. The roar of an engine coming to life reached Adi's ears. In swift succession, Abasi's weapon barked twice, but it was too late. The white SUV squealed its tires as it raced away.

Abasi pulled out a whistle, sounded three short blasts, and waved at his two groups of men. He made a circling motion over his head with his arm and pumped his fist up and down twice to signal, *Assemble*! *Hurry*!

□ □ □

Stephanos, a key player in this unfolding drama, raised his cellphone to his ear. "Yes, Nabeel?"

While Stephanos listened, Rahm studied the Order of Protection. He pulled out his notebook and scribbled some notes. *If the Prophet's protection preserved Sinaiticus, how could the Bible get corrupted like the imams say?*

Stephanos spoke into his phone. "Abasi wants us to shelter in place? Then that is what we will do. Thank you." With a beckoning gesture, Stephanos motioned toward Rahm's chair and sat down himself. "So, where were did we leave off?"

Rahm's eyes darted toward the parking lot, curiosity and anxiety etched on his face, "What's happening out there?"

"Abasi's team successfully eliminated a sniper. The other assailants left. Abasi called for reinforcements and insisted that the monastery gate remain locked until things are safe."

"So, we wait?" Rahm mused, his thoughts shrouded in a cloud of uncertainty.

"Yes." Stephanos looked down, scratched the back of his head, then rubbed his neck. After a pause, he looked intently at Rahm.

Silence ensued until Rahm eventually said, "The Professor was like a father to me. He was a good man."

Puzzled by the enigma of Dr. Schwalm's murder, Stephanos inquired, "I don't understand. If Dr. Schwalm was the man you describe, why would anyone want to harm him?"

Rahm hesitated, gauging how much he could divulge to the Greek cleric. However, a sense of trust had formed, allowing him to speak more freely. "Did you hear about the attack on our van?"

Stephanos nodded in acknowledgment. "Yes, I had a conversation with Dr. Schwalm shortly after you arrived."

Rahm wrestled with his emotions, choosing his words carefully. "I gave the flash drive the Russian had given me to Adi. The Professor was protecting her. She should never have come here!" Rahm's voice broke.

"What drive? And she who? Your traveling companion? I'm lost."

Rahm couldn't disclose everything. He certainly wouldn't mention that Adi was Mossad. That was for sure. "Well, when the van was attacked, the Russian man who died at the scene handed me a flash drive."

Stephanos stood. "Are you telling me all this trouble could have been avoided if," he shuffled through some papers on his desk, then continued, "Did Miss Ovitz know something that would have allowed her to foresee this?"

Rahm, wrestling with his inner demons, tried to refocus the conversation. "I guess I was just looking for someone to blame. I don't really know if there was a way to avoid all this. The fact is that it has happened." He sighed heavily. "The pressing issue is Captain Abasi. He'll want to know what we intend to do with the Professor's remains."

Offering his condolences and sitting down, Stepanos said, "I am truly so sorry for your loss." Then hurried on, "My predecessor believed the Urim and Thummim were a pair of large jewels. One an emerald and the other a diamond of identical size, weight, and shape. The Jewish high priest would ask a binary question, one that could be answered with a simple 'yes' or 'no,' or 'guilty' or 'innocent.' Then he would pray, reach into the breast piece of his garb, and, depending on which stone came out, he would have his answer. The word Thummim means *innocent*. Urim means *cursed*. The Thummim was the diamond."

Puzzled by the connection between this revelation and the murder of Dr. Schwalm, Rahm's curiosity led him to ask, "What does that have to do with the Professor?"

Stephanos silently gazed at Rahm with a knowing look.

Rahm fidgeted in his seat.

"When you touch the ring, do you feel a tingling sensation?"

This revelation took Rahm aback. "How could you know about that?" His voice quivered, overwhelmed by the sudden revelation. Stunned, Rahm said, "What are you talking about?"

Stephanos smiled, revealing a depth of understanding. "As a student of ancient manuscripts, I work at being observant, noticing details, and piecing together fragments of information."

Intrigued by the implications, Rahm probed further. "Like?"

"First, you tell me that Dr. Schwalm was shot in the Charnel House at the entrance to the Bone Room. Second, you were alone with him there." Rahm started to speak, but Stephanos held up his hand. "Third, your demeanor has a very intense focus and underlying serenity about it. The clues are subtle but very familiar."

Rahm squirmed in his seat, the weight of his secrets pressing down upon him. “What have you concluded from these random pieces of information?”

Stephanos’s words resonated with conviction. “Facts are never random. The facts force me to conclude two things. Number one, either Dr. Schwalm or perhaps you discovered the Seal where I hid it. And number two, you’ve touched it.”

CHAPTER THIRTY-SEVEN
CONFESSION

"The weak can never forgive. Forgiveness is the attribute of the strong."
Mahatma Gandhi

Present

Rahm faced Stephanos across his ancient carved desk. The man lived in a monastery that had been around for nearly fifteen centuries. He spent his career working with old manuscripts and artifacts, honing his powers of observation. It probably shouldn't have surprised him that Stephanos had been two steps ahead of him. "You hid the ring in the Charnel House?" He asked, his voice laced with astonishment.

Stephanos, the enigmatic guardian of the monastery's secrets, nodded affirmatively. "Yes, back in 1976."

The room tilted off-center as Rahm scrambled to make sense of the confession. Once the shock had settled in, he delved deeper into the mystery, "What's the connection between the Urim and Thummim and the ring?"

With a sagacious nod, Stephanos wove the threads of history and myth together. "How much do you know about the history of the Jews as recorded in the Bible?"

Rahm admitted, "Not much."

Stephanos delved into a labyrinth of ancient tales and wisdom. “When Solomon ascended to the throne, he named Zadok High Priest. According to tradition, Zadok was eager to see Solomon’s position as the new king be solidified. So, he gave the stones to Solomon.”

This cryptic narrative befuddled Rahm. “You’re speaking in riddles. What stones?”

“The Urim and Thummim,” Stephanos clarified.

"Are the ring and the stones connected?" Rahm probed, his intrigue deepening.

Stephanos beamed. “Yes! I believe the ring in your possession is Solomon’s Seal. I’ve pieced together the fragments of a complex puzzle. It includes the previous Abbot’s words and tidbits from the Bible. I gathered material from the Quran, and a variety of Islamic and Jewish legends, too. Then, mixing all of that with my experience, I arrived at some conclusions.

“First, I conclude Solomon fashioned the ring or had it fashioned. Second, when Zadok gave it to him, Solomon made the Thummim the ring’s centerpiece. Then cut the Urim into twelve smaller emeralds, one for each of Israel’s tribes. Those are the stones you see at the outer edge of the ring’s face. Third, that the Seal has the power to influence the wearer’s thoughts and destiny. Although the exact nature of this power remains elusive. I have experienced it. Fourth, one should exercise extreme caution when handling an object of such profound potency.”

Rahm’s jaw muscles clenched. “Careful? Why? What can it do?”

"I never took seriously any of the tales I had heard about Solomon's Seal. Like granting him power over demons or the ability to speak to animals. But there is something supernatural about it. God gave the Urim and Thummim to the high priest to help provide guidance. Those stones symbolized revelation and truth, respectively. Because of the ways the priests used them, they have a different effect on the guilty than on the innocent."

Rahm remained skeptical. "I cannot see how an ancient piece of jewelry could have such abilities."

"I understand. But 1 Samuel 28 reports that when Saul attempted to get an answer from God by using the Urim and Thummim, God refused to answer him. After that, things went from bad to worse for Saul."

Rahm shook his head in apparent unfamiliarity. "I am not well-versed in the stories of the Bible."

"He was the king who preceded King David. I assume you know of him."

"Of course," Rahm said. "The Quran says that Dawud was given revelation. You think this happened because of the Urim and Thummim?"

Stephanos shrugged. "I don't know. All I can say is that my conviction has grown in the decades since I found the Seal."

"How could a jeweled ring be used as a seal?"

"That is puzzling. But only a few of the legends involve Solomon using it as a signet or to seal documents. Usually, they focus on its mystical qualities."

Curiosity piqued, Rahm questioned Stephanos's decision to part with the Seal. "Why didn't you just keep it?"

The old cleric's voice trembled with earnestness. "I worried about its power. My unease stemmed from two ancient texts, one by a Yemeni rabbi and another by Jeremiah. Rabbi Avraham Salem, one of Solomon's advisors sent to Ma'rib with the Queen of Sheba, wrote: 'This ring exposes folly and reveals wisdom. It will bring curses upon those who are evil. But the Almighty will add blessings to men of integrity.' "

Rahm absorbed this information, concern tinging his features. "Am I in danger, then?"

Stephanos continued, "Jeremiah wrote, 'The heart is deceitful above all things and beyond cure. Who can understand it?' "

"You believe that?"

Stephanos affirmed his conviction. "Yes," I believe both Jeremiah and Rabbi Salem. Many legends mention misfortune coming from misusing the Seal. In 1975, when I found them, the Seal and pouch wrapped in a piece of Yemeni newsprint dated 1952. It wasn't until much later I discovered a messenger had come here from an excavation in Yemen, Ma'rib, that year. The previous Abbot said that the messenger fell terribly ill and died from an injury shortly after arriving. I now believe that messenger must have brought the Seal here and suffered the fate Rabbi Salem warned about.

"I am also convinced that we all have an incredible capacity for evil. I don't just mean people like those who killed Dr. Schwalm. Evil is not something outside these walls. It is something in which I have participated."

"But you're a deeply religious man!" Rahm protested.

Stephanos acknowledged the dual nature of humanity. "You are correct on both counts. I am devout, but I am also a man. Jeremiah's words ring true to me, do they not to you?"

Rahm hesitated but finally admitted, "No. We Muslims believe just the opposite. We believe that we have inherited fitra, the same innocence God gave Adam."

Stephanos leaned forward and pointed a bony finger at Rahm. "You may have Adam's innocence, but you, my young friend, must face reality. You are capable of great evil."

Rahm leaned back and grappled with this unsettling notion.

Stephanos pointed at his own head. "Tell me, what thoughts come to mind when you think about the man who killed your friend? What feelings are stirred in here?" He patted his chest.

Rahm's hands sweat.

"The devil is afoot," Stephanos said. "I can see it in your eyes. The evil one has already planted the seed of revenge. You must face the truth. You are capable of the same level of malevolence that caused your friend's death."

"But, what about 'an eye for an eye'?"

"But nothing. To the degree you reject reality, to that degree, you are living in a fantasy world. If you are to be the keeper of the Seal, even if only for a season, you will need to guard your heart against such darkness."

Rahm wanted to protest, but the old man had a point.

Stephanos stroked his white beard. "May I tell you a story?"

Rahm gave a small nod.

"A couple had a son. At age 19, he was killed while riding home from work on his motorcycle. A drunk driver had crossed the center line and hit him head-on. When the drunk went to trial, the parents worried he would get off lightly. Eventually, the judge found the accused guilty and sentenced him to five years. The parents were relieved and felt justice had been served."

Rahm furrowed his brow, questioning the significance of this tale. "Five years is not very long. A drunk driver in Ramallah got fifteen years. That's not much of a story."

Stephanos's eyes glinted with a hidden truth. "The beauty of the story lies in what the parents did next. "During the drive home from the courthouse, the wife claimed to have heard God's voice guiding her. She shared her revelation with her husband, and together, they contacted the judge. The judge was astounded. In all his years on the bench, he had never encountered victims' families making such a request. He agreed to hear them out in court. The following morning, they sat in the courtroom next to the man who had taken their son's life."

Rahm couldn't fathom such an act of forgiveness. "Hold it." He held up his hand in protest. "That's not believable. Where I come from, no good parent would sit next to their child's killer."

"Parents don't behave that way in Greece either," Stephanos said. "You should know that I met Charles and Jeri years ago during my graduate studies. They were part of the school's host program. They had me at their home for several meals."

Rahm's confusion deepened. "This is a true story? I thought—"

Stephanos opened a drawer and pulled out a file folder. He thumbed through it, letting it fall open. He picked up a yellowed piece of newsprint. "They sent this in their letter. Before I show it to you, I would like to finish the story."

Rahm nodded, captivated by the unfolding narrative.

"They told the judge that the hardest part of their son Brian's death was that his body was so badly mangled that they never got the chance to tell him goodbye. They revealed that the convicted man also had a son, a little boy aged five, named Bryan. Little Bryan had a terminal heart condition and was expected to live only a few more months. Jeri asked the judge to delay imposing the killer's sentence until the man could say goodbye to his son. The judge warned them that if they went ahead with their request, the convicted man's sentence be reduced from five years to six months. After struggling with a reduction being just or not, they finally agreed."

Rahm shook his head, incredulous. "That can't be real."

"They mailed me a copy of the front page." Stephanos unfolded the yellowed newsprint. The headline bore testimony to the truth of the unbelievable tale: "Forgiveness Has Its Day in Court." *

*See Author's Note "Brian and Bryan"

CHAPTER THIRTY-EIGHT
GUIDED

"The greatest discoveries will be along spiritual lines. This is the field where miracles are going to happen. Spiritual power is the greatest underdeveloped power and has the greatest future."
Thomas A. Edison

St. Catherine Monastery
Present

Rahm sat in stunned silence, trying to sort things out. He closed his eyes. The image of the Professor dying in his arms flashed on the screen in his head. That settled it. Handing the yellowed piece of newsprint back to Stephanos, Rahm stood. "Sentimental stories are nice. But I can't forgive. What Qatal did was inexcusable."

"Please sit down," Stephanos urged gently. "Mercy is not easy. It's costly—a burden. Almost too much to bear. But Charles and Jeri told me that the moment they hung up the phone after calling the judge, they experienced a tremendous sense of release."

"That sounds wonderful. But I just don't see it."

Stephanos sat quietly, his hands folded in his lap. "It's a process, not something we do, and then it's over. It's a choice. We sometimes have to go back and decide for mercy again."

"What does that have to do with the Seal?"

"It is easy for me to yield to darkness. I hid the Seal because I was afraid that either its power was too much for me or, like that drunk driver, that my own depravity would lead me astray. I worried I would misuse the enhancements that the ring produced. I wanted to avoid the misfortunes that Rabbi Salem wrote about. So, I hid it where you found it."

"You're telling me I *am* in danger."

"Based on the Rabbi's warning, I conclude you are free to make choices about how to respond to your circumstances. But not free from the consequences that follow a choice."

A heavy silence hung in the room like a thundercloud until Rahm spoke. "You mentioned enhancements? What enhancements?"

Stephanos folded his hands on his desk and studied Rahm. After taking a deep breath and exhaling through his nose, he asked, "You haven't noticed?"

Rahm hesitated, then said, "Do you mean the feeling I get that I am smarter when I touch it?"

"Is that all?"

"No. I always feel more focused and calmer. Something like the meds they gave me before surgery."

Stephanos' brow furrowed. "You feel sedated?"

"Not at all. Just peaceful." He held up his right hand. "They didn't put me under for the repair on this hand. But they made sure I wasn't agitated during the procedure."

"Do you consider the Seal's influence positive or negative?"

"Positive, Extremely positive!"

"How much time have you spent in physical contact with the ring?"

"A few minutes. Why?"

"Over several months," Stephanos said, "I experimented. If I wore it for more than a few minutes, I felt completely drained."

"That's strange because when I touched it, I felt energized."

"I felt the same way at first. But with longer exposures, I became more and more fatigued."

"Was it because it made your brain work overtime?" Rahm asked. "Because while I was touching it, my mind was racing."

"I honestly don't understand it. Some effects still linger, even after all these years. The ability to focus stands out."

"I don't understand it either," Rahm said. "But I definitely like it. And I'm also way more focused. But I'm surprised. You've never had the desire to use it again?"

Stephanos blushed. “Only once when I was being considered for abbot. But I resisted the urge.” He leaned forward. "Can’t you see how seductive it is?"

"Yes. So, is that what you were afraid of?"

Stephanos leaned back in his chair and scanned the stuccoed ceiling ten feet overhead as if an answer were written there. "I'm not sure what it is. I prefer to think of myself as cautious rather than fearful. A big part of what makes me cautious is that I feel like the Seal found me rather than the other way around."

Rahm sat still for several heartbeats. "I feel the same way. My problem is that I can't imagine how that could be true. An even bigger mystery is *why* it would be true. Regardless, if you hid the ring, then it must be yours. I should give it back."

Stephanos stood and paced while responding. "That was the kind of thing I had hoped to hear you say."

Rahm grimaced. "Meaning?"

"I worried about who might be in possession of the Seal. Your willingness to surrender it is healthy. Solomon probably felt a sense of ownership. Maybe he gave it to the Queen of Sheba because he had the same experience." The Bible says he was the wisest man to ever live. At any rate, one thing I am certain of is that it does not belong to me. And it never did. It's more like it chose me, so maybe it found you, too. Or maybe it's more accurate to say that we were guided to it. As soon as it was in my possession, I stumbled onto some remarkable manuscripts, including the missing pages of Sinaiticus, the oldest New Testament in the world. This has shaped my entire career, my life."

"But if it has anything to do with God, why me?" Rahm asked. "I'm not a Jew like Solomon, nor a Christian like you. I'm not even a good Muslim."

"When it found me, I was young and brash and full of myself," Stephanos said. "But here are the facts as I see them. The Russian gave you a drive containing weaponized software, something the terrorists will stop at nothing to get. The code on that drive may have been written in Saudi Arabia, where the Captain said the Russian worked. Hamas, Iran, Libya, Syria, the Houthi Group of Yemen, Hezbollah of Lebanon, and the Israelis are all enemies of the Saudi government. Therefore, they are potential targets, and you are in great danger. Furthermore, your mentor was murdered over the drive at the very spot where the Seal was hidden." Stephanos stopped pacing, sat, and gazed intently across the desk. "Was that a coincidence?"

Rahm leaned back. "I thought you were the expert. I have no idea."

"There is danger from misusing the Seal and from those who would kill to get the drive. So, why you? This is pure speculation, but perhaps you were guided to the Seal because of that drive."

"What's the connection?"

"Two other facts come to mind. You are a Palestinian traveling in the company of an Israeli. Maybe Israel is the target of that software. After all, Solomon, king of Israel, created the Seal."

"Hostility between them would be surprising." Rahm scratched his eyebrow. "There have been behind-the-scenes negotiations between the Israelis and the Saudis. They're pursuing their mutual interest in dealing with Iran. It would make more sense for the target to be Iran."

"Maybe so. Whoever is involved, this second attack on this holy place is linked to your presence. I'm going to have to ask you and your Israeli friend to leave the premises. But before you go, you should know that as difficult as it is, if you embrace forgiveness, it will change you."

Rahm nodded and stood. As he was formulating a response, the silence was broken by the sound of two distant gunshots.

Stephanos rushed to the window. “Dear God. Now what?”

CHAPTER THIRTY-NINE
THE SEAL'S POWER

"There are more things in Heaven and Earth, Horatio, than are dreamt of in your philosophy."
William Shakespeare

St. Catherine Monastery
Present

Rahm's stomach tightened. "Will the Seal help me deal with those terrorists and all this shooting?"

Stephanos turned away from the window and faced him. "Mr. Khalidi, the ring's power is most of all about clarity of thought. It will not obviate the outcomes that flow from any choices you make while under its influence. I mean no disrespect, but I am convinced that the power of the ring is supernatural, not magical."

Rahm swept his hand around the room, and his eyes opened wide. "You're telling me that with all these crosses, icons, and statues, none of these things are magic in any way?"

"Exactly."

"This morning, I saw someone bowing their head to an icon in the chapel as if they were praying," Rahm said. "You're telling me they *weren't* worshiping?"

"When a soldier salutes an officer, or when children say a pledge to a flag, would you consider that worship?"

Rahm shrugged. "No, but If the Thummim isn't magical, and if Solomon's Seal isn't either, then why do I feel the buzz in my head when I touch it?" Rahm rubbed his forehead. "What caused my brain to speed up as it did?"

"I don't know." Stephanos scratched his chin with his arthritic fingers and said, "But consider this possibility. What if the reason you were led to the Seal was the land disputes between the Israelis and the Palestinians? This is what most of the conflicts are about, right?"

"Great!" Rahm snorted. "Solomon, the great Jewish king's ring, comes to the rescue, and we have another miracle for Israel. Right?"

Stephanos pushed his black hat forward a little and scratched the back of his head. "Where did that come from? Hasn't it occurred to you that God loves Palestinians as much as he loves Israelis?"

"A fat lot of good that's doing us!"

Stephanos stroked his beard. "Meaning?"

"If God loves Palestinians, then why is this slow-motion train wreck happening to us? Why are 1.5 million of my people still living in U.N. refugee camps? Why do we keep losing land to new settlements every year? Maybe God should find someone else to show his affection to. Pretty soon, all our lands will be gone. There'll be no Palestine left."

"So, your theory is that if God cares, life should go well?"

"Shouldn't it?"

"I played basketball in my school days. My teammate, Nikolas, used to complain about our coach. 'He's always yelling. He's on me all the time.' I told him, 'Why do you think he yells at you and not at me? He yells at you because he knows you have talent. He ignores me because I have none.' "

"Things go from bad to worse with you. You're trying to tell me that God punishes us because he likes us so much?"

"Maybe it's not punishment." Stephanos pointed at the crucifix on his office wall. "God's favorite Palestinian *was* crucified."

"Just when I was getting to like you, you start preaching? Unbelievable!"

"Please forgive me," Stephanos said. "What I am trying to say is that I was guided to the Seal at a critical point in my life. My discovery of those remaining pages of Sinaiticus and all those other manuscripts had worldwide implications for biblical scholarship. Therefore, I wouldn't be surprised if you finding the Seal had something to do with the disputes in the Holy Land. What if you could help change the relationship between the two nations?"

"What did finding the Seal have to do with finding those pages?"

"Think about it. I found the ring hidden in the basilica wall. Then, a few feet away, I caused a cave-in that revealed the forgotten room of lost manuscripts. That wasn't a coincidence any more than I believe it was a coincidence that your friend died where he did."

Rahm stood to his feet, seething. "Wait just a minute! You think God had the Professor killed so I would find the ring? What kind of God would do that? That's sick!"

Stephanos motioned for Rahm to sit. "Calm yourself. I wouldn't worry about God going around killing people. Human beings do quite enough of that without his help. I believe the convergence has something to do with God and the power of the ring. Whatever it is, I must conclude that the reason you were guided to it is because of something big. Whatever it is, it must be significant not just for you, but for the rest of the world as well."

CHAPTER FORTY
CALL A CAB

"The man who has experienced shipwreck shudders even at a calm sea."
Ovid

St. Catherine Monastery
Present

The mountains were sullen and threatening as Rahm left Stephanos' office. The peaks loomed larger and closer as the early afternoon shadows lengthened. At Stephanos' suggestion, he went to the first aid station, had his head wound bandaged, and then proceeded to his room. On his way, he found Adi sitting in the courtyard nearby. Rahm felt strangely happy to see her. "How did it go after I left?" he asked.

Adi briefed him on the elimination of the sniper and told him about the officer who had been shot in the leg. "They took him to the hospital," she said.

Rahm looked around and lowered his voice. "While I was inside, the Abbot seemed to think that Israel may have been Danilov's target when he wrote that software."

"What a brilliant deduction! Why do you think I'm here?" Adi waved her hand dismissively. "Oh. Before I forget." She pulled out a slip of paper and offered it to him, her tone softer. "I'm sorry about the Professor. I know he meant a lot to you."

"What is this?" He took the paper.

"You dropped it when Abasi questioned you by the Charnel House."

Rahm read the letterhead. It was from an oncology office in Jerusalem.

"I think," Adi said, "we know now why the Professor gave you his house. Six months to live. Stage four pancreatic cancer. Did you notice it was dated five months ago?"

Rahm looked at the note again. "No, I had no idea. No wonder he was so insistent about taking this trip now." Rahm's eyes moistened. "He never mentioned being sick."

Adi glanced over Rahm's shoulder. "We have company."

Rahm turned and was confronted by an approaching policeman who strode purposefully across the flagstone courtyard. He pointed at Rahm. "You come."

"Yes, one moment."

The cop frowned, did an about-face, and marched away.

Rahm whispered to Adi, "You'd better find a safe place to hide that thumb drive."

The officer looked over his shoulder and barked, "You come!" When he saw Rahm moving, he headed for the parking lot.

Rahm followed. When he got to the head of the ramp, he saw Captain Abasi standing next to an ambulance in the parking lot. The stretcher near his feet held a draped corpse.

"Mr. Khalidi," Abasi said as Rahm approached. "This is the sniper. He had no identification papers on him. But from the Persian lions tattooed on his chest, he appears to be Iranian VAJA." Abasi reached down and pulled the sheet back. "Do you recognize him?"

Rahm studied the face and the tattoos on the man's chest and shook his head no. Despite having seen more than his share of dead people, he shuddered at the sight of the corpse's ugly head wound.

Abasi faced Rahm. "The rest of his team escaped. But I will capture them soon. The voice on the bullhorn insisted you had a drive. It was too bad that you forced me to crack you on the head. But I was under tremendous pressure. The next time I give you a direct order, I expect obedience."

"Captain Abasi, while I was in the abbot's office, I borrowed his phone and took some pictures of the gash on my head."

"I see. Then I will need to confiscate the abbot's phone and the drive." Abasi held out his hand.

"As I told you earlier, I do not have whatever that madman wanted. You should know that I've already sent two of the clearest photos of my wound to my editor and deleted all the remaining photos from the abbot's phone. There is no need to confiscate it."

"So, I suppose you will write about Egyptian police brutality?" Abasi's left eyebrow arched.

"I'm not looking to cause you any trouble, captain. But I believe there is a story behind this attack. I need to impress my boss after my last submission didn't make print or online editions. Could I interview you?"

Abasi squinted. "Why should I talk to you?"

"If I could get an interview, I could make sure those pictures disappear."

"An interesting proposal. Show me your passport."

"I already—"

"Give it here!" Abasi said through clenched teeth.

Rahm looked into the Captain's dark eyes and realized he was not in a position to offer resistance. He handed over his passport.

Abasi's foot nudged the corpse. "I need to file a report and join the pursuit of this dog's accomplices. Before you leave tomorrow, come to the station, and I will return your passport. We will discuss your request then."

□ □ □

Rahm went looking for Adi. "Abasi told me to come by the police station in St. Catherine City. He took my passport when I tried to persuade him to give me an interview."

"You did what?"

He patted his forehead. "I told him I took some pictures of this and sent them to my editor. I said I would gladly make them go away if he gave me the interview."

"You tried blackmailing him?" Adi opened her eyes wide. "Egyptian cops are the worst!"

"That's why I thought a little leverage would offer us a little protection. He ordered me to come to the station in St. Catherine City tomorrow."

"Are you crazy? We've got to get out of here. Go get your things. We're leaving now."

"He took my papers. If we leave, I'll never get them back. I'm a freelance journalist. I need to be able to move freely from one place to another."

"I sent a text to HQ and asked for backup. But with the trouble in Gaza, our resources are still spread thin. They ordered me to evacuate. I am to report to Eilat with the drive as soon as possible. If we stay here, between Qatal and Abasi, we'll be dead by morning. What value will your precious papers be, then?" She pulled out a cell phone and asked, "Do you still have that taxi driver's card?"

"Where did you get that phone?" Rahm asked.

"If you must know, from that nice Bedouin nurse at the hospital. She could afford to buy two phones with what I gave her. Do you have that card or not?" She held out her hand.

Rahm nodded and rummaged through his pockets. Where does she get off being so demanding? He finally fished the business card out of his back pocket. "Here!" He smacked the card into her palm a little harder than he had intended. "The Abbot ordered us to leave."

She jerked the card away and glared. "That settles it!" She focused her attention on the card and tapped out the number. After a long pause, she turned her back on Rahm. "Hello? Habib? Yesterday, you picked us up at the hospital and dropped the three of us off at the monastery. We need a ride to Nuweiba."

She listened for a few moments, then looked at her watch. "No! I mean, right now. We will pay you well. But you must come to the monastery right away."

She listened again. "Yes, right where you dropped us off, but on the far side of the parking lot that can't be seen from the gate. And don't be late. Twelve-thirty or we get someone else." She clicked off her phone, then said to Rahm in a whisper, "Go get anything you absolutely must have. But leave your backpack. People think we're staying for another day. Let's keep them thinking that way. We don't want anyone alerting Abasi. You heard what I said to the driver. Be down here in the parking lot in fifteen minutes. Not a minute sooner."

CHAPTER FORTY-ONE
THE TIDE IS TURNING!

"If dogs are governing a country, what can you hear every day other than horrible barking noises?"
Mehmet Murat Ildan

St. Catherine Monastery
Present

As Adi slipped into the taxi, "Did you tell anyone about where we were going?"

Habib's thick accent delivered chilling news through lips that smiled into the cab's rearview mirror. "Habib, call brozer for place for Habib stay. Brozer live in Dahab. After Nuweiba, Habib drive Dahab. Brozer tell no one."

Adi's shook her head. "After Iranian attacks on the road and here at the monastery--"

Habib held up his right hand, his gesture showing understanding. "Must take much care, yes? Habib happy zhe police let you go."

Adi and Rahm looked at each other, silently sinking lower in the taxi's rear seats.

"Ahh!" Habib grinned. "No worry. Police arrest Habib uncle for grow poppy. Habib have no love for zhem. We escape Abasi's guys." He stopped the car and made a quick U-turn.

Rahm's forehead creased. "Your uncle is selling drugs?"

Habib shrugged. “When zhe tourist come, uncle use zhe camel and take zhem to mountain. Uncle has band zhat play Bedouin music for tourist. Now no tourist. No business. No problem, poppies sell good in Sharm al Sheik. We go back road. Habib sink police look you in Nuweiba. Come Dahab wis Habib. Yes? Dahab more safe.”

Adi asked, “Isn’t that a longer drive than to Nuweiba?”

“Zhe back road more slow. But no police. Dahab just ten minute more. You like.”

“Okay,” Adi looked at Rahm, who nodded. She continued, “Let’s go to Dahab.”

“Habib brozer take to Aqaba on boat. Yes?”

Rahm nodded. “Yes, thank you, Habib. I think that’s a great idea.”

Adi snapped, “You can go to Jordan if you want. I’m going to Eilat. Our tech people are waiting for me there.”

Rahm spoke, but Habib held up his free hand. “No worry, please. Brozer go where lady say. Habib send text.” He tapped a message on his phone, hoping these fares would help the family’s struggling business.

□ □ □

Habib honked the horn as they slid to a stop in the sand and gravel patch that served as a parking lot at Dahab’s southernmost moorage. “Here brozer house!” A sign in English, Arabic, and Hebrew read “Daily Glass Boat Excursions.” Overhead, yellow and blue plastic pennants applauded as a dust devil danced through the lot.

A boy about twelve years old came running out, “Uncle! How you are? Fazer say attack on Nuweiba Road. Fazer worry?”

“We okay, Omar.”

The boy asked, “Are zhese people for boat?”

Adi’s face paled. “So, your brother tells no one? Even this child knows about us?”

Habib laughed and held his forefinger to his lips and said to his nephew. “Shh! Yes, zhese my friends. Please take to boat.” Glancing up at the sea, he added, “Hurry, tide is turn.”

Motioning for Adi and Rahm to follow, the boy trotted toward the end of the dock.

□ □ □

Gulf of Aqaba
Present

“The sign said, ‘Glass Bottom Boat,” Rahm shouted over the thrumming motors.

The boat’s captain tapped the chrome speedometer recessed in the matte black dash and winked. “Habib say you hurry. Zhis Destiny. Dive boat. She more fast!”

Baki, Habib’s brother, wore a hideous Hawaiian shirt with large magenta and yellow flowers.

Baki pointed at the speedometer. "We go Aqaba more fast, wis zhis boat." Baki scanned the water ahead and glanced at Rahm whenever he spoke. "Destiny have two big engine. She go fast all day when water like zhis."

Rahm hoped the afternoon chop would hold off until they got there. "Hurry is the right word. We need to get there as soon as possible. But don't forget Eilat. Then we can head to Aqaba. Thank you!" Rahm enjoyed the view from the high-profile wheelhouse. He watched the white wake spread out behind them, leaving a shimmering trail on the water. It felt good to be skimming across the surface of the gulf, away from danger. After the dusty heat of the desert, the fresh scent of the sea was delicious. When he stood up, he could see the aft deck. Adi lounged there on a cushioned bench, blonde hair whipping in the breeze, relaxed and unguarded. *She's so beautiful!*

"How long before we arrive?" he asked Baki.

Baki checked his watch, then held up two fingers. "If sea flat, go more fast. Two hour."

Rahm excused himself and climbed down the deck, and made his way aft. "Feel better?"

Adi looked up and brushed a strand of blond hair out of her face.

When she did, Rahm saw her eyes scanning the distant horizon behind them.

"I'll feel better when I can hand Danilov's drive over to our technical people in Eilat."

□□□

Dahab Moorage
Present

A white SUV sprayed gravel as it slid to a halt next to Habib's taxi. Saeed Qatal jumped out and saw a fast-moving white boat a quarter mile away heading north. He spoke to a boy walking back from the dock. "Were a Jewish woman and an Arab man on that boat?" he asked.

The boy hesitated, then shrugged.

Qatal snarled at his two men, "If they escape with that drive, you will answer for this--"

"Major, look!" his lieutenant said.

Qatal turned. He saw it moored at a dock fifty yards away. It had six outboard motors, each with a large number 400 printed below the word *Racing*. He guessed it to be about fifteen meters long. The name printed on the side in bold red and gold letters, *Rapid Transit*. The red leather upholstery and the sleek lines of the black cigarette boat made it look fast even while moored and bobbing at the dock. A smile played on Qatal's face.

□□□

Rahm sat across from Adi on the rear-facing bench of Baki's boat. He closed his eyes and inhaled through his nose. "Just what I needed, some vitamin sea."

Adi yelled over the engine's roar, "What?"

Rahm raised his voice. "I love being on the water and the feel of the spray. I've been thinking about what it would be like to live in America. I can't get over the Professor's generosity. It boggles my brain. Inside I feel freer, hopeful even."

Adi jumped up. "Don't get too comfortable, Khalidi. We're not there yet." She pointed at the southern horizon. "That looks like the cigarette boat that was at the dock, and it's closing fast!"

CHAPTER FORTY-TWO
CHASING DESTINY

"Whoever pursues evil will die."
Solomon

Gulf of Aqaba
Present

Saeed Qatal and his two men, Javad and Farbod, raced north on the Gulf of Aqaba in the high-performance boat called Rapid Transit. Its six outboard motors roaring.

Javad's stringy black hair whipped in the wind as he struggled with the controls of the commandeered craft.

Less than two miles ahead, Qatal spied a white and blue boat cruising north down the middle of the twelve-mile-wide Gulf. The sea was calm, and they were quickly overtaking the other boat. But even with his seat's specialized suspension, Qatal bounced and jostled with each tiny ripple on the water's surface until the pain in his back was too much. Old injuries reminded him he wasn't young anymore. He glanced at the speedometer and was surprised that even though the throttle wasn't maxed; it read 60 knots. The Rapid Transit was well-named. He gestured for Javad to slow down.

As they approached the high-profile white boat, Qatal could see a name painted on the transom: *Destiny*. Anticipation rose inside. "Pull alongside," he shouted to Javad.

Javad steered left.

Qatal saw three people onboard. When they got closer, the Destiny swerved and dodged. Qatal pulled his pistol and stood but plopped down when they hit the Destiny's wake.

Javad slowed to match the white boat's speed. He steered within twenty feet.

Qatal showed his Browning HP semi-auto and shouted, "Stop, or I'll shoot!"

The Destiny swerved at the low-slung cigarette boat.

Javad steered hard left and sped away.

Meanwhile, the Destiny did a looping right turn.

Racing to catch up to the Destiny, Qatal's boat crossed her wake again. At that speed, the black boat's nose lifted and threatened to flip over. Javad jerked the throttle back. A moment later, the cigarette boat's long hull slammed against the sea's surface.

Qatal cried out. The pain in his back brought tears to his eyes that were already stinging from the salt spray.

Farbod fell on the aft deck from the force of the impact.

Javad recovered control and pushed the throttle forward. They jetted ahead and were alongside the Destiny in two heartbeats.

Baki's taller white boat made another aggressive move. This time, Javad was ready.

Qatal fired a warning shot over Baki's head. When that failed to slow him, Qatal aimed to kill. But an accurate shot was impossible with the incessant jouncing. Qatal holstered his gun and shouted at Javad, "Ram them!"

Javad accelerated into a wide turn and roared at the fleeing Destiny.

□ □ □

Rahm saw the long-nosed black boat that had veered away swing back and race in their direction. He yelled at Adi. "Hang on!"

Adi shouted, "He's crazy!"

The collision was like a Corvette hitting a bus. Fiberglass exploded. The heftier speed boat cut the white dive boat in half. Destiny's wheelhouse crashed down onto the front of the cigarette boat, and Rahm lost sight of Baki.

Split amidships, the Destiny started sinking immediately.

Their momentum threw Rahm and Adi clear, and both plunged underwater. Adi surfaced and started treading water, coughing, and sputtering. Rahm, who was in his element, closed the gap between them with a few powerful strokes. "Are you okay?" he asked.

"I'm fine." Adi looked around and nodded at the Saudi coast a few hundred meters away. "We'd better swim for it."

"You go ahead," Rahm said. He turned toward the shattered wreckage. The front half of the Destiny was listing badly to one side, and the stern half was sinking. "I'll see what's up with Baki."

"Watch yourself," she said, nodding toward the limping cigarette boat. "Those guys mean business."

□ □ □

On the Rapid Transit, Qatal picked himself up off the teak deck, and checked himself for injuries. No blood. And as far as he could tell, nothing was broken. Behind him, he saw both halves of the dive boat sinking. An oil slick formed around the stern portion.

"Javad, can't you do anything right? I said, ram them, not sink them. We need to recover that drive. We'll be lucky to find it now."

With a frightened look on his face, Javad protested, "I thought—"

"Let me do the thinking," Qatal growled. Then he pointed to their forward deck. "See if you and Farbod can clear away that wreckage." He looked at where Farbod had been earlier. "Where is he?"

"I don't know."

Qatal moved to the rear of the boat, shouting, "Farbod?" No answer. He noticed the black keffiyeh Farbod had been wearing floating in the water a few meters away and decided that he must have been lost in the crash. He moved back toward the cabin, staggered, and nearly fell. "Javad, the deck is tilting. Take us closer to the land. We're sinking!"

Javad steered toward shore. "Major, look." Then he pointed ashore.

Qatal saw Adi Ovitz on the beach, motioning to someone in the water. He then noticed a swimmer who looked like . . . Was that

Rahm Khalidi swimming toward the woman? He said, "Don't let them escape." Qatal pointed at the sandy shoreline. "Go!"

□ □ □

Wadi Tayyib Al Ism, on the Saudi Arabian Coast

Saeed Qatal stood on the beach at the mouth of the narrow canyon that sliced through the mountains and drained Saudi Arabia's interior. Sheer cliffs soared a hundred feet overhead. Where the wadi widened, a grove of scruffy-looking palm trees stood in a jumble at the base of the bluffs on either side. A two-lane asphalt road ran north and south, hugging the coast along the improbably narrow strip of real estate at the rugged mountains' fringe. No wonder the Saudis called the range "al Hejaz," "the Barrier."

They were stranded. The dive boat was already gone, and the speedboat bobbed with the tide, nose up out of the sea, with the aft section with its six engines submerged. Qatal held his gun on a water-logged duo. "Get on the ground."

Adi Ovitz, eyes blazing with anger, knelt on the sand. Rahm Khalidi looked belligerent but complied.

Qatal relished the hatred he saw in their eyes. *They all look the same when I have the upper hand.* "All the way down. I am a reasonable man. I do not want to shoot. But . . ." He shrugged.

They both sprawled on the sand.

"Javad, frisk them. I want that drive and anything else of value."

Qatal watched as Javad searched Rahm and found some cash and a leather pouch. In Adi's pocket, there was a cell phone that dripped water. Javad pulled out what looked like a multi-blade knife in a sealed plastic bag. It was the thumb drive. *Yes!* "Bring those to me. Now!"

Javad handed the items over.

"Agent Ovitz, how clever to carry an evidence bag with you." Qatal held up the bag. "Otherwise, the drive would have been destroyed by the saltwater. Thank you very much for your thoughtfulness. Too bad about your phone, though." Qatal examined the cell phone, threw it aside, and smirked. "Good thing mine is waterproof. You'll be glad to know I will call to request an extraction team to take us back to Tehran. If you behave, you and your friend can come along."

"Good luck," she said. "Our navy patrols these waters constantly, and our OFEK satellite watches from above."

Qatal smiled broadly. "Thank you for the reminder, Miss Ovitz. I will relay that to headquarters so we can avoid both."

CHAPTER FORTY-THREE
NO FALSE MOVES!

"Shame is a soul eating emotion."
Karl Jung

Gulf of Aqaba
Present

Qatal stood over the duo prostrated on the sand. "Miss Ovitz, we are quite aware of Israel's naval capabilities in the gulf. OFEK's synthetic aperture radar is impressive. But, my dear, you know that satellites have their limits. Their overhead passes are quite predictable." Then, glancing at his watch, he dialed his phone. As he waited for a connection, he held up the leather pouch. "What do we have here, Mr. Khalidi?"

Rahm stared, his jaws tight.

"We need an emergency extraction for two team members and two prisoners. The boat we were using is out of commission," Qatal spoke confidently into his phone. "When a location has been chosen, send the coordinates to this number." Then he ended the call and opened the pouch. Looking inside, he said, "Oh my, a gift for your lady friend? How sweet!" He reached inside the pouch to remove the ring but dropped it back into the bag when his touch resulted in a jolt of energy coursing through his hand and arm. He looked down, startled and puzzled. Looking up at Rahm, he demanded, "What is this?"

"It's what the Americans call a mood ring," Rahm said. "Have you ever heard of those?"

Qatal reached into the pouch and removed the ring. Strange energy surged through his entire body again. Confusion settled over his mind like morning a fog. Holding the ring between his thumb and index finger, he lifted it to the light. His dark eyes stared off into the middle distance, lips parted, and lines formed between his brows. Holding the ring at arm's length, he studied it, then put it back into the pouch. For almost a full minute, he looked at the pouch. He put the leather bag in his pocket and began shuffling back and forth, as if uncertain of which direction to go.

"Major?" Javad bit his lower lip. "Are you okay?"

Qatal shook his head as if to clear it, "Silence, fool! I'm thinking." After shaking his head two more times, he barked, "What are you waiting for? Cuff them both. The woman first. We may want to amuse ourselves with her later."

Javad approached Adi. "Spread your arms out to the side and cross your ankles."

She glared up at him.

Javad kicked her in the ribs and shouted, "Do not look at me!"

She turned her head, and he grabbed her left hand and put her in a wristlock. Keeping her arm twisted, he knelt on her shoulder and cuffed her left wrist. Then twisted her cuffed arm behind her back.

Adi groaned.

"Stop complaining," Javad said. "Give me your other hand."

Adi put her right hand behind her back.

Javad cuffed her wrists together, smacked her across the back of her head, smirked, then bent low, and whispered something in her ear.

When Javad hit her, Rahm moved to intervene.

Qatal pointed his gun at him. "Don't even think about it!"

Rahm froze in place.

Qatal could see him seething. "Don't worry," he said, leering and winking. "We're saving the fun part for later. She might enjoy it. Isn't that right, Javad?"

Javad looked exasperated, but chuckled and stood. "Not when I'm done with her."

"Leave her alone!" Rahm shouted.

Qatal sneered. "Go ahead, rush to the rescue. I dare you. I'll drop you where you stand."

□ □ □

Rahm's head swiveled back and forth between Adi struggling and the business end of Qatal's handgun.

"What's it going to be, Mr. Khalidi?"

Qatal's mocking stung. Rahm shouted, "Stop it!"

Qatal stepped closer, pressed his gun to Rahm's forehead, and snarled, "Go ahead! Try it!"

Rahm glared at Qatal and trembled with rage for a few moments. Then his shoulders sagged, and he looked down.

"That's what I thought. Khalidi, you're pitiful! Given a choice, you saved your own pathetic skin? You make me sick. I'm not sure which is worse, your incompetence or your unwillingness to try. You could have at least died trying and salvaged a little dignity. If you weren't useful for managing Miss Ovitz, I would put you out of your misery right now."

Rahm's eyes met Adi's. She studied him as if waiting for him to do something. Her earlier words came back like a sledgehammer—*Poor little Palestinian*. He looked away and hung his head in shame.

"Assume your natural position," Qatal said.

Rahm frowned.

"Kneel, fool!"

Rahm obeyed and closed his eyes.

□ □ □

Qatal shook his head and glanced at his watch. "Javad, we're on a tight schedule. Come and cuff the hero."

Javad strutted over, kicked Rahm in the back, and knocked him to the ground. "Okay, *hero*, you saw how it's done. Spread your arms out, cross your ankles, and look away. He cuffed Rahm's left hand, but before he could restrain the right, the sound of an approaching vehicle interrupted. He jumped to his feet and shouted, "Major, we have company!"

Hearing the commotion, Rahm stood and faced Javad, keeping both hands behind him.

A black Mercedes SUV came around the corner on the coast highway. Pointing at Adi and Rahm, Qatal growled, "Watch them." Then he marched toward the SUV, his gun pointed at the driver.

When the Mercedes got closer, its tires screeched on the pavement as it lurched to a stop. The driver and his passenger held up their hands.

Qatal waggled his weapon, indicating they should get out.

"I-I have money," the driver said. "I will give it to you. Don't hurt us."

"Put it in park and leave the engine running."

The kid exited the vehicle and said, "It's push button start. The fob is in my pocket."

"Both of you. Step away and keep your hands up." Qatal kept his gun trained on the driver. "Now, very slowly, reach into your pocket. When you have the key, throw it here. One false move, and you will see paradise before your time. I am a very good shot."

The driver kept his left hand in the air. It trembled above his head. With his right, he reached into his designer jeans' front pocket.

Qatal cocked his gun. "Careful!"

The young man pulled the fob out and dangled it for Qatal to see. "It's jus-just a fob. See?"

"Throw it here," Qatal said. When the kid obeyed, Qatal caught it in mid-air and said, "Thank you very much. You should go now. I would hate for something worse to happen."

"But--"

"I am very reasonable. But my trigger finger doesn't always cooperate. I think you should run."

When they hesitated, Qatal shot the pavement near the driver's feet.

The pair sprinted north, out of sight.

Qatal got into the Mercedes, pulled forward, and parked with its nose pointed into the wadi, then got back out and said to Javad, "Put them in the car one at a time. Start with the woman." He eyed his watch. "We must hurry."

Javad grabbed Adi and wrestled her toward the SUV, but she stomped on his foot, then kneed him in the groin.

Javad fell to the ground, groaning and writhing in pain.

Adi kicked him in the head.

"Stop!" Qatal shouted, pointing his gun at Adi. "Javad. Get up!"

Javad staggered to his feet, glowering.

“Take her to the car, and while you’re at it, check the fuel level.” He turned to Adi. “If you act out again, I will put a bullet in your friend.”

Javad took his time while belting her in.

Qatal held up the pouch for Rahm to see. “What is this? It does strange things to my head.”

“I found it in the Charnel House where you killed the Professor. You animal!”

“And?”

“And I saw its face was a twelve-pointed star.”

“Twelve points? A Jewish ring?” Qatal dug the ring back out and studied it. From the look on the Iranian’s face, Rahm guessed that confusion was clouding his thoughts again.

It surprised Rahm when Qatal started staring at the ring because he let the point of the gun drift downward. *It must distract him.*

Seeing the effect the seal was having on Qatal gave Rahm new hope, although he wasn’t sure why. He grabbed the loose end of the handcuffs with his left hand and took a small step backward.

Qatal looked up but didn’t react. His gaze returned to the ring.

Rahm took two steps. *No reaction. Now!* He turned and ran toward the beached cigarette boat.

□ □ □

Qatal's voice sliced through the air, "Stop!" He aimed his gun and dropped the ring, looked down for a moment, then shook his head. And his eyes cleared. His focus now razor-sharp, he aimed at the fleeing hostage and fired twice. But missed both times.

Rahm ran, juking left and right. The sound of bullets whizzing past his head added desperation to his pace. He hit the water, took three swift steps, and dove out of sight, using the beached speedboat as cover.

□ □ □

Javad came running and started firing at the hostage whenever he surfaced to snatch a breath.

Qatal said, "Forget him. He's your sidearm is ineffective at this distance. We have the drive and the woman. Let's go." He stopped to search for the ring. After a few moments, he found it, picked it up, studied it briefly, deliberately returned it to the pouch, then headed for the vehicle.

The door of the Mercedes swung open as Qatal checked on Adi. Placing the bag on top of the Mercedes, he reached in to secure Adi's seatbelt. "We can't have our guest of honor making any foolish attempts to escape," he said with a sneer.

As Qatal reached across her body, Adi slammed her head into his right ear.

Stunned, Qatal swore and retaliated with a brutal backhand. Then he viciously punched her in the head until she was unconscious. He unbuckled her seatbelt, laid her across the back seat, ran one seat belt between her cuffed hands and clicked it closed. Then he wrapped the other belt around her legs.

Qatal yelled, "Javad, let's go!"

Javad climbed in, slammed the Mercedes into gear, and stomped on the accelerator. The vehicle surged forward into the wadi. On its roof, a tiny leather pouch bounced once, then slide off and fell to the ground.

CHAPTER FORTY-FOUR
INTO SHADOWS

"The true soldier fights not because he hates what is in front of him, but because he loves what is behind him."
G.K. Chesterton

Saudi Arabian Coast
Present

Lungs bursting, Rahm Khalidi resurfaced in the cold blue waters of the Gulf of Aqaba, gasping for air. Silence replaced the earlier gunfire. Leaving Rahm cautious, but out of immediate danger from the two men who were holding Adi hostage. Rahm stayed safely out of range, just in case. At this distance, he couldn't see what was happening onshore.

While considering how long he could keep treading water without attracting the attention of sharks, the Mercedes' driver's door opened and closed. Then he heard the ominous sound of the engine starting. A moment later, Wadi Tayyib Al-Ism's imposing cliffs swallowed the SUV, leaving Rahm alone with echoing uncertain. Did they take her?

Warily paddling toward shore, Rahm remained vigilant, watching to be sure Qatal was really gone. Keeping an eye on the cavernous opening to the wadi shrouded in afternoon shadows. Rahm paddled toward the shore. The beach appeared abandoned. But Rahm's instincts urged caution. Set back thirty or forty meters from the water, a small grove of palm trees clung to either side of the path that led into the wadi.

Searching for signs of ambush among the palm groves, Rahm found none. No one was there, including Adi. Relieved, he waded ashore, casting furtive glances to insure he was alone.

He scurried across the road and moved into the palm grove on the north side of the wadi. He hid in the shadows to watch and listen. Satisfied that he was alone, he let out a long breath.

It wasn't until that moment that he noticed his left wrist rubbed raw by the handcuffs. Stripping down, he wrung the seawater from his clothes.

While putting them back on, he studied the bit of the road that led north. He longed to be Adi's savior. Yet felt inadequate. *Qatal is always one step ahead of me.* An abyss of confusion fissured his brain. Or was it his heart? He was caving in on himself, torn, afraid, and angry. *Every time I try to help, I make things worse for Adi. Face it. She'd be better off if I followed those two kids north. She's right. "Poor little Palestinian!"* He cringed as thickness filled his throat. He wanted to run away. Just escape. His face flushed with shame at the thought of abandoning Adi.

I should forget trying to be a hero and go home. Taking the route to Aqaba was probably the smart move. He bit the inside of his cheek. The problem with that idea was that Aqaba was almost fifty miles away. It would not be an easy trip if he was on foot. He hoped that someone would come along and give him a ride, but he couldn't be sure when or if that might happen.

Then he walked over to where he could see the road that led south. The southern coast appeared just as desolate and offered the same challenges. *That doesn't make any sense.*

Rahm then recalled Javad mentioning that there was fresh water in the wadi and his mouth was already dry, and his thirst intensifying.

The thought of what Qatal, and the leering Javad, had in mind for Adi was intolerable. *I have to try!* Leaving the beach; he headed inland. A few yards beyond the divots left by the fleeing Mercedes, Rahm spotted something in the sand. His heartbeat ramped up as he got closer. Lying there was the familiar leather pouch. He stooped to pick it up. Then, suddenly suspicious, stopped, stood up, and scanned the canyon and its rim.

A puff of breeze from the Gulf rattled the fronds of a palm. Rahm spun in that direction. His pulse soared. But there was nothing. No one. He was alone. "Get a grip, Khalidi," he muttered. "Get a grip!"

Stooping, he picked up the pouch, and opened it. Taking out the seal, he slipped it on. The customary buzz brought a tremendous sense of clarity and resolve. *Adi is in danger. Why am I hesitating?* With his jaw set, he took off the ring, put it away, and marched into the wadi's shadows only to halt abruptly, when he heard footsteps behind him.

□ □ □

Wadi Tayyib Al-Ism

With one eye on Javad driving along the wadi's twisting road, Qatal looked over his shoulder and said to Adi, "Israelis take so much pride in saying that Israel is God's chosen. If it is, then why do they persecute the Palestinian minority?"

"There is no such thing as a Palestinian. The British invented that name. They're Arabs, most of them Bedouins."

"Ha!" Qatal mocked. "Israelis have been using that line since Golda Meir's days. Arguing over labels doesn't change the facts."

Adi winced when she angrily clenched her jaws. Qatal's beating left her left eye swollen shut and her lower lip split in three places. But anger flashed from her one open eye.

"Your parliament has ruled that Arabs living in Israel are second-class citizens," Qatal continued. "Your own holy book speaks against such treatment of people. You certainly aren't acting like you're God's people, are you?"

Adi just shook her head.

Qatal sneered, "No answer? Nothing? Here is what Moses said, 'Do not oppress a foreigner.' Can you tell me how you Israelis can claim that your nation follows the teachings of Prophet Moses when you frequently violate . . ." Qatal waved his hand as if trying to erase his own words. "No. The right word is constantly. You constantly violate the rights of Palestinians. Is that following the teachings of Moses? Is that Jewish?"

"We defend ourselves against terrorists," Adi said.

Qatal shook his head. "That is the biggest lie of all!"

"They . . ."

Qatal screamed at her, "Stop it! You steal the land of Palestinians, and then when one of them dares to protest or throw rocks, you attack with tanks and automatic weapons."

"The nation of Israel is a miracle from God. He defends her!" Adi shouted.

Qatal hissed, "There is no miracle in an uneven fight. Is it a supernatural event when a Jew in a Black Hawk gunship triumphs over a Palestinian teenager with a slingshot? Is it a miracle when a Merkava tank destroys a Palestinian house?"

Adi was unfazed. "Israel is surrounded by enemies. We continue to survive against all odds."

"You survive because you are puppets of the American regime. They send you weapons and three billion dollars a year. If God were your savior, you wouldn't need the devils in the American Congress funding your war machine?"

"Let's talk about what's unfair," Adi snarled. "Four hundred million Muslims who want us obliterated surround seven million Jews. Besides their humanitarian interests, we're America's greatest ally in the region. Why wouldn't American leaders want to defend us?"

"We will see how your master does when we unleash this on you and them," Qatal smirked, holding up Danilov's drive.

"We *are* God's chosen people. Of course, God protects his chosen." Wincing, Adi's swollen eye twitched. "He has and will always defend us."

CHAPTER FORTY-FIVE
FIRAS

"Do not withhold good from those who deserve it,
when it is in your power to act."
Jewish Proverb

Saudi Arabian Coast
Present

The two kids from the Mercedes approached Rahm. The driver said, "Wa 'alaikum as salaam. My name is Firas, and this is my friend Othman. Where is my father's Mercedes?"

"They took Adi and the car." Rahm pointed east. "They went inland. I have to help her."

Firas patted his chest and then pointed at Othman. "We know people. We can help." With that, he pulled out his phone and held it up to the sky. Then shook his head. "No coverage between these cliffs. The wadi turns in about a kilometer. We should get a signal there." With a wink, he added, "My uncle will send one of my cousins to come and pick us up."

"Then let's go. Hurry!" Rahm gestured for the duo to follow and hurried off.

The two Saudis followed, and the trio jogged into the wadi, warily scanning the surroundings.

"Thank you . . . for your help. . . But these men . . . are dangerous," Rahm said between breaths.

Firas pulled a pistol from a concealed carry holster tucked inside his designer jeans and with a sinister grin said, “So are we.”

“Why didn’t you use it back there?” Rahm asked, attempting to understand his young companions.

“There were two of them,” Firas replied displaying some tactical finesse. “We had only this one weapon, and it looked like they were well-trained. I was worried they might kill one of you or us if I resisted. I may be young, but I am not foolish. What’s going on? Who are those guys?”

“It’s a long story,” Rahm confided, unraveling the intrigue. “They’re Iranian VAJA agents, like the US CIA or the Saudi GIP. I heard the leader talking about extraction, I assume by helicopter or airplane. I need to catch them before they leave. What are you two doing out here, anyway?”

In a subdued tone, Firas revealed, “The winter rains washed out the footbridge near the mouth of the wadi. Othman and I thought we might make it through all the way to the coast road this way. If not, we would walk from the bridge. But the bridge was out. When we got to the coast road, we headed north. There is a better spot for swimming up the coast. We were heading back when they stole the Mercedes. You know the rest.”

The wadi made a sharp turn to the right. While watching for trouble, Rahm jogged around the corner. A cluster of palm trees materialized. Although the calendar whispered March, the heat felt more like a Ramallah summer. I wonder what summer must be like in this place.

The steepest wadi walls were now behind them, gentle slopes surrounded them, and he had a clear view of the southern sky. There was no shade here except among the palms.

Firas climbed a low hill, then shouted down, “I have a signal!”

Rahm heard Firas talking excitedly. But he couldn’t make out much of the conversation until there was an outburst near the end.

“Yes, that’s my car. Keep them there if you can. Tell Karim to hurry!” Firas came running down the slope and joined the others in the shadow of a tall palm. “My uncle says the Mercedes has the hood up at his gas station. He will offer his help and try to delay them. My cousin, Karim saw my car being driven by strangers and got worried. He’s already on his way.”

The road in the wadi floor bent around a gravel mound covered in large rocks and palms. The three scrambled up the slight incline and sat down under a tree to wait in the shade.

Moments later, a blue Volvo SUV came hurtling around the corner.

Firas ran out and waved his arms, smiling, “It’s Karim. He made good time. Come on.”

The vehicle slid, spraying sand and gravel, and came to a stop thirty yards away. Karim swiveled, his head bug-eyed, apparently inspecting the wadi and surrounding rocks for danger. After a thorough sweep, the Volvo crept forward.

“No worries,” Firas said. “The bad guys are gone.”

Rahm called out with a big smile, “Kaifa alhal?” *How are you?*

The Volvo stopped, and Karim put down his window. His eyes wide, he looked ready to race away if necessary. Firas ran to the front passenger door, opened it, and got in. Othman ran toward the SUV and waved Rahm forward. "You come. Hurry."

When Rahm climbed into the back seat, Firas handed him a bottle of cold water.

"Shukran!" Rahm said. He accepted it and greedily gulped it down.

Karim slammed the Volvo into gear, made a U-turn, spraying gravel, sand, and dust as he sped east.

"Rahm Khalidi, why are you in Saudi Arabia?" Firas asked.

"I'm a journalist. from Ramallah. We were trying to get away from the Iranians in a boat."

"We saw the wrecked boat. But how did the Iranians get here?"

"Our boat is on the bottom of the Gulf. The wreck you saw was their boat. They rammed ours and killed the captain."

"The guy who shot at us had cold eyes," Firas said.

"His name is Qatal. He's ruthless."

"That's his name? Murderer?"

Rahm nodded and said, "Yes! They're both murderers. They killed several people in Egypt, too."

"The woman they took is in danger."

"I worry about what they will do to her." Rahm rubbed his eyebrow.

Firas said, “My uncle’s gas station is north of Al Bad on Highway 5. If the Mercedes’ hood is up, it must be damaged,” He then turned to his cousin and asked, “Did you see them doing any work on the Mercedes? Did they say anything?”

“Yes,” Karim said as he steered around a half-buried bolder in the middle of the wadi. “The older guy was yelling something about delays. There were two men and a woman. I noticed her because she wore no hijab, and it looked like someone had given her a beating. So, I figured you were in trouble and came to find you.”

“Why didn’t uncle shoot them?”

Karim shrugged, “Maybe worried about the woman.”

“He hit her? That must be them! Qatal threatened Adi when she wouldn’t get in the car. I need to catch them. “Thank you for coming, Karim. I will gladly pay you for the ride.”

Sitting taller, Firas placed his right hand over his chest and said, “My name is Firas al Ali al Haramain from Al Bad. My father is a leader in our tribe, and so is Karim’s father. They would disown us if I violated our family’s honor and took your money!”

Rahm leaned back in the seat, looked at the clock on the dash, and closed his eyes. I hope I’m not too late.

CHAPTER FORTY-SIX
FOLLOWING THE CLOUD

"Men go abroad to wonder at the heights of mountains, at the huge waves of the sea, at the long courses of the rivers, at the vast compass of the ocean, at the circular motions of the stars, and they pass by themselves without wondering."
Saint Augustine

Saudi Arabia
Present

"Sir, where are we going?" Saeed Qatal spoke into his encrypted phone, trying to sound like he was an employee talking with his boss in case anyone monitored his call.

"From your current location, proceed southeast," General Barzan's authoritative voice commanded.

Qatal listened and entered the encoded coordinates into his phone's GPS function. A map showed on his screen. "Sir, why are we moving deeper inland? We have the drive. We are wasting time." His eyes narrowed to slits as he listened. The General had stayed on past his retirement. He must have nothing better to do. He had been standing in the way of younger men having the opportunity for promotion for years.

"You're moving away from the Gulf, so your transport can avoid interfering with air traffic."

"Sir, we have an extra guest, a female. I hope our transport can handle that."

"Is it that the woman we discussed yesterday?"

"Yes, sir."

"Excellent work Saeed. I will make sure they are prepared to handle another guest."

"Thank you, sir. One more thing, we have seen no air traffic."

"You aren't suggesting that my judgment is impaired, are you?"

"No, sir. Not at all. I'm trying to understand."

"You don't need to understand!" the general barked. "You just need to follow orders. I see things you cannot. What really matters is that you stay out of trouble and do not put the company's equipment in danger. By the way, your transport has been waiting for you. We can't hold in that location much longer. I assume you've solved the problems with the vehicle?"

"Yes, sir. Javad assures me it's just a small oil leak on the manifold. We should be there in a few minutes. We're leaving now." Qatal terminated the call and waved Javad on.

The black Mercedes left the gas station with a dramatic screech of tires and headed northeast along a dusty trail between rocky ridges that rose on either side of a wide valley. A rooster tail of dust and black smoke traced their path.

Qatal, vigilant and calculating, repeatedly looked over his shoulder, left and right, then said to Javad. "It's only seventeen more kilometers. Take that fork to the left."

The revelation that his transport was standing by ignited a triumphant smile on Qatal's face. The mission had encountered some unexpected wrinkles, that had cost some team members. But it was still a remarkable success. Not only did he have the jump drive that contained the Russian's malware, but the general was pleased with the news about capturing a Mossad agent who might provide important intelligence about Israeli defenses. "VAJA can interrogate her after I'm done with her." Qatal mused.

As the SUV raced to their extraction point, Qatal leaned his seat back and closed his eyes. The rest of the brass, even his enemies, would be reminded of his commitment and usefulness to the Revolution. He imagined a hero's welcome—maybe even a promotion.

He was deep into the fantasy when he jolted upright, dialing General Barzan. Being careful to maintain the charade, but knowing the general would understand. "Sir, one thought. When we upload the new softward, what if we gave our Palestinian friends all the credit?"

"Brilliant!" General Barzan replied. "Our founder would applaud that idea! I think you can expect a bonus if all goes well."

"Thank you, sir." Qatal, ending the call, turned to Karim and said, "Maybe you should start calling me Colonel."

□ □ □

The blue Volvo XC90 bounced onto the Saudi two-lane Route 5M that ran between Haqi and al Bad and rolled to a stop at the service station crowned with the distinctive blue and green Aramco sign.

Rahm jumped out and surveyed the desolate surroundings. To the north, the highway curved around a low hill and disappeared. South, the highway ran between ridges on both sides of the road—not a single vehicle. No buildings. No trees. Nothing but sand, rocks and mountains. Where did they go? When he gazed northeast, he saw a plume of dusty smoke that indicated something or someone had just disappeared around the corner of a distant rocky outcrop.

"What's over there?" he asked Firas, who had also exited the Volvo and walked to where Rahm stood.

"Jebal al Lawz is there." Firas pointed northeast. "That's the mountain where Allah spoke to Prophet Moses. Just north of al Lawz, there is a giant rock formation called the Rock of Horeb and some ancient petroglyphs. Not much else. It's a remote spot. We never had many visitors in the past. But since the Crown Prince is pushing tourism, online videos describing the vicinity have attracted a lot of attention. Tourists have started showing up. Uncle had to add new pumps.."

When Firas pointed, Rahm spotted the pistol in a holster tucked inside his jeans in the small of his back. A sudden realization—I've got to stop Qatal! Who knows what might happen to Adi? A momentary hesitation and then Rahm grabbed the gun. "I'm sorry, Firas." He held up the weapon. "I need to borrow this and your cousin's car." He motioned with the weapon for the others to get out of the vehicle.

"What are you doing?" Firas protested.

Rahm pointed at the plume of dust. "It looks like they went that way."

"You can't go after them by yourself!"

"I have to try," Rahm said as he jumped into the Volvo.

"They have my father's car. I need to get it back. I should go with you. You said she—the woman—is yours?"

"I wish!" Rahm said.

"She is in danger. Let us go with you. You need help," Firas grinned. "My uncle owns this station. He has guns inside. Besides, there are two of them. We'll go with you. I told you we were looking for an adventure."

"I can't wait, and I don't want anyone else to die." He slammed the door and sped away. In the rearview mirror, he spotted the young men run after him. Firas pausing abruptly, turned, and dashed back toward the service station.

Rahm grinned at his naivete and enthusiasm. Young guys always think they're made of steel.

He turned his attention to the road, pushed Volvo to its limits, and chased the rapidly disappearing dust cloud. He drove the Volvo as fast as he dared on the vague hint of a road. Bouncing along, recollections of the calming touch of Solomon's Seal flashed in his mind. He pulled it out, put it on, felt the usual buzz in his head, and released a long breath.

At the spot where the dust had just about settled, the valley took a sharp turn to the north. The barren hills closed in as he entered the shadows cast by the setting sun. Around the corner, two narrow valleys split off to his left. In the fading light, Rahm slowed to look for the distinctive Mercedes tracks in the Saudi sand. Reassured by spotting their trail, he followed the central valley that now curved sharply to the right.

Zig-zagging around a clump of four-foot salt bushes he steered through the twists and turns of the path.

Contemplating impending confrontation with Qatal, he fumbled with the Glock 40 caliber handgun. It offered limited firepower. Steering with his knees, he released the clip and found it full—nine in the clip but none in the chamber. "Not enough!" He reinserted the clip and put the weapon in the center console tray.

He was going up against two trained experts. Javad and Qatal had familiar weapons and lots of experience. It had been a long time since Rahm's college days when he'd done a lot of shooting with his friends. They shot at targets and silhouettes that didn't shoot back. With limited firepower, and even less confidence, doubts haunted him. But he had to try. At a wide straight spot, he steered with his knees, picked up the gun, chambered a round, and prayed. *Please, don't let me be too late!*

CHAPTER FORTY-SEVEN

SHOOT HIM!

"I learned that courage was not the absence of fear but the triumph over it. The brave man is not he who does not feel afraid, but he who conquers that fear." Nelson Mandela

Saudi Arabia
Present

Rahm's shoulders slumped under the weight of the moment. He leaned forward while steering the Volvo along the twisting wadi. Somewhere ahead, Adi was captive in the backseat of a sinister black SUV in Saeed Qatal's custody.

Rahm felt a bone-deep weariness, a cocktail of stress and trauma. The residue of watching the Professor die. Maybe it was the mystifying effect of wearing the Seal that Stephanos had mentioned. Despite the calm and clarity it produced, Rahm reluctantly slipped the ring off and stowed it in his pocket.

Amid the pursuit, he brought a shaky hand to his forehead. A lightning bolt jolted him. Despite the fatigue, Rahm had an unfamiliar lucidity well up inside. Was it the Seal? Or the aftermath of the Professor's murder?

He drove on, deep in thought. Regardless, there was absolute clarity about what he wanted. The list was short—protect Adi, stop Qatal, and avenge the Professor. If he was going to accomplish those goals, and be more than a poor little Palestinian, something had to change. Gasping, he saw everything in a new light. I'm too passive. It's me! I need to change.

One thing was sure. When he thought of Adi, he wanted to do better—be better. Why had he resented her? More clarity—the loss his family and people had experienced. Was that her fault? She worked for Mossad, but a lot of good people did. The Professor was right. Retaliation did no good.

But her being Israeli didn't matter now. Her combination of toughness and savvy drew him to her. A slight smile curled the corner of his mouth. Her being gorgeous may have influenced his change of perspective. He white-knuckled the steering wheel and pushed the Volvo harder.

As he drove farther inland, the hills grew taller and more formidable. Mountain peaks loomed beyond. Looking right and left, he strained to see which one was al Lawz.

The Volvo slid around the shoulder of a low hill and slalomed around another bend in the wadi. Suddenly, there they were. The black Mercedes sat a hundred meters from an idling helicopter painted in desert camouflage. The Mercedes' front doors stood open. Javad and Qatal were getting out.

When Qatal looked up, his eyes met Rahm's, and his mouth opened wide. He whirled, breaking into a sprint. Rahm heard the whining engine winding up. It sounded like the aircraft was preparing to lift off. Stop!

Qatal ran straight into the dust cloud stirred up by the helicopter's spinning blades.

Rahm stomped on the gas, and the Volvo sprang forward. *Adi wants that drive!* Rahm steered after the fleeing man, who ducked under the whirling rotors and shielded his eyes as he raced into a billowing dust storm.

As Rahm thundered past the Mercedes, he saw Qatal's thug, Javad, jerk open the door behind the driver's seat and pull Adi out. His foot eased off the gas, but only for a single heartbeat. He looked back and forth between Qatal and Adi, swallowed hard, gritted his teeth, and accelerated again.

Rahm was closing when a hail of bullets shattered his windshield. Who's shooting? He ducked and swerved, but pressed on. As he got closer, the Sahed 285 helicopter burst into view. It loomed like a monster—the windows looked like eyes, its machine-gun snout stitching a trail of destruction in his direction. His pulse surged.

Qatal reached the helicopter and jumped in. Two heartbeats later, the rotors stirred, and the aircraft vanished in a growing cloud of dust, as it lifted and pivoted north.

Rahm pushed the gas harder. Then realized it was already on the floor. The Volvo's roof hit the landing skid with a loud crash. As he'd hoped, the craft's center of gravity shifted. The car shot under the lifting helicopter. Then churning rotors dug into the desert, barely missing the speeding car. The rotors shattered, and debris filled the air. Pieces skittered across the sand. An eight-foot section of the rotor bayonetted the sand five meters to his left.

Rahm slammed on the brakes, slid to a stop in a swirl of dust, and took a breath. In the mirror, he spotted Qatal at the door of the helicopter. Incredibly, the aircraft rolled on its side, throwing him clear an instant before the fuselage slammed to the ground. Fuel splashed onto the engine's exhaust, causing a huge fireball. A column of oily smoke and flame roiled skyward.

Qatal hobbled away from the wreckage. Bullets pinged off the rear of the Volvo, and Rahm twisted his head around. Qatal's henchman was firing as he retreated through the clouds of smoke stinking of burning rubber. Javad dragged Adi back toward the Mercedes. When she resisted, he punched her in the face.

Rahm's rage surged. "No!" His fists clenched the steering wheel. His jaws clenched—the taste of loathing boiling up. More bullets pinged. Every instinct screamed, Escape! But Adi was in danger. He spun the steering wheel and accelerated. "Hang on, Adi. I'm here!" He pressed the horn, held it down, and sped up, pursuing Javad as the thug ran across the sand toward the Mercedes, pulling Adi in his wake. Rahm could see the muzzle flashes from Javad's gun and heard bullets pinging off his vehicle. One burst through the window next to him. Shifting the steering wheel left and right, praying that he wouldn't guess wrong. Stop it! You animal!

More shots slammed against the Volvo. The hood flew up with a loud bang, fracturing the remains of the windshield. The dislodged hood flew over the roof. Rahm could barely see the Mercedes' doors close. He yelled, "Adi!"

As Javad swerved in a wide turn away from him, Rahm saw an opening and rammed the black SUV. They collided. The Volvo's airbag deployed in Rahm's face.

In the stillness that followed, Rahm briefly wondered if he was alive. The report of gunshots sounded far away. But he realized he wouldn't be alive for long if he didn't move. Coughing and spitting, he pushed aside the deflated airbag. A cloud of dust stirred. It tasted like bitter chalk. When Rahm's view cleared, the Mercedes lay inverted on its roof, its wheels still spinning like pinwheels, futilely seeking traction.

Hanging upside down, Javad was firing at Rahm from behind the steering wheel.

The Volvo stalled on impact and refused to start. Rahm searched for the Glock, and after a panicky moment, he found it on the floor in front of the passenger seat. He considered returning fire but with his rusty skills he couldn't risk hitting Adi.

Through the shattered driver's window, Rahm heard a voice. "I'll take that."

A chill ran down Rahm's back. He turned left and saw Qatal's oil smudged and sweaty face looming above the barrel of a gun.

"I always get the job done," Qatal smirked. "Always! Now hand me that weapon."

Rahm surrendered the Glock. "You'll pay for this."

Now a gun in each fist, Qatal said, "No, my young friend. They will blame you and will pay me a great deal of money when I return with the drive, and it has fulfilled its destiny. They might even have a parade down Khomeini Boulevard in my honor."

Over Qatal's shoulder, Javad scrambled out of the totaled Mercedes and limped in Rahm's direction.

Qatal turned when he heard his aide approaching. “Is the woman still alive?”

“I’ll check.” Javad walked back toward the wrecked Mercedes, opened the rear door, and hauled Adi out.

When Rahm saw Adi’s face, he gasped. Her left eye had swollen shut, and her lower lip split in multiple places. Dried blood caked above her right eye.

His sanity edged toward extinction as old feelings of helplessness overwhelmed him. Qatal always seemed to have the upper hand.

What was even worse, instead of helping, everything Rahm tried caused Adi more trouble. Just then, movement in the Volvo’s side mirror caught Rahm’s attention. He saw an approaching white pickup loaded with men waving guns. One looked familiar.

Javad obviously saw them too. He released Adi and ran.

Qatal glanced at the approaching vehicle and shouted at Javad, “You deserter! Come back here!” He raised the Glock and fired at the retreating coward.

Javad fell. Blood flowed from his hip. He struggled to his feet and limped away.

Qatal smirked and raised the Glock again, but when the oncoming truck sounded its horn, he turned and took aim.

Rahm shouted, “No!” Putting all his fury and weight behind the Volvo door, he slammed it open into Qatal’s side. Qatal’s own weapon went flying. He fell to the ground with a thud. Firas' Glock dropped to the ground at Qatal's feet.

Rahm scrambled out of the Volvo and scooped it up. With a gun in his hand, his face lit up in a triumphant smile. "Stay down!" Rahm kept his eyes on Qatal while he bent to pick up the other handgun.

When he did, Qatal jumped up and looked ready to pounce.

Rahm stood with both barrels pointed at Qatal. "Stop, you psychopath! It's over."

Qatal crossed his arms. "My, my, how does it feel to be the hero?" His laugh sounded forced and lasted a beat too long. Despite a nervous twitch around his mouth, he said, "It's *not* over while I'm still breathing."

The white pickup slid to a stop behind Qatal. Firas was standing in the truck's bed, holding onto a roll bar and gripping an AK-47. He winked. "Didn't I tell you? You need help. You've got this one," he said, pointing at Qatal. "I'll get that one." He left to pursue Javad.

As the pickup sped away, Adi stepped forward.

"Are you okay?" Rahm asked.

"I'll be fine. Why didn't you shoot the pig? He's right, you know. The problem is he's still breathing." She held out her hand. "Do you mind?"

"Huh?" Rahm saw the look on Adi's face and said, "You wouldn't actually. . ."

"I'd shoot him where he stands." She nodded at Qatal. "But it is my duty to take this animal into custody."

"Be my guest," Rahm said.

As Adi stepped forward, reaching to accept the weapon, Qatal grabbed her and put a knife to her throat.

Rahm pointed both barrels at Qatal.

"Put those down," Qatal snarled, "or I will cut her throat, and you can watch her and bleed out join your American friend in hell."

"Shoot him!" Adi shouted.

Rahm hesitated.

"Shoot!" Adi repeated. "What are you waiting for?"

CHAPTER FORTY-EIGHT
LOOK WHAT WE FOUND

"An arrogant person considers himself perfect. This is the chief harm of arrogance. It interferes with a person's main task in life - becoming a better person."
Leo Tolstoy

Saudi Arabia
Present

Rahm's pulse pounded in his ears. His grip on the gun aimed at Qatal wavered, his hand shook like a palsied senior citizen.

Qatal remained defiant. "You think you can finish me with one shot?" Tightening his grip on Adi's neck with his left hand, his knife's gleaming blade slashing ominously close to Adi's throat. "Go ahead, pull the trigger. But know this, my trained reflexes will finish her, and it will be as if you killed her yourself. Go ahead, hero. Shoot! I dare you."

"Do it!" Adi shouted.

When Rahm wavered, the familiar disdainful look flitted across her face. His thoughts replayed the stinging phrase that had cut so deep: "Poor little Palestinian."

Adi's eyes communicated disappointment, as Rahm hesitated met his and her hands crept up, reaching for Qatal's knife-hand. She's lost confidence in me. She's going to get hurt. He had to do something. He inhaled; a sudden sense of calm settled over him.

Rage boiled up and his trebling hand stilled. He took aim and fired. The bullet hit Qatal in the right elbow, shattering bone and tendons.

As threatened, Qatal's knife hand jerked toward Adi's neck. She grabbed his arm. Ripping it away from her neck, she stepped left and jerked down.

Qatal bellowed in pain and bent forward. Adi kicked him in the face, sending him sprawling and the knife flying away.

"Impressive!" Rahm grinned, his earlier hesitation replaced with newfound confidence.

"Not bad yourself. That was a great shot!" Adi said. "When you finally got around to it."

Rahm noticed a cut on her neck. The color drained from his face. "You're hurt."

Adi reached up and probed her wound. "It's a nick. Very superficial."

"Superficial or not, I think you need to keep pressure on it."

"Yes, Daddy," Adi said, her voice dripping sarcasm. But she complied.

Rahm grinned. "Captain Ovitz doesn't enjoy taking orders?"

Meanwhile, Qatal was writhing in pain, blood flowing from his nose and draining from his wounded arm. He let loose with a string of angry words Rahm could only assume were Farsi expletives.

The sight of so much blood made Rahm queasy, a stark contrast to his war zone demeanor. He'd covered lots of stories involving mayhem. But he had inflicted Qatal's wounds. Logical or not, it was different. Shaking slightly, he handed Adi the Glock and felt an immense sense of relief.

She took the weapon and aimed it at the Iranian.

Defiance ruled Qatal's face. "Go ahead. Shoot."

"I would love to oblige, but I think Mr. Khalidi has taken care of that," Adi said, her good eye twinkling. She gestured with the gun. "You and I are going back to Egypt to see Captain Abasi. You have some crimes to answer for in the Sinai. Give me that drive."

"Come and get it," he snarled.

"I think not. Throw it here."

When Qatal refused, Adi turned to Rahm. "Would you mind?"

"Not at all," he said, sounding far more confident than he felt. The sight of Qatal's grisly wound made him uncomfortable, but he reached into Qatal's pocket and got the drive. He handed it to Adi.

Once she had it in her possession, Adi threw a pair of handcuffs at Rahm. "Here, you can put these on the prisoner."

Rahm held up the cuffs and noticed his hands were still shaking. "Where did you get these?"

"They're his. Our training at the institute included lots of basic stuff, like escaping from handcuffs and dealing with knife-wielding thugs."

As he moved to cuff Qatal, Rahm said over his shoulder, "Won't he be able to get out of these as easily as you did?"

Adi smirked, "Not with one hand, he won't. He won't be doing anything with that right arm for a long time. Just be sure to cuff his hands behind his back."

When Rahm moved his wounded right arm, Qatal screamed in pain.

Once he had the cuffs on, Rahm felt safer. He dusted off his hands and looked down at Qatal, and said, "I'd say it's over now, wouldn't you?"

Qatal glared defiantly.

With a grim expression and a short, disgusted grunt, Rahm said, "I sure hope that isn't uncomfortable."

Rahm heard whooping and hollering. He spun in the sound's direction. He saw Firas and his friends rolling up in the white pickup. Javad was sitting in the bed of the truck with his arms behind him. His back was to the tailgate. One of Firas' buddies had a gun pointed at Javad's head.

"Look what we found," Firas said with a triumphant gleam in his eye.

Before he could respond, Rahm felt Adi's hand tapping him on the shoulder.

She pointed to the right. "Oh my gosh, the Professor was right. Look at that." A few hundred yards away, a monolithic rock formation stood on a small boulder-strewn hill. The monolith was at least sixty feet tall.

Rahm turned. He saw it, but things didn't click immediately. It looked familiar. Then it hit him. "The Split Rock of Horeb." He jerked the leather pouch out of his pocket. Whoever burned that brand into the leather had seen what he was now looking at. He held up the pouch for comparison. The drawing on the bag bore a remarkable resemblance to the gigantic formation. Whoever did the sketch must have been standing right here. Who sketched it, and why? What's the connection between the Seal and this?

Firas looked where Adi had pointed. "Yes! Rahm, I told you it was it here. Prophet Moses hit that rock, and Allah sent water gushing up through it."

Rahm immediately pivoted and started scanning the horizon. To the southeast, maybe eight kilometers away, he saw a mountain. Its peak was taller than anything else and appeared to have a shadow over its peak, even though there were no clouds in the sky. He turned to Adi, "Is that Mt. Sinai?"

Adi looked in the direction he was pointing. "I don't know. But wouldn't that be amazing?"

"We call it Jabel al Lawz," Firas said. "Allah spoke to Prophet Moses. Ask anybody who lives around here."

Rahm's gaze returned to the leather pouch in his hand, and he held it up. Why is the Seal in a bag with an image of that rock branded on it?

Qatal growled, "Could we forget the geography lesson? I need medical attention."

"Hey!" Firas howled. "Is that my dad's Mercedes?" He pointed at the upside-down wreck that used to be a luxury SUV. "He's going to kill me. What happened?"

Rahm said with a grim tone, "We can tell you all about it on the way. But right now, we need to take these two men to a hospital to get medical attention—I think it should be at one of those nice *Egyptian* hospitals."

CHAPTER FORTY-NINE
TORA PRISON

"But I tell you, love your enemies and pray for those who persecute you, that you may be children of your Father in heaven."
Jesus

Cairo, Egypt
Present

"The Scorpion" was the name inmates whispered to each other. On the southern outskirts of Cairo, Tora was notorious. A place where many who entered were never seen again.

Rahm Khalidi interviewed people leaving. He heard reports that guards routinely welcomed new inmates with a beating. They claimed that squalid conditions, torture, medical neglect, and extended solitary confinement were customary.

One woman sobbed out her story to Rahm. She said the police had arrested her two sons for opposing the regime. Several times, authorities had rejected her application to visit them over the last three years, despite her offer of substantial bribes. She was returning from her very first visit with her younger son. He told his mother that thirty-eight men were crammed into a cell designed for ten. Worse, his older brother had paid the ultimate price under dubious circumstances.

Those reports made Rahm nervous as he approached the gate. But waving an order signed by the Inspector General and a fistful of cash got him through. When he entered the jammed visitor's center, the cacophony of despairing voices was overwhelming. He heard pleading wives and families cajoling prison staff, mixing with their harsh rebuffs.

The swampy humidity and malicious conditions made the Israeli prison Rahm had endured look like a resort. He absentmindedly rubbed the scar on his hand, then wiped the sweat from his brow and neck. After jostling his way through the throng, a rude officer finally ushered him to a place along a fence and told him to wait.

He watched through the double mesh wire as two guards dragged Qatal to a spot across from his position.

The older guard said something and turned to leave.

"What?" Rahm asked. "I couldn't hear you."

"Ten minutes."

"But the Inspector General said I had thirty."

"Nine minutes," the guard made a show of checking his watch, then smirked, daring Rahm to protest.

Rahm didn't respond. Both guards swaggered twenty feet away to slouch against a grimy wall and gave a disdainful look. Rahm imagined every guard practicing that sneer in a mirror at home.

He turned to Qatal through the mesh. The prisoner's clothes were grubby and smelled of body odor. Rahm thought he should feel *something*—hatred for this shell of a man who could casually kill or savagely beat a fellow human without remorse—sympathy for an old man whose right arm looked like it still hadn't healed properly—shame for not forgiving him. After all, the Professor had made an extravagant gift. But his chest was empty. *What's wrong with me? Why don't I feel anything?* A shudder shook his soul. He worried he was becoming like the creature that stood across from him. He brushed that shadow aside with an almost imperceptible head shake and heard himself say, "The Grand Mufti met with me after they found you guilty."

"So?" Qatal scoffed.

That's what's wrong, and it's not all me! Rahm shook off the realization and said, "The Penal Code says they should give you the death penalty. You deserve it."

"Is this going somewhere?"

"Since you're from Iran, you may not understand Egyptian law. The code stipulates the death penalty for murder. But before pronouncing a death sentence, the Mufti must review the case. I had only ten days."

"For?"

"If the Mufti does not object, the Court pronounces its decision. I got an emergency hearing with the Mufti on the ninth day."

"And?"

"I told him about the Professor's final request for mercy."

Qatal just stared.

"What you *did* was inexcusable, and who you *are* is worse. I promised the Professor I would send you to hell for it. But he asked me to forgive you. So, I met with the Mufti. As the Professor was dying, he gave me the deed to his house to pay me to forgive." Rahm leaned closer. "Do you have any idea what it means to me?"

Qatal folded his arms. "It means that he wasted his charity on you. There is no forgiveness in your eyes—none in your words."

"The Professor knew Israel plowed down my family's home. While he was dying, he gave me a fresh start. I went online and looked at the pictures. I was stunned."

"Like I said, he wasted his generosity on you."

"You're right. I'm not sure I will ever forgive you. But because of his request, I went to the Mufti and begged him to change your sentence to life in prison. I came here so you'd know what my friend did for you."

"What did the Mufti say?"

"He said in the last nine years, he's handled over 1,700 capital cases and hasn't overturned any of them. Nor had he ever heard of anyone being as forgiving as Dr. Schwalm. He recommended the court show mercy. This morning, they changed your sentence to life in prison. You won't be executed."

"Your friend's gift was wasted. I would rather *die* than spend my life in this hell hole."

Rahm forced a smile and said, "Inshallah! This feels more like the justice you deserve. But I want to thank you. Because you are what you are, you have given me an opportunity to work on forgiveness. I'm not there yet. That's obvious because I despise you, and I'm glad you're stuck here. Maybe someday you'll realize your mistakes." Then he turned and walked out, the echoes of Tora's suffering lingering in his ears.

□ □ □

St. Catherine's Monastery
Sinai

As Rahm swam through a crowd of tourists heading toward a waiting tour bus, he glimpsed Stephanos standing in the morning sun in the courtyard between the monastery's gate and The Charnel House.

"Good morning, Mr. Khalidi. I am delighted to see you!"

"Good morning." Rahm leaned in to accept the warmth of the old man's hug and breathed a heavy sigh. He felt safe with this man, despite the horrifying events that had happened a few months ago.

"Let's go to my office, where we can talk privately. Would you like a cup of tea?" Stephanos asked. "You look tired."

"Yes, I would. Thank you very much." When they moved into the shadows of the monastery's walls, a shiver shook Rahm's whole body. *This T-shirt doesn't cut it.* As he climbed the stairs behind Stephanos, he opened his backpack, pulled out a windbreaker, and slipped it on.

Stephanos opened his office door. "Please come in and have a seat." While Rahm got comfortable, Stephanos plugged in a well-used teapot that soon rumbled. "Black or green?" Stephanos dangled two tea bags.

"Black, please. By the way, from the number of people leaving, it looks like tourism has picked up."

"Yes, *t*here have been no problems in South Sinai for months. The authorities have settled some grievances with opposition groups." Stephanos turned to prepare a brass tray with two teacups, some sugar, and two spoons, then asked, "You said you had some things you wanted to discuss?"

"I don't know how to forgive," Rahm said. "But I think it would please the Professor that the court had mercy on Qatal because of my efforts."

As Stephanos carried the clattering tray toward his desk with trembling hands, he chuckled. "Just one of the indignities imposed on the old. The doctor calls it 'essential tremor.' I told him I thought it a poor name for something so *non*-essential." He put the tray on the desk in front of Rahm and pointed. "This one is yours."

"Thank you. I wanted to talk about my visit to Tora Prison."

Stephanos reached for his own cup but froze when he heard the name of the infamous place. "Tora, the Scorpion? You weren't—"

"Oh, no. I'm sorry. I visited Qatal there to report on my visit with the Grand Mufti."

Stephanos' mouth fell open. "The Grand Mufti himself? How?" He plopped into his chair.

After describing his visit with the Mufti, Rahm said, "He's like Egypt's Islamic Pope."

"Yes, St. Catherine reports to his office annually."

"Excuse me. Of course. Anyway, when the verdict was in," Rahm took a sip of his tea and winced when the bitter brew burned his tongue. "I immediately tried to get an audience with the Mufti. I pulled every string I could, making dozens of calls. Finally, with the Palestinian embassy's help, I got a visit on the ninth day."

"I'm surprised you got in at all." Stephanos studied Rahm intently. "You realize that sending a man to Tora is not terribly merciful. How do you feel about that?"

"Conflicted. I'm glad Qatal was convicted and sent to Tora. I feel good about fulfilling part of the Professor's request. And I'm struggling to fulfill the hardest part. I don't know how to let it go. I was tough on Qatal. When he said he would rather die than live at Tora, I basically wished him dead. On the way here, it haunted me. I haven't slept in two days. I keep seeing the Professor lying there. His life ebbing away. He forgave Qatal and thought of me. I don't understand. I don't have a category for that kind of compassion and mercy. I've tried to forgive. I want to. But I can't."

"I cannot judge another man's heart," Stephanos said. "But looking at your actions, I . . . I think, somewhere deep inside, you have shifted your thinking. I would encourage you to investigate this change. Embrace it. You wouldn't be struggling if something wasn't going on inside."

Rahm squirmed in his seat. "Maybe so."

"Let's go," Stephanos stood. "I want to show you Dr. Schwalm's grave."

CHAPTER FIFTY
THE KEY

"I am the light of the world. Whoever follows me will not walk in darkness but will have the light of life."
Jesus

Saint Catherine's Monastery
Present

Six crosses marked six graves. There wasn't room for many more. The monastery's cemetery was tiny. The ground at the base of the mountain was so rocky that when they built the monastery, the monks had to import soil for the cemetery and the garden. Four grave markers had epitaphs written in Greek, one was in Arabic, and one in English. Stephanos pointed at the simple iron cross in the corner with the English text. "Your friend will rest there for three years. Then—"

"I understand the process." Rahm stepped toward the grave, carefully stepping between grave plots, a lump in his throat. "Thank you for that." Someone had engraved the cross with the Professor's name, dates, and the slogan he had requested. "He followed Jesus. Not well. But gladly."

Rahm sighed heavily, knelt, and traced the inscription with his finger. A wistful smile twisted his face. "By following, you led a better life than anyone I've ever known." He drew a ragged breath. "Thank you for being my friend. I'm here to make a trade."

Wiping a tear away, he pulled the key out from under his shirt. "I promised to take this and return to our family's land. But there's no going back. It's gone. I want to make a trade." He lifted the gold chain from around his neck. "My vision for yours. Instead of clinging to my hatred, I want to work at making peace with others. I suppose that includes Qatal. But I have a feeling it involves something bigger." He carefully draped the chain over the center of the cross and gently placed the key, so it hung below the inscription. He kissed two fingers and touched the key.

Rahm stood, hesitated for a moment, then said to Stephanos, "Thank you, dear friend." Then he turned to leave. "Habib's in the cab waiting."

Stephanos said, "Before you go, could I ask a question?"

"Of course."

"I couldn't hear everything you said to the Professor, but I think I heard you say something about working for peace. Could I ask what you hope to do?"

Rahm rubbed the nape of his neck. "I haven't worked it all out. But last night, I was exhausted over my struggle with forgiveness. I was desperate for some sleep. I wondered if the Seal could calm me down, and I put it on."

"But you didn't sleep?"

"No, I was hit with the idea that peacemaking might need to be done between individuals first rather than starting with nations."

"If you wore the ring long enough, wouldn't that eventually exhaust you?" Stephanos asked.

"You would think, wouldn't you? Instead, the burst of energy and clarity kept my head spinning. I got online and saw some videos of a guy interviewing people on the streets in New York City. The stories were of ordinary people and their lives. It was fascinating stuff. It gave me an idea. I think I can use my journalism skills and connections to tell some honest stories that could leverage the goodwill that my Jewish and Palestinian neighbors have for each other."

Stephanos smiled. "You sound hopeful."

"Hopeful might be a little overstated. Maybe it's cautious optimism."

"That sounds like a good place to start. I will pray that God gives you wisdom."

"Thank you. I sure need it—wisdom, I mean."

Stephanos chuckled. "Don't we all? Did I hear you say Habib is back?"

Rahm shrugged. "Maybe. I called him from Nuweiba and asked him to bring me here. He said he's still living in Dahab with his family. But when he saw the buses and tourists, he called his brother. They were talking about Habib moving back here. I missed the rest."

Stephanos pointed at the cross. "When we move his remains to the Charnel House, I will see that it is to a place of honor. His cross and your key will hang where you will see them when you visit."

Rahm grabbed Stephanos and gave him a big hug. "Thank you!"

"Speaking of bones, be careful with mine," Stephanos said.

Rahm was confused. "I'm sorry."

Stephanos laughed. "I'm full of arthritis. Your hug felt good and bad at the same time. God bless you, Rahm. Your friend is in good hands."

Looking around, Rahm said, "Yes." Then pointing up. "In every way possible."

Stephanos gazed at him, and Rahm felt like the old man was reading his deepest thoughts.

Rahm said, "The Professor came to Ramallah to work for peace. I used to think he was naïve. I told him so to his face. I said, 'There is no peace in this crazy world.' He didn't skip a beat. He patted his chest and said, 'There is in here.' I couldn't see it then. But as he lay dying, I could. There was no hatred or resentment—only a last plea for mercy. Rahm turned and pointed at the grave. "I came here" o trade my resentment for something better. Clinging to that key has been draining the life out of me. I've been hanging onto hate, keeping me stuck in the past and poisoning my future. That key symbolized escape. It was as if I imagined the ancient olive trees and that grand old house could bring me peace."

"How do you feel about letting go?"

"Better."

"Peaceful?"

Rahm rubbed the closely cropped stubble on his chin. "Yes, that's it. Peaceful."

The monk and the reporter headed toward the parking lot. It surprised Rahm how spryly Stephanos climbed the stairs from the cemetery to the courtyard. Then they walked side by side down the ramp to the waiting taxi. Rahm had to keep up. His respect for Stephanos just kept growing.

At the vehicle, Rahm bent down, speaking through the open window, and held up one finger to Habib. "One moment." He straightened, turned to Stephanos, and said, "Knowing you has changed my life."

"I think you have your friend and the Seal to thank for that."

"Interesting that you would bring this up." Rahm reached into his pocket and took out the pouch. "Before I go, I have two questions. How did the Seal get to St. Catherine's? And why does this bag have the image of this rock on the outside?"

"It's a rock? Could I look at that drawing again?"

Rahm held the bag by the drawstring, with the sketch facing Stephanos. "This is the proper orientation. Take it." When Stephanos held out his hand, Rahm released it. When he let it go, a sense of relief flooded over him. *What is that?* While Stephanos studied the drawing, Rahm said, "On our way here, before we were attacked, the Professor said that if the Exodus crossing happened at Nuweiba, then Mount Sinai and the Split Rock should be on the Saudi side of the Gulf."

"The rock at Horeb?" Stephanos handed the pouch back.

When he did, Rahm felt the heaviness return. His shoulders drooped. Then it hit him. He knew what he needed to do.

"Wasn't Dr. Schwalm," Stephanos continued, "aware that very few scholars agree with any of the Exodus events happening in Saudi?"

"He said the public seemed enamored with the idea but that academics preferred this location or Har Karkom near Kadesh in Israel. But I *saw* this rock. I wish the Professor had lived long enough to see it himself."

Stephanos paced. "For over 1,500 years, Greek monks have lived and labored here." He pointed at the peak behind the monastery. "Believing *this mountain* is the biblical Sinai. But I know that all the ancient accounts said that Sinai is in Midian. I recently read Bill Dever's claim that the area you just visited is Midian."

He could see Stephanos was struggling but pressed on. "What about the fact that the rock formation matched the brand on the bag?"

"I have no idea," Stephanos said. "I've puzzled over that sketch myself. However, I'm not convinced that the Saudi rock formation has anything to do with the Exodus. It could just be an interesting geological feature." He shook his head. "It doesn't make sense that Moses received the Jewish law in Saudi Arabia." He stopped pacing. "Here are the facts I can confirm," he ticked them off on his fingers. "First, I found the Seal inside that pouch in 1975. Second, the Seal must have come from Ma'rib because the American Archaeological Trust was simultaneously doing a dig at Ma'rib and doing a manuscript cataloging project at St. Catherine's in 1952. Third, the pouch was wrapped in a Yemeni newspaper dated 1952. Finally, the Egyptian supervisor of the Ma'rib dig died in 1952 here at St. Catherine's at the precise spot where I found the Seal."

The two men stood in silence, both looking into the distance.

Rahm shrugged. "Here's what I know." He counted on his fingers. "One, this image on the pouch looks like an exact drawing of the giant split rock I saw in Saudi. Two, the Seal and that rock connect somehow. Three, when you were holding the pouch a few moments ago, it felt like it was the right thing." He patted his chest. "I felt it in here. Four, I am convinced you handled this better than I ever did." He handed the pouch back to Stephanos. "Please put the Seal somewhere safe."

Stephanos hesitated. "I'm not so sure about handling it well. I am not sure I want people even imagining Sinai is in the Saudi Kingdom. Tourism to this place would evaporate. While that might be good for the monastery, it would devastate the local economy." He reached out and accepted it. "You're sure about this?"

Rahm nodded, "Yes, I'm sure. St. Catherine's has become my letting go place. Besides, I think the Professor would urge me to let it go along with my resentment and hatred. Thank you for everything. Your questions helped me see so much. One more hug? I'll be careful."

Stephanos stretched out his arms. "Please."

While they embraced, Rahm said, "I'll be back."

Rahm got into the front seat of the cab.

Stephanos leaned down and spoke through the cab's open window. "Habib, I hear we may be blessed to have you as a neighbor again."

"Yes! Uncle say Habib live wis him."

Rahm then said to Stephanos, "I almost forgot. I want to donate to the monastery. But I don't have much cash on me."

"Don't worry about that now."

"Thank you, Stephanos. Well, Habib. Let's head to Nuweiba. I need to catch the ferry to Aqaba. I have a date in Ramallah."

Habib grinned and poked Rahm. "Wis ze blonde lady, yes?"

CHAPTER FIFTY-ONE
THE VISION

"Vision is the ability to see what is invisible to others."
Jonathan Swift

Jerusalem
Present

A two-bar sea bream with a yellow tail swam lazily in the large aquarium that separated two seating sections of the second-floor restaurant. When the tank's small shark moved in his direction, the yellow-tailed fish scooted away.

Linens graced the tables. Wait staff in crisp black shirts and red aprons moved briskly around the room. The clatter of dishes punctuated the buzz of happy chatter.

Across the table, Rahm gazed into Adi's brown eyes.

Adi grinned and leaned in. "My commander says that he is lobbying to recognize your heroism. As far as I know, Israel has never awarded the President's Medal to a Palestinian. Conservatives don't like your articles. And say it wouldn't be right to recognize someone who is no friend of Israel. However, others say, 'Actions speak louder than words.' And I agree."

"I don't need medals. I certainly don't want to cause trouble," Rahm said. "I *do* want something from you, though."

Adi's head tilted. "Yes?"

"Well." Rahm rubbed his palms on his pants. "I need to apologize."

"You don't need to—"

Rahm hung his head, then looked up. "I need to ask you to forgive me. When we first met, I blamed you for all the wrongs done to my family, but you didn't do any of those things. That was wrong. I've done some reading lately. I agree with Viktor Frankl; there is no such thing as collective guilt. Please forgive me."

Adi stuttered, "I. I mean. I just don't know what to say."

"I was hoping you would say, 'I forgive you.'"

"Of course. But I'm not sure I treated you any better."

"I wanted to clear the air." Rahm gazed out the window at the lights illuminating the street below. His mind rehearsed their encounters with their Iranian pursuers. He often felt second-rate during those confrontations compared to how Adi had handled them. He looked back at her. "About the medal. I really don't deserve one. You were the one who captured Qatal."

"Are you kidding? He had a knife to my throat!"

"You were going to handle it."

"Rahm, you saved my life."

"Whatever. Here's what I really need. I need to stop believing that my problems are someone else's responsibility."

Adi's mouth opened, but a few beats passed before she finally said, "That's profound. You sound more and more like the Professor. My commander's report said you deserve a medal. His report noted that I was doing my job. He wrote you're a foreign national who risked his life to save me and prevent great harm to Israel, doing it voluntarily and at significant risk to himself. Politicians might haggle, but no one is disputing those facts."

"As I remember it, you saved me more often than I saved you."

"You showed real courage."

"The things I did endangered you more often than they helped."

"When you rammed that Mercedes, you freaked me out."

"Exactly!" Rahm said. "That's what I mean."

"It was risky." Adi winked. "But it worked. And that's *my* point. Anyway, Israel's leaders will do what they think is best. I'm curious about why you invited me here tonight."

Rahm scooted his chair closer to the table. "Besides clearing the air, I wanted to ask you to help me put something together. But first, I need to tell you about my visit to St. Catherine's."

"You went back?" Her eyes searched his. "I'll bet that was tough."

"It got emotional when I visited the Professor's grave. I knelt by it and made an exchange. I told him I wanted to trade my vision for his."

"Vision?"

"Mine was to return and find a way to punish Israel. His was peace. I gave him my key."

Her eyebrows raised, and she gasped. "Wait! The key? When the van was under attack, I tried to get you to take cover, and you wouldn't leave without that key. You seemed ready to die for it."

"I was. I promised my mother that no matter how long it took, I would go home. But I took the chain from around my neck and hung it on the cross."

"I don't understand," Adi said. "What were you trading it for? He already gave you his house."

Rahm's voice trembled. "I traded my vision for his."

"Meaning?"

"When I returned to Ramallah, I looked up the Professor's house online. I learned that it's worth a little over a million dollars."

"The Professor was rich?"

"Not really, but in the last 20 years, the housing market boomed, especially in places with acreage. I'm thinking of selling it."

"Why? The Professor wanted you to have a place you could call home."

A waiter stopped at their table to hand them menus. Beaming, he asked, "How are we tonight?"

Adi looked up at the waiter and smiled with a twinkle in her eye. "You're fine. How am *I*?"

Obviously flustered, the waiter said, "Our special tonight is the Zibdiyit Gambari. It's a spicy shrimp stew with sesame seeds and plum tomatoes. May I take your drink orders?"

"I'll have water," Adi said, "with a slice of lime, please."

Rahm nodded. "Make it two."

"Certainly. I'll be back to take your dinner orders." The waiter made a slight bow and hurried away.

"When I saw the pictures of the Professor's house, I was stunned," Rahm continued.

"It's beautiful and has a fantastic view. I could immediately see myself living there. I tried to imagine getting away from all the insanity here." He swept his hand in a gesture toward the panorama outside their window. "I suppose the Professor would like it if I did move there. But I've thought about this a lot. I think what he wanted most was that I would be at home wherever I might be. When I think about how to best honor his memory, other things come to mind."

Adi's frown scrunched her eyebrows together. "Things?"

The sizzle of a seafood dish being prepared nearby caught Rahm's attention. He inhaled the aroma. "By the way, order anything you want. It's on me. The seafood here is amazing." He pointed at the steamy platter. "I'm going to have that. Scallops, prawns, and salmon. I'll bet it's delicious."

"My mother wouldn't approve." Adi wrinkled her nose. "Not kosher. I think I'll have the sea bass."

"I'm sorry. I should know better."

Adi held up her hand. "Don't worry about it. Tell me more about honoring the Professor."

"He moved to Ramallah because he wanted to be a peacemaker. A slogan he often repeated in class was, 'I'm Pro-Israel, pro-Palestine, pro-peace, and pro-Jesus.' He rented his Oregon home so he could invest in his vision of peace. He took no salary from the school. Sorry for going on about him. This sounds like a eulogy, but when I think about how he lived his life and how he died, I'm inspired. By contrast, I spent my career as a journalist with a chip on my shoulder. I tried to hold individuals, businesses, and governments accountable. Expose everything I saw that was wrong, you know?"

"You said you were trading your vision for his?"

The waiter returned. "Excuse me," the waiter said. "Are we " He glanced nervously at Adi, and his face turned the color of his apron. "Are *you* ready to order?"

"Yes," Rahm said, "the lady will have the sea bass, and I will have what that table over there has—the scallops, prawns, and salmon."

"Excellent choices. Would you like something else to drink with dinner? Perhaps some wine? We have a delightful Chardonnay, and the Pinot Grigio pairs nicely with your fish."

Adi shook her head. "Not for me. I would like more water, though."

"I'll stick with water as well," Rahm said. The waiter left, and Rahm sat up straighter. "I want to start an institute or foundation in his honor and use the proceeds from the sale of his property to fund it. What do you think?"

"I think you sound exactly like the Professor—noble but very naïve."

"What if it's powerful and not naïve at all? Do you remember what the Professor said the day we were attacked? 'The most powerful thing in the world is love, and the most powerful kind of love is love for your enemy.'"

"I remember brushing the idea aside as nonsense." Adi chuckled ruefully.

"So did I. But nonsensical or not, think about it. Love's the one thing we haven't tried. We've tried war, skirmishes, negotiations, blaming, threats, ceasefires, and treaties. None of it has worked. I believe the Professor was right. Peace is possible. I would like this to be a joint venture, with Israelis and Palestinians working together. I want to see us living in peace and safety as an extended family, as cousins at the grassroots level, like mother said it used to be. Peace is relational and starts with one person intentionally reaching out. I want to celebrate individuals or groups who embody peace through simple good deeds." Rahm took a deep breath. "I want you to help me."

"Why me? I can be incredibly rude and offensive, you know."

"I want your help because you're a velvet-covered brick."

Adi raised her eyebrows. "What?"

"See? You're tough. Hard as a brick."

Adi laughed.

"But you have a soft side. I believe making peace, the way the Professor spoke of it, and lived it, is going to be dangerous and difficult. It will take strength to push through. Even though you hide it, there's a tenderness there. I think his work will require sensitivity. Maybe you're more like a kosher armored marshmallow. Your tough exterior shields your tenderness."

"I think that's the nicest thing anyone has ever said to me." A small smile came to her lips.

"I respect you and would like to spend a lot more time with you."

"You would?"

"Yes." Rahm grinned. "I'm thinking of calling the foundation Holy Land Harmony. It could promote good neighbor relationships between all the people living in the land, Jews, Christians, Muslims, atheists, and secularists. I already went online and paid for a year for the domain name HolyLandHarmony.org. I would like to feature videos submitted by neighbors who've been on the receiving end of good deeds, especially from people of other faiths. Maybe even offer a Kaarl Schwalm Peace Prize every year."

"You really have done a lot of thinking."

"Do you remember when Qatal held up that ring on the beach in Saudi?"

"How could I forget? It was beautiful."

"I believe it's Solomon's Seal. Somehow, Solomon has been in the middle of this entire experience. The pillar. The ring."

Adi blinked rapidly and gave her head a little shake. "What?"

"I found the ring at St. Catherine's in the Charnel House when the Professor . . . I'm sorry. I . . ." He blinked back tears.

Adi reached out her hand and squeezed his.

"Anyway, I carried the Seal with me and found that it made my brain shift into a higher gear and calmed me. Stephanos told me he had hidden the ring there in 1976. He thinks it's the Seal too. When I went back to visit, I gave it back to him."

"If it helped so much, why give it up?"

"It felt to me like it belonged there, at least for now. When I handed it to Stephanos, I felt lighter, like someone lifted a load off my shoulders."

Adi smoothed a strand of hair from her forehead. "I see the link between your vision and the Professor's, but are you sure there's not some connection with the ring?"

Rahm nodded. "I'm sure there is. It definitely helped me clarify what's really important."

"That's it?"

"I'm sure there is more to it than I understand now. Maybe I'll understand better in the future."

"Can you work on this foundation and still keep your job?"

"Whether or not I carry a press pass, I think I will always be a journalist. I'll always look for the next story. But instead of peddling bad news, I want to share the good news. I'll probably keep working at The Breaking News for a while. At least at first, but I could see this really taking off."

After a long silence, Adi leaned forward and grinned. "I can too."

"Excuse me." The waiter was back. "I believe the lady had the bass, and the gentleman had the seafood platter."

"Dig in," Rahm said. "Let me know how the bass is." He speared a scallop, cut it in half, popped a bite in his mouth, and munched happily. Gesturing with his fork, he said, "Long term, I would like to flip the old journalistic mantra, 'If it bleeds, it leads," to where the news we offer is about acts of kindness. If we could show neighbors doing good deeds to people they're supposed to hate, maybe we could make a difference. I know what I'm suggesting is idealistic, but I want you to think about it."

"One condition." Adi put down her fork and held up a finger.

"Condition?"

"You accept Israel's Presidential Medal." She smiled.

Rahm reached across the table and shook her hand. "Deal."

ABOUT THE AUTHOR

J. Michael Corley's journey from humble beginnings to a life of exploration and imagination is as captivating as the stories he weaves. Born into a drinking-class family in California, his early education in the public school system provided the fertile ground for his creative spirit to take root. It was in the third grade that he first picked up a pen to write stories, setting the stage for a lifelong passion.

During his college years, fate led him to cross paths with a Middle Eastern man who would forever alter the course of his life. This fateful encounter led him to join the man's organization, diverting his attention to the world of a global enterprise. As a result, his passport bears the marks of a well-traveled influencer, with stamps and visas from Western and Eastern Europe, South and Central America, Asia, Turkey, Armenia, and the Middle East. Global encounters left an indelible mark on his worldview and inspired him to return to his true calling—writing stories.

J. Michael Corley writes between the lines of history, delving into the realms of fantasy and speculation to explore what might have been. His narratives are imbued with a sense of wonder and curiosity, inviting readers to question the boundaries of reality and fiction.

Today, he and his wife make their home in the enchanting landscapes of the Pacific Northwest, where the natural beauty of the region continues to fuel his creativity. He invites you to join him on a journey through the corridors of history, where fact and imagination converge to create stories that captivate the mind and touch the heart.

GLOSSARY

9mm: The world's most widely used military cartridge.

ABNI: Arabic word meaning "my son."

ADEN: Yemen's principal port city located near the mouth of the Red Sea.

ALLAH: The Arabic word for God.

AHMED III: Sultan of the Ottoman Empire 1703-1730.

ALIYA: The Arab name given to the Queen of Sheba, whose capital was at Ma'rib, Yemen.

AQABA, GULF OF: The arm of the Red Sea that runs along the east coast of the Sinai Peninsula.

ASKARI: During the colonial period, a local soldier hired to serve an outside, typically western, government or organization.

BABA JOON: Farsi phrase that is similar in meaning to the English "papa," but with an added dimension of deep respect.

BCE: Academic date designation "Before Common (sometimes Current) Era." This is a neutral replacement of B.C. (in this system, C.E. also replaces A.D.).

BEDOUIN: A nomadic, tent-dwelling Arab.

BEGIN, MENACHEM: Zionist freedom fighter, politician, and Prime Minister (1977-1983) of Israel.

CORAL RESORT NUWEIBA: An amazingly affordable resort property owned by Hilton Worldwide.

DAHAB: A Sinai resort town on the western shore of the Red Sea's Gulf of Aqaba, lying 55 miles north of the southern tip of the Sinai Peninsula.

DEIR YASSIN: A Holy Land village that was the site of the April 1948 massacre of 117 Palestinians, many of whom were reported to be women and children.

DIG: Used as a noun, the word means an archaeological excavation.

EUSEBIUS OF CAESAREA: Fourth-century scholar and Christian bishop

FATAH: A Palestinian political party and wing of the Palestinian Liberation Organization. Factions within the party have often been linked with terrorism.

'ILIHI: Arabic for "my God."

INSHALLAH: Arabic for "if God wills it."

INTERNATIONAL BACCALAUREATE ORGANIZATION: An educational foundation based in Geneva, Switzerland, offering educational programs for students ages 3-19.

JALEH SQUARE: A city square in Tehran, Iran, and the site of the Black Friday Massacre, September 1978. Where as many as 15,000 Iranians were killed.

JAMBIYA: An ornate Arab dagger with a sharply curved blade.

KAFIR: Arabic for infidel.

KEFFIYEH: Arab head scarf with many uses, including dust and sun protection.

KING DAVID HOTEL: During the British Mandate, the headquarters of the British armed forces, which was bombed on July 22, 1946, by the Zionist underground Irgun, led by Menachem Begin. Ninety-one people were killed and 46 injured.

KING, MARTIN LUTHER JR, An African American minister and civil rights activist.

KIPPAH, a brimless cap typically made of cloth, worn by many Jewish males (a.k.a. yarmulke).

LEAGUE OF NATIONS: An international organization founded after World War I and dedicated to preserving world peace. It was replaced with the founding of the United Nations.

MAHRAM BILQIS: Ma'rib's Temple of the Moon, otherwise known as "the Temple of the Queen of Sheba."

MENNONITE: A protestant Christian denomination founded by Menno Simons in the 16th century. The group tends to be committed to hard work, social action, disciple, nonresistance, and pacifism.

MONASTERY OF ST. ANTHONY: A Coptic Orthodox monastery located deep in the Red Sea Mountains south of Cairo built 298-300 C.E.

MOSQUE: An Islamic place of worship.

MOSSAD: The national security agency of Israel.

MUEZZIN: The man at the Islamic mosque who recites the call to prayer (usually from the tower or minaret—often through a public address system).

MUFTI: A legal scholar who interprets and gives non-binding opinions to the court system regarding Islamic law (Sharia).

MUSLIM: The Arabic word (meaning "submitted" or "submitter") for a follower of Islam.

NATIONAL SCIENCE FOUNDATION: Also known as NSF, it is a U.S. government research agency founded in 1950 during the Truman administration.

NETANYA CENTER BOMBING: Also known as the Passover Massacre, occurred in 2002 during a Passover meal. Hamas claimed responsibility for the thirty civilian causalities and 140 who were injured.

NUWEIBA: A Sinai resort town on the western shore of the Red Sea's Gulf of Aqaba, lying 40 miles south of the Israeli port of Eilat.

PEDER: Farsi word for father.

QURAN: Islam's holy book.

RPG: A handheld rocket launcher (rocket-propelled grenade).

SAFA: A Palestinian village in the West Bank territory.

SAINT CATHERINE CITY: A South Sinai city on the outskirts of the El Tur Mountains where the traditional location of Mt. Sinai is found.

SANAA: Capital city of Yemen.

SINAITICUS: A 4th-century Greek manuscript (copied 3225-350 CE) of the Bible, also known as the "Sinai Bible."

SOLOMON: King of Israel from 970-931 BCE is also regarded as a prophet in Islam.

SOLOMON'S SEAL: a legendary ring said to have been created by King Solomon of Israel, also known by its Hebrew name, "Khatam Shlomo," or its Arabic name, "Khatam Sulayman."

TEMPLE OF THE MOON: The ancient ruins of a pre-Islamic temple in Yemen near Ma'rib. It is also known as "The Throne of Aliya."

TORAH: Torah can mean the five books of Moses and is often used interchangeably with the more technical term, Tanakh, for all 24 books of the Hebrew Bible.

VON TISCHENDORF, COUNT CONSTANTIN: A 19th-century German biblical scholar remembered primarily for his discovery of the Sinaiticus manuscript of the Bible at St. Catherine's Monastery in the Sinai desert.

ZIONISM: A political movement launched in the late 19th century among Jewish people that advocated the establishment of a modern nation-state in the territory called "Palestine," or "the Holy Land." "Zionist" is sometimes used as a pejorative label.

AUTHOR'S NOTES

AMERICAN TRUST FOR THE STUDY OF MAN— Is a pseudonym for the American Foundation for the Study of Man that conducted an excavation at Ma'rib, Yemen, in 1952 at Mahram Bilqis (Temple of the Queen of Sheba). Details of this expedition led by Wendell Phillips can be found in the pages of *Qataban and Sheba: Exploring the Ancient Kingdoms on the Biblical Spice Routes of Arabia*, Harcourt, Brace and Company, New York, 1955. At the same time, a team from AFSM was working on cataloging manuscripts at St. Catherine's Monastery in the Sinai. Learn more at www.afms.org

BRIAN AND BRYAN—The Brian Boley story refers to actual events that were reported on the front page of Oregon's principal statewide newspaper, The Oregonian, on May 18, 1984.

CODEX SINAITICUS-- Codex Sinaiticus is dated from the mid-fourth century and is arguably one of the most important books in the world. Handwritten well over 1600 years ago, the manuscript contains the Christian Bible in Greek, including the oldest complete copy of the New Testament. It came to the attention of western scholars when it was discovered at St. Catherine's Monastery in the mid-nineteenth century by Constantin Von Tischendorf. Tischendorf took most of Sinaiticus to St. Petersburg and presented the Tsar, Peter II of Russia. Currently, the bulk of the manuscript is at British Library in London, with a few pages at the Russian National Library in St. Petersburg and others at the Leipzig University Library. Twelve complete leaves of Sinaiticus were discovered in an abandoned room at St. Catherine's Monastery in 1975. Further detail is available at www.codexsinaiticus.org.

ISRAELI COMMITTEE AGAINST HOUSE DEMOLITIONS—An Israeli non-profit that opposes Israeli settlements and the Israeli government's policy of demolishing Palestinian homes. https://icahd.org

MA'RIB—The capital city of the Sabaean kingdom, also known as Sheba. It was the largest city in pre-Islamic Arabia and featured five-story buildings. Nearby was the Temple of the Moon, where the god Almaqah was worshiped. The economy of the city was based on trading spices like frankincense and myrrh. The Ma'rib Dam captured the runoff from torrential summer rains and provided irrigation to 25,000 acres of farmland.

QUEEN OF SHEBA—Although she is mentioned in the Hebrew scriptures, the New Testament, and the Quran, archaeological evidence of her existence remains elusive. However, legends abound.

RAMALLAH FRIENDS SCHOOL—Founded in October 1889, Friends Girls School opened as "The Girls Training Home of Ramallah." Fifteen students enrolled in the first year. Six years later, the first class graduated. Recent graduating classes have seen an average of 95% attending top-rated colleges and universities locally and abroad. In 2019 the school celebrated its 150th anniversary. Learn more at www.rfs.edu.ps

SCORPION, THE—Tora El Mahkoum, also known as the Scorpion, is a notorious super-maximum security prison located on the south side of Cairo, Egypt.

SINAI, MOUNT—Scholars disagree about the exact locations of Mt. Sinai, the Red Sea crossing, and the split rock of Horeb. Some believe the real Mount Sinai is in Saudi Arabia, where the locals call it Jabal al Lawz.

SOLOMON'S PILLAR—A twenty-foot pillar located above the Nuweiba Beach, about half a mile from the Gulf of Aqaba. It can be seen on Google Earth, where the Dahab Highway turns away from the beach into Wadi Watir. Latitude: 29° 0'50.73"N Longitude 34°38'46.90"E

SPLIT ROCK OF HOREB—Although there is a large rock formation in Saudi Arabia, an image of which can be seen at https://www.youtube.com/watch?v=ssG7_maFk2s, it cannot be confirmed that this is the rock Moses struck producing a well of water to satisfy the thirst of the Exodus Hebrews. This formation is found less than six miles from Jabal al Lawz, which the locals believe is the mountain on which Moses received the Ten Commandments.

URIM AND THUMMIM—Although the exact nature of these objects is not mentioned, they were prescribed as part of the High Priest's "breast piece of judgment" in Exodus 28:30. Their use is described in 1 Samuel 14:41. They disappeared after Ezra mentions their use.w

VAJA—The Ministry of Intelligence of the Islamic Republic of Iran is the primary intelligence of Iran.

WADI TAYYIB AL-ISM—drains rainwater from the Saudi Arabian interior. However, it is entirely impassable to vehicle traffic.

WENDELL PHILLIPS—may have been the inspiration for the Indiana Jones character featured in Raiders of the Lost Ark. Phillips was an American archaeologist and oil tycoon. He led archaeological expeditions into Africa and later into Arabian Peninsula in the early

1950s. He went to the ancient city of Ma'rib, Yemen, in search of the biblical Queen of Sheba. There he excavated the Temple of the Moon, where eight pillars marked the entrance to the local place of worship. In 1952 he barely escaped with his life when relations with the local tribal leaders broke down. In 1975 his oil holdings were valued at $120,000,000.

ACKNOWLEDGMENTS

I am indebted to so many who have helped with this project.

Charles and Jeri Boley have financially supported my attendance at writer's conferences.

Since 2019, the friends at Red Sands Writers' Circle plowed through the story and offered insightful suggestions, and put up with my bad habits. I especially want to thank our gifted and patient Saturday morning leader, Mike Oppenheim, who has described our group as "a smart room." He was referring to the band of writers that includes Gennie, George, Glenn, Margot, Mark, Olivia, Rachel, Robin, Sander, Sandy, and Vin.

Our Saturday sessions were hosted by the good people at Jarrod's Coffee, Tea, and Gallery at 154 W. Main, Mesa, Arizona.

Justin Tate is not only the founder of Red Sands Writers Circle but also skillfully guides the Wednesday night virtual sessions that starting in the fall of 2021, have also joined in the critiquing process. Bob, Mess Mike, and Patrick made invaluable recommendations.

I also have gotten some great help from the Power Road Critique group that meets at the Queen Creek Library. The guru of that group is Craig Mazur, and he is joined by Elvis, Janice, Mariann, and Sylvia. They sharpened me a bunch.

Beta readers Jean and Jesse offered strong encouragement. The person who has been my biggest help and rock has been my gifted and delightful wife, Lynetta. Thank you, sweetie!

Made in the USA
Coppell, TX
20 April 2026

75983861R10197